FROZEN

HEART OF DREAD

BOOK ONE

Melissa de la Cruz
and
Michael Johnston

ORCHARD

FROZEN

HEART OF DREAD

BOOK ONE

ORCHARD BOOKS
338 Euston Road, London NW1 3BH
Orchard Books Australia
Level 17/207 Kent Street, Sydney, NSW 2000

First published in 2013 in the United States by G. P. Putnam's Sons, an
imprint of Penguin Young Readers Group, a division of The Penguin
Group (USA) Inc.

This edition published in Great Britain in 2014 by Orchard Books

ISBN 978 1 40833 466 9

A CIP catalogue record for this book is available
from the British Library.

10 9 8 7 6 5 4 3 2 1

Printed in Great Britain

Orchard Books is a division of Hachette Children's Books,
an Hachette UK company.

www.hachette.co.uk

For Mattie

Some say the world will end in fire,
Some say in ice.
From what I've tasted of desire
I hold with those who favor fire.
But if it had to perish twice,
I think I know enough of hate
To say that for destruction ice
Is also great
And would suffice.

—ROBERT FROST, "Fire and Ice"

It's time to begin.

—IMAGINE DRAGONS, "It's Time"

THE VOICE OF THE MONSTER

They were coming for her. She could hear their heavy footsteps echoing in the concrete hallway. In a way, the sound was a relief. For days upon days she had been left in the room, alone, in total silence, with little food and water, the weight of solitude becoming ever more oppressive, the silence a heaviness that she could not shake, punishment for refusing to do as she was told, punishment for being what she was.

She had forgotten how many days, how many months, she had been left here, alone with only her thoughts for company.

But not quite alone.

I warned you about waiting, *rumbled the voice in her head. The voice that she heard in her dreams, whose words echoed like thunder, thunder and ash, smoke and flame. When it spoke, she saw a beast through the inferno, carrying her aloft on black wings through dark skies as it rained fire upon its enemies. The fire that raged within* her. *The fire that destroyed and consumed. The fire that would destroy and consume her if she let it.*

Her destiny. A destiny of rage and ruin.

Fire and pain.

The voice in her head was the reason her eyes were not brown or gray. Her clear tiger eyes—hazel-green with golden pupils—told the world she carried a mark on her skin, one that she kept hidden, one that was shaped like a flame and hurt like a burn, right above her heart. The reason she was imprisoned, the reason they wanted her to do as she was told.

The girl did not want to be different. She did not want to be marked. She did not want to be what the voice said she was. What the commander and the doctors believed she was. A freak. A monster.

Let me go—*she had implored the first time she had been brought to this place*—I'm not what you think I am. *She had insisted they were wrong about her from the beginning of her captivity.*

What is your talent? *they had demanded.* Show us.

I have none, *she had told them.* I have no ability. I can do nothing. Let me go. You're wrong. Let me go.

She never told them about the voice in her head.

But they found ways to use her anyway.

Now they were coming, their heavy footsteps plodding against the stone. They would make her do what they wanted, and she would not be able to refuse. It was always this way. She resisted at first, they punished her for it, and finally she gave in.

Unless…

Unless she listened to the voice.

When it spoke to her, it always said the same thing: I have been searching for you, but now it is you who must find me. The time has come for us to be one. The map has been found. Leave this place. Journey to the Blue.

Like others she had heard the legends of a secret doorway in the middle of the ruined Pacific that led to a place where the air was warm and the water was turquoise. But the way was impossible—the dark oceans treacherous, and many had perished attempting to find it.

But perhaps there was hope. Perhaps she would find a way to do what it sought.

Out there.

In New Vegas.

Outside her window, far away, she could see the glittering lights of the city shining through the gray. Before the ice, night skies were supposedly black and infinite, dotted with stars that shone as sharp as diamonds against velvet. Looking up into that dark expanse you could imagine traveling to distant lands, experiencing the vastness of the universe, and understanding your own small part in it. But now the sky was glassy and opaque at night, a reflection of the bright white snow that covered the ground and swirled in the atmosphere. Even the brightest of stars appeared only as faint, distant glimmers in the blurry firmament.

There were no more stars. There was only New Vegas, glowing, a beacon in the darkness.

The city lights stopped abruptly at a long arcing line just a few miles out. Beyond the line, beyond the border, everything was black, Garbage Country, a place where light had disappeared—a no-man's-land of terrors—and past that, the toxic sea. And somewhere, hidden in that ocean, if she believed what the voice said, she would find a way to another world.

They were closer and closer. She could hear their voices outside, arguing.

The guards were opening the door.

She didn't have much time…

Panic rose in her throat.

What would they ask her to do now…what did they want…the children most likely…always the children…

They were here.

The window! *the voice bellowed.* Now!

Glass smashed, broken, sharp icicles falling to the floor. The door burst open, but the girl was already on the ledge, the cold air whipping against her cheeks. She shivered in her thin pajamas, the arctic winds blowing sharp as daggers as she dangled on the knife-edge, two hundred stories in the air.

Fly!

I will hold you.

Her mark was burning like a hot ember against her skin. It had awakened, as a rush of power, electric as the sparks that lit up the sky, snaked through her limbs, and she was warm, so warm, as if she was bathed in fire. She was burning, burning, the mark above her heart pressing on her like a brand, scorching her with its heat.

Let us be one.

You are mine.

No, never! *She shook her head, but they were inside now, the commander and his men, raising their guns, training their sights on her.*

"STOP!" The commander stared her down. "REMAIN WHERE YOU ARE!"

GO!

She was dead either way. Fire and pain. Rage and ruin.

She turned from the room and toward the city lights, toward New Vegas, frozen city of impossible delights, a world where everything and anything could be bought and sold, the pulsing, decadent, greedy heart of the new republic. New Vegas: a place where she could hide, a place where she could find passage, out to the water, into the Blue.

The commander was screaming. He aimed and pressed the trigger.

She held her breath. There was only one way to go.

Out and down.

Up and away.

Fly! *roared the monster in her head.*

The girl jumped from the ledge and into the void.

PART THE FIRST

LEAVING NEW VEGAS

Am I just in Heaven or Las Vegas?

—Cocteau Twins, "Heaven or Las Vegas"

ONE

It was the start of the weekend, amateur night; her table was crowded with conventioneers, rich kids flashing platinum chips, a pair of soldiers on leave—honeymooners nuzzling between drinks, nervous first-timers laying down their bets with trembling fingers. Nat shuffled the cards and dealt the next hand. The name she used had come to her in a fragment from a dream she could not place, and could not remember, but it seemed to fit. She was Nat now. Familiar with numbers and cards, she had easily landed a job as a blackjack dealer at the Loss—what everyone called the Wynn since the Big Freeze. Some days she could pretend that was all she was, just another Vegas dreamer, trying to make ends meet, hoping to get lucky on a bet.

She could pretend that she had never run, that she had never stepped out of that window, although "fall" wasn't the right word; she had glided, flying through the air as if she had wings. Nat had landed hard in a snowbank, disarming the perimeter guards who had surrounded her, stealing a heat vest to keep herself warm. She followed the lights of the Strip and once she arrived in the city it was easy enough to trade in the vest for lenses to hide her eyes, allowing her to find work in the nearest casino.

New Vegas had lived up to her hopes. While the rest of the country chafed under martial law, the western frontier town was the same as it ever was—the place where the rules were often bent, and where the world came to play. Nothing kept the crowds away. Not the constant threat of violence, not the fear of the marked, not even the rumors of dark sorcery at work in the city's shadows.

Since her freedom, the voice in her head was exultant, and her dreams were growing darker. Almost every day she woke to the smell of smoke and the sound of screams. Some days, the dreams were so vivid she did not know if she was sleeping or awake. Dreams of fire and ruin, the smoldering wreckage, the air thick with smoke, the blood on the walls…

The sound of screams…

"Hit me."

Nat blinked. She had seen it so clearly. The explosion, the flashing bright-white light, the black hole in the ceiling, the bodies slumped on the floor.

But all around her, it was business as usual. The casino hummed with noise, from the blaring pop song over the stereo, the craps dealers barking numbers as they raked in die, video poker screens beeping, slot machines ringing, players impatient for their cards. The fifteen-year-old bride was the one who had asked for another. "Hit me," she said again.

"You've got sixteen, you should hold," Nat advised. "Let the house bust, dealer hits on sixteen, which I'm showing."

"You think?" she asked with a hopeful smile. The child bride and her equally young husband, both soldiers, wouldn't see anything like the main floor of a luxury casino for a long time. Tomorrow they would ship back out to their distant patrol assignments, controlling the drones that policed the country's far-flung borders, or the seekers that roamed the forbidden wastelands.

Nat nodded, flipped up the next card and showed the newly-weds...an eight, dealer busted, and she paid out their winnings. "Let it ride!" The bride whooped. They would keep their chips in play to see if they could double their holdings.

It was a terrible idea, but Nat couldn't dissuade them. She dealt the next round. "Good luck," she said, giving them the usual Vegas blessing before she showed them her cards. She was sighing—*Twenty-one, the house always wins, there goes their wedding bonus*—when the first bomb exploded.

One moment she was collecting chips, and the next she was thrown against the wall.

Nat blinked. Her head buzzed and her ears rang, but at least she was still in one piece. She knew to take it slow, gingerly wiggling fingers and toes to see if everything still worked, the tears in her eyes washing away the soot. Her lenses hurt, they felt stuck, heavy and itchy, but she kept them on just to be safe.

So her dream had been real after all.

"Drau bomb," she heard people mutter, people who had never seen a drau—let alone a sylph—in their lives. Ice trash. Monsters.

Nat picked herself up, trying to orient herself in the chaos of the broken casino. The explosion had blown a hole in the ceiling and pulverized the big plate-glass windows, sending incandescent shards tumbling down fifty stories to the sidewalks below.

Everyone at her blackjack table was dead. Some had died still clutching their cards, while the newlyweds were slumped together on the floor, blood pooling around their bodies. She felt sick to her stomach, remembering their happy faces.

Screams echoed over the fire alarms. But the power was still on, so pop music from overhead speakers lent a jarring, upbeat soundtrack to the casino's swift fall into chaos, as patrons stumbled about, reeling and dazed, covered in ashes and dust. Looters reached for chips while dealers and pit bosses fended them off with guns and threats. Police in riot gear arrived, moving from room to room, rounding up the rest of the survivors, looking for conspirators rather than helping victims.

Not too far from where she was standing, she heard a

different sort of screaming—the sound of an animal cornered, of a person begging for his life.

She turned to see who was making that terrible noise. It was one of the roulette dealers. Military police surrounded him, their guns trained on his head. He was kneeling on the floor, cowering. "Please," he cried, collapsing into heart-wrenching sobs. "Don't shoot, don't shoot, please don't shoot!" he begged, and when he looked up, Nat could see what was wrong. His eyes. They were blue, a startling, iridescent hue. His lenses must have slipped off, or he'd taken them off when they burned from the smoke, as she almost did hers. The blue-eyed ones were said to be able to control minds, create illusions. Apparently, this one didn't have the ability to control minds, or his tears.

He tried to hide his face, tried to cover his eyes with his hands. "Please!"

It was no use.

He died with his blue eyes open, his uniform splattered with blood.

Executed.

In public.

And no one cared.

"It's all right, everyone, move on, the danger's passed now. Move along," the guards said, ushering the survivors to the side, away from the corpses in the middle of the broken casino, as a sanitation and recovery team began cleaning up the mess, moving the tables back upright.

Nat followed the stream of people herded in a corner, knowing what would come next—ret scans and security checks, standard procedure after a disturbance. "Ladies and gentlemen, you know the drill," an officer announced, holding up his laser.

"Don't blink," security officers warned as they flashed their lights. Patrons lined up quietly—this wasn't the first bombing they'd survived—and several were impatient to get back to their games. Already the craps dealers were calling out numbers again. It was just another day in New Vegas, just another bomb.

"I can't get a read, you're going to have to come with us, ma'am," a guard said to an unfortunate soul slumped by the slot machines. The sallow-faced woman was led to a separate line. Those who failed the scans or carried suspect documentation would be thrown into lockdowns. They would be left to the mercy of the system, left to rot, forgotten, unless a celebrity took a shine to their cause, but lately the mega-rockers were all agitating to restore the ozone. The only magic they believed in was their own charisma.

It was her turn next.

"Evening," Nat said, as she looked straight into the small red light, willing her voice to remain calm. She told herself she had nothing to fear, nothing to hide. Her eyes were the same as the rest.

The officer was roughly her age—sixteen. He had a row of pimples across his forehead, but his tone was world-weary. Tired as an old man. He kept the beam focused on her eyes until she had no choice but to blink and he had to start over.

"Sorry," she said, crossing her arms against her chest and struggling to keep her breathing steady. Why was it taking so long? Did he see something she didn't? She would hunt down the lockhead who'd conjured her rets if he'd proven her false.

The officer finally switched off the light.

"Everything all right?" she asked, as she flipped her long dark hair over one shoulder.

"Perfect." He leaned closely to read her name tag. "Natasha Kestal. Pretty name for a pretty girl."

"You're too kind." She smiled, thankful for the invisible gray lenses that allowed her to pass the scan.

Nat had gotten the job with fake papers and a favor, and as they waved her through to the employee lockers so she could change into a clean uniform and get back to work, she thanked the unseen stars above, because for now, she was safe.

TWO

"I can't take this job." Wes pushed the slim manila folder across the table without opening it. Sixteen, with soft, sandy-brown hair and warm brown eyes, he was muscular but lean and wearing a tattered down vest over a threadbare sweater and torn jeans. His face was hard, but his eyes were kind—although more often than not he had a smirk on his face.

He had one now. Wes knew all he needed to about the assignment just from the words PACIFIC RECON typed in boldface Courier across the cover. Lately all the work was in the black waters. There was nothing else. He sighed, leaning back on the plush leather chair. He had been looking forward to a real meal, but the chances of that were slim now that he'd turned down the offer. There were white tablecloths and real silverware. But it was still inside a gambling hall and every corner blinked with tiny lights as slots clinked and beeped and coins dropped into buckets.

Wes was from New Vegas and found the sound of

casino clamor soothing. The Loss was still recovering from that spectacular bombing that had torn the place in half a few weeks before. A grid of gas heaters were strung across the ceiling as a temporary fix; their fiery glow the only defense against the never-ending winter outside. Snow was coming down hard, and Wes watched the dense flakes vaporize, each flake sizzling like oil in a frying pan as it hit the grid. He brushed back his hair as an errant snowflake drifted through the mesh to land on his nose.

He shivered—he never could get used to the cold; even as a boy he'd been teased for being too warm-blooded. He was wearing several layers of shirts underneath his sweater, the ghetto way to keep warm when you couldn't afford self-heating clothing powered by a fusion battery. "I'm sorry," he said. "But I can't."

Bradley ignored him and motioned the waitress over. "Two steaks. Tuscan style, Wagyu. The biggest you got," he ordered. "I like my beef massaged," he told Wes.

Beef was a rarity, unaffordable to the general population. Sure, there was a lot of meat around—whale, walrus, reindeer, if you could stomach it—but only the heat-elite ate beef anymore. Especially since the only cattle left were nurtured in expensive temperature-controlled stables. The cow that died to make his steak probably lived a better life than he did, Wes thought. It had probably been warm.

He locked eyes with his dinner companion. "You need

25

another CEO kidnapped? I'm your boy. But I can't do this."

As a former Marine sergeant, Wes had headed one of the most sought-after mercenary teams in the city. Correction: one of the *formerly* most sought-after teams. He'd done well in the casino wars until he got on the bad side of one of the bosses for refusing to torch a rival's hotel during Mardi Gras. Since then, all the work came from the secret divisions of the military: protection, intimidation, kidnapping and rescue (more often than not Wes found himself on both sides). He'd been hoping for one of those gigs.

"Wesson, be reasonable," Bradley said, his voice icy. "You know you need this job. Take it. You're one of the best we've ever had, especially after that victory in Texas. Shame you left us so soon. I've got a hundred guys champing at the bit to take this gig, but I thought I'd throw you a bone. Heard you haven't worked in a while."

Wes smiled, acknowledging the truth of the man's words. "Except some assignments aren't worth the trouble," he said. "Even I need to be able to sleep at night." He'd learned as much from his stint in the army, especially after what happened in Santonio.

"These marked factions who resist treatment and registration continue to pose a danger, and they need to be dealt with accordingly," the older man said. "Look what they did to this place."

Wes grunted. Sure looked like they found someone to

do the casino hit he'd turned down, but what did he know. He only knew as much as the rest of them—that after the ice came, dark hair and dark eyes were the norm, and the rare blue- or green- or yellow-eyed babies were born with strange marks on their bodies.

Mages' marks, the gypsies whispered, fortune-tellers who read palms and tarot in Vegas's dark alleys. *It's started. Others will come out of the ice and into our world.*

This is the end.

The end of the beginning. The beginning of the end.

The marked children could do things—read minds, make things move without touching them, sometimes even predict the future. Enchanters, they were called, warlocks, "lockheads" and "chanters" in the popular slang.

The others who came out of the ice were smallmen, grown men the size of toddlers who were gifted with rare talents for survival, able to hide in plain sight or forage for food where none could be found; sylphs, a race of beings of luminous beauty and awesome power, it was said their hair was the color of the sun that was no more and their voices were the sound of the birds that no longer flew across the land; and finally the terrifying drau— silver-haired sylphs with white eyes and dark purpose. Drau were said to be able to kill with their minds alone, that their very hearts were made of ice.

The smallmen were rumored to live openly with their taller brethren in New Pangaea, but the sylphs and the drau kept to themselves, hidden in their remote mountain glaciers. Many doubted they truly existed, as very few had ever seen one.

In the past, the military had drafted the marked into its ranks, along with an elusive sylph or a smallman or two, but ever since that program ended in abject failure during the battle for Texas, government policy evolved to its current state of registration, containment, and blame. The marked were deemed dangerous, and people were taught to fear them.

But Wes was a Vegas native, and the city had always been a conglomeration of misfits living peacefully together for more than a hundred years since the world had been buried in sheets of ice. "It's not that I don't need the work, I do," he said. "But not this."

The stern-faced captain reached for the folder and flipped it open, paging through the documents. "I don't see what the problem is," he said, sliding it back across the table. "We're not asking for much, just someone to lead the hired guns to clean up the rubbish in the Pacific. Someone like you, who knows the lay of the land—or the lay of the water, so to speak."

The price was good, and Wes had done dangerous work before, sure, running people in and out of the Trash Pile, no questions asked. As Bradley said, he knew his way around the ruined seas, playing coyote to citizens seeking illegal passage all the way to the Xian Empire; or if they were particularly delusional, they'd ask him to find the Blue, the fabled nirvana that the pilgrims sought and no one had ever found, least of all Wes. But lately work had dried up for runners, as fewer and fewer chose to brave the difficulty of a dire ocean crossing, and even Wes was having second thoughts about his calling. He was desperate, and Bradley knew it.

"Come on, you haven't even opened the folder," his former captain said. "At least check out the mission."

Wes sighed, opened the folder, and skimmed through the document. The text was redacted, black bars covered most of the words, but he got the gist of the assignment.

It was just as he'd guessed.

Dirty work.

Murder.

The waitress swung back with a couple of beers in frosted, oversize mugs. Bradley knocked his back while Wes finished reading the pages. This wasn't his usual operation, a one-way ticket into the Pile where if anyone got hurt it was him and his boys. He could deal with that. A good run could keep his team out of the food lines for a month.

This was different. He'd done a lot to survive, but he wasn't a paid killer.

Bradley waited patiently. No smile, no change in expression. His shirt was tucked a little too tight, hair clipped a little too short for a civilian. Even out of uniform, he had military written all over him. But the

United States of America was not what it once was—no wonder everyone called it the "Remaining States of America" instead. The RSA: a handful of surviving states, and aside from its massive military machine that kept gobbling up new terrain, the country had nothing else and was hocked lock, stock, and barrel to its debtors.

The captain smiled as he wiped the froth from his lips. "Cakewalk, right?"

Wes shrugged as he closed the folder. Bradley was a hard man, one who wouldn't blink twice before giving a kill order. Most of the time Wes followed those orders. But not this time.

In any other world, Wes might have grown up to be something else: a musician maybe, or a sculptor, a carpenter, someone who worked with his hands. But he lived in this world, in New Vegas; he had a team that counted on him, and he was cold and hungry.

When the waitress came back, she was wheeling a silver cart holding two wide platters, each one bearing a fat steak, charred on top and dripping juice over a bed of mashed potatoes. The smell of melted butter and smoke was tantalizing.

It was a far cry from the MRSs he was used to: Meals Ready to Squeeze. It was all he and his boys could afford lately: pizza squeezers, Thanksgiving dinner in a can. Some of it wasn't even food, it came out of aerosol containers; you sprayed it directly into your mouth and called it dinner. Wes couldn't remember the last time he'd had a hamburger, much less a steak, that smelled this good.

"So, you taking the job or not? Listen, these are hard times. Don't sweat it. Everyone needs to eat. You should be thanking me for this opportunity. I came to you first."

Wes shook his head, tried to get the smell of the steak out of his mind. "I told you, try someone else. You've got the wrong guy," he said.

If Bradley thought he could buy him for the price of a meal, he was wrong. Wes styled himself after Paleolithic hunters he'd learned about in school, who kept their eyes trained on the horizon, always scanning, always searching for that elusive prize that would mean survival. But the tribesmen would fast for days rather than consume the meat of sacred animals. Wes liked that idea; it allowed him feel better about himself, that he wasn't a vulture, one of those people who would do anything for a heat lamp. Wes didn't have much, but he had his integrity.

The army captain scowled. "You really want me to send this back to the kitchen? I bet you haven't eaten anything but mush for weeks."

"Throw it in the garbage, what do I care," Wes said as he tossed the folder back across the table.

Bradley straightened his lapels and shot him a withering look. "Get used to starving then."

THREE

The casino was buzzing as usual when Nat arrived for work that evening. It had never even closed, not for a day, not for an hour; management didn't care that there was a hole in the roof as long as the slot machines kept ringing. She nodded to Old Joe as she walked in and the wizened card shark smiled in greeting, his eyes disappearing into his cheeks. Joe was an anomaly, a rare bird, a man who had lived past his fiftieth birthday. He was also a legend at the casinos. Supposedly he'd been one of the smartest and most successful card sharks, and one of the most elusive—he'd brought down many a gambling hall, decimating coffers, staying just one step ahead of security. When he made his way to the Strip, the Loss offered him a job on the inside, rather than watch him walk away with their profits.

"You remind me of my niece who died in 'Tonio," Joe had said when he'd hired her right off the felt, a skinny, starving thing who was on a winning streak at the poker tables. "She was like you—too smart for her own good." Joe made her the same deal he gave all his fellow card counters. Work for me, help us turn in the other pros, I'll give you a decent salary and keep you from getting beat up by the casino goons. He didn't ask any questions about how she came to Vegas or what she was doing before, but he'd made good on his word, and got her set up.

Ask him, the voice ordered. *Ask him about the stone. Do what we came here for. You have delayed long enough. The Map has been found*, the voice kept telling her. *Hurry, it is time.*

What map? she had asked, even if she had a feeling she already knew the answer. The pilgrims called it Anaximander's Map; it was said to provide safe passage through the rocky, perilous waters of Hell Strait to the island doorway that led to the Blue.

"Joe?" she asked. "You got a sec?"

"What's up?"

"Can we talk privately?"

"Sure," he said, motioning that she should follow him to a quiet corner, where a group of tourists were robotically feeding credits into the video poker stations. The smell of smoke was overpowering, and it reminded her of her dreams.

Joe crossed his meaty arms. "What's on your mind?"

"What is that?" she asked, pointing to the stone he wore around his wrinkled neck. The one she had noticed the first time they had met, the one that the voice in her head demanded she ask him about the moment she had set foot in the city, and in this casino. She had put off the voice for as long as she could, fearing what would happen if she did as she was told.

"This?" the old man asked, lifting the stone to the light, where it shone brightly against the dim cocoon of the gambling hall.

That is the one! Take it! Take the stone. Kill him if you must. It is ours! The voice was frenetic, excited, she could feel the monster's need thrumming in her veins.

"No!" she said aloud, shocking herself and startling a nearby gambler who dropped her token.

"What?" Joe asked, still admiring the shining stone.

"Nothing," she said. "It's pretty."

"I won it at a card game a while back," he said with a dismissive wave. "It's supposed to be some kind of map, but it's nothing."

Take it! Take it! Take it from him!

"Can I hold it?" she asked, her voice quavering.

"Sure," Joe said, slowly removing it from his neck. He hesitated for a moment before handing it to her. It was warm in her palm.

She studied the small blue stone in her hand. It was the weight and color of a sapphire, a round stone with a circle in the middle of it. She put it up to her eye and jumped back, startled.

"What happened? You see something?" Joe asked excitedly.

"No—no...nothing," Nat lied. For a moment, the casino had disappeared and through the hole in the stone, all she could see was blue water, shimmering and clean. She peered into it again. There it was. Blue water.

That wasn't all. Upon closer inspection she saw there was more, an image of a charted course, a jagged line between obstacles, a way forward, through the rocky and whirlpool waters of the Hellespont Strait.

The stone contains the map to Arem, the doorway to Vallonis, the voice murmured reverently.

This was why the voice had led her to New Vegas, to the Loss, and to Joe. It had facilitated her escape, it had brought her freedom, and it was relentlessly pushing her forward.

Come to me.

You are mine.

It is time we are one.

"There's nothing," she told Joe.

His shoulders slumped. "Yeah, that's what I thought. It's just a fake."

She closed her fist around it, unsure of what would happen next, afraid of what she'd do if Joe asked for it back and hoping that he wouldn't.

She stared down the casino boss. The monster in her head was seething. *What are you waiting for! Take it and run! Kill him if he stops you!*

"Give it to me," she whispered, and somehow she knew he would do as told.

Joe flinched as if she'd hurt him. "Keep it," he said finally, and walked away from her quickly.

Nat leaned against the wall in relief, glad for Joe's sake that he had given it freely.

Later that evening she was awoken by the sound of a scuffle. Joe lived two rooms down from her, and she heard them—military police? Casino security? Bounty hunters? Whoever had come had kicked open his door and was taking him from his bed. She heard the old man begging, screaming and crying, but no one came to his aid. No neighbors dared to peer down the hallway, no one even asked what the matter was. Tomorrow no one would talk about what happened either, or what they had heard. Joe would simply be gone, and nothing more would be said. She huddled in her thick blankets as she heard them tearing his room apart, throwing open closet doors, upending tables, looking...looking... for something...for the cold blue stone that she now held in her hand?

If they had found Joe, it wouldn't be long before they found her as well.

Then what? She could not look back, she had nothing to go back to, but if she kept moving forward...She shuddered, and her mouth tasted of ashes and cinder.

She held the stone in her hand. The map to Arem, doorway to Vallonis.

From the window, she saw them take Joe away in a straitjacket, and she knew what awaited her if she stayed.

They would send her back to where she came from, back to those solitary rooms, back to those dark assignments.

No. She could not stay. She had to leave New Vegas, and soon.

What are you waiting for?

FOUR

His mother had been a showgirl. One of the prettiest in the business, his dad had liked to say, and Wes was sure he was right. Dad had been a cop. They were good people, fine citizens of New Vegas. Neither of them was still alive, each succumbing to the big C years ago. Cancer was a disease that was a matter of when, not why, and his parents had been no exception. But Wes knew they had died long before; they were empty shells after what happened to Eliza. His little sister whom no one could save.

He had his parents to thank for his good looks and his sharp wits, but not much else. As Wes walked away from the four-star meal, he was angry with himself for turning down Bradley's offer, but angrier that it was the only avenue open to the likes of him. He could starve, he had starved before, but he hated the boys going hungry. They were the only family he had left.

When he was little, his mother would make him tomato soup and grilled cheese sandwiches. It didn't happen often—she worked late nights and wasn't usually awake when he was home from school. But once in a while, she would appear, last night's makeup faint on her cheeks, smelling of perfume and sweat, and she would turn on the stove and the smell of butter—real butter, she always insisted they save up for it—would fill their small house.

The sandwich would be gooey on the inside and crisp on the outside and the soup—thin and red—was tart and flavorful, even if it was from a can. Wes wondered if he missed his mother or those sandwiches more. She had hid her disease from them, beneath the makeup. She had worked until the end, and one day, had doubled over, vomiting blood backstage. Dead in a matter of days.

Dad had tried to keep it together for a while, and his girlfriends—cocktail waitresses with outlaw accents, the occasional lap-girl from the clubs—(his mother would never have approved, she was a *performer*, a *dancer*, not a cheap grab-and-grope-girl) had been kind to Wes, but it was never the same.

When his father died in hospice, a shriveled twenty-nine-year-old man, Wes was orphaned.

He was nine years old and alone.

The world had ended long before the snows came, his father liked to say. It had ended after the Great Wars, ended after the Black Floods, the Big Freeze only the latest catastrophe. The world was always ending. The point was to survive whatever came next.

Wes had promised his boys work, had promised them food, had promised them they would eat tonight. He had also promised himself he would never go back there, never do anything so stupid and dangerous again. But there he was. Back at the death races, so named because to drive one of the beat-up jalopies in the game was to risk everything. The tracks ran through the carcasses of old casinos on the street level. The cars were patched-up wrecks with souped-up engines, although once in a while they were able to find an old Ferrari or a Porsche with an engine that could still zoom.

"Thought you said you were done," said Dre, the gangster who ran the track, when he saw Wes.

"Things change," Wes said grimly. "How much?"

"Ten if you win, nickel if you place. Nothing if you don't."

"Fine." He'd always been good at being fast. He could drive fast, he could run fast, he even talked fast. In a way, it was a relief to do something that came easily to him.

Wes got in a car. No helmet, no seat belt. No rules except to try to stay alive, to try not to crash into one of the walls, or into the glass panels, or to flip off the ice onto another car. The cars were named for the great racehorses of old. Ajax. Man o' War. Cigar. Barbaro. Secretariat. He looked up at the boards that would broadcast the race to the OTB network—his odds were low and he felt gratified at that, that the bookies remembered him, that they bet that he would live. When the checkered flag was raised, Wes revved up the engine and flew down the course.

The course took him past the city's relics, the Olden Ugg, Rah's, and R Queens, ending on the corner where the neon cowboy waved his hat.

There were a few cars ahead of him, and Wes decided to keep up with the pack, make his move on the final round, best not to be the lead car—somehow the lead always ended up in fourth place. Finally, it was time. Only one more car in front of him. The yellow flag was flying, meaning to use caution; the ice was probably more slippery than usual. He slammed the gas pedal and muscled his way to the lead. The other driver saw it coming and tried to block his way, but his wheels slipped on the ice and his car slammed against Wes's, sending both of them against the wall. Wes's car scraped the ice on its right wheels, and flipped up once, twice, and he hit his head on the roof and fell back to his seat with a crash. The other car was a fireball at the end of the lane, but since his own car was still running, Wes gunned the engine and the car reared up and shot across the finish line.

The race was over. The engine finally died, sputtering, the wheels spinning on ice, but it was all right.

He'd survived.

Wes slid out through the window, his cheeks red, his heart pumping. That was close. Too close. For a moment there he hadn't thought he'd make it.

"Nice work. See you tomorrow?"

Wes shook his head as he counted the hard-won watts in his hand, barely enough to buy the boys dinner. He couldn't do this again. He would have to think of another way to feed his crew. His friend Carlos at the Loss owed him one. After all, Wes had refused to torch the place earlier in the year, and it wasn't his fault their rivals had found someone else to take the job. Maybe it was time to try his luck at the casino tables again.

In Vegas, there was always another game.

FIVE

"Hey, Manny," Nat called, motioning to her pit boss.

"Yeah?" Manny counted out a roll of five hundred watts as he approached. There was the New Vegas that was run by the real-estate overlords and their ambiguous military connections, and then there was the Vegas that was still Vegas—run by the mob, by the gangsters, by people like Manny, who kept the place packed, the patrons happy, the drinks potent.

"You know anyone with a connection to a ship?" she whispered. "A runner?"

Manny shook his head and wet his finger with his tongue, continuing to count the money. "Why you wanna leave New Veg? You just got here. This is the best place around," he said, motioning to the busy casino. "Where else is there?"

The man had a point. After the world ended, in a rush to dominate the earth's remaining resources, the country had expanded its borders, colonizing and renaming regions as it did so. Africa became New Rhodes, Australia divided into Upper Pangaea and New Crete, South America—a wasteland called simply Nuevo Residuos. There were a few independent sectors left, like the Xian Empire, of course, the only country that had the foresight to preserve its agricultural industry by spearheading the indoor-farming movement before the ice came. But what was left of the rest of the world— swaths of Russia and most of Europe—was overrun by pirates and led by madmen.

Visas were more expensive than a working space heater, more costly than clean water. Acquiring one was near impossible, not to mention the endless blizzards that made travel precarious and expensive.

Nat shrugged. "C'mon, Manny, you know everyone in this snow globe." She had asked around, but her dealer friends laughed in her face. They all did, from the valets from Nuevo Cabo, to the waitresses from Mesa Sol, to the topless dancers from nearby Henderson. There was no way. They all told her to forget about it, those who tried to jump the borders were crazy, and you never saw them again. The only thing the Vegas hands knew was that jumpers were unlucky, and unlucky had no place in the casinos.

The pit boss tucked the roll into his back pocket, sucked his teeth, and worked a toothpick through his molars. "No, baby. Not gonna happen, don't want to see you shot in the head, floating in that black water. There's pirates—scavengers—out there, too, don't you know?

Taking slaves, selling 'em to the outlaw territories." He shook his head. "Besides, remember what happened to Joe? Bounty hunters find out you're itching to jump, they'll turn you in for the reward for snitching." That was what everyone believed—that Joe had been turned in for blood money. Jumper watt, someone had snitched. "Besides, you need mucho credit to pay a runner."

She sighed, counting her small stack. Tips had been steady all evening. She had almost twenty credits, not enough for a proper heat suit, but maybe a pair of those seal-fur gloves or a cup of real chicken soup. She dealt the next hand. All day she'd had a good, steady stream of players, a group celebrating a bachelor party, a few pros who made their living from the tables.

"Slow night?" a voice asked.

Nat looked up to see a guy standing across from her. Tall, with caramel-colored hair and honey-brown eyes. He smiled and she thought she recognized him from somewhere. Her breath caught at the sight of his handsome face, with his kind eyes and somewhat familiar mien. She swore she knew him but couldn't remember where from. He was dressed in layers, and she noted the worn edges of his sleeves, and the burns on his jeans that could only have come from driving the blood tracks. She didn't think she knew any of the death-wish boys, but she could be wrong. Whoever he was, she sensed mischief from the way he hovered around the edges of her table.

"Can I deal you in?" she asked in her crisp dealer tone.

"If not, you'll have to step back. Casino rules, sorry."

"Maybe. What's the ante?" he drawled, even though the neon sign was blinking on the table. Fifty heat credits to play.

She pointed at it with a frown.

"That all?" he asked, all smooth and suave. "Maybe I'll stay, make sure these clowns here don't give you a hard time." He smiled as he motioned to the players seated around her table.

"I can take care of myself, thanks," Nat said coolly. She knew the type. She had no patience for pretty boys. He probably broke a dozen hearts just by walking across the casino floor. If he thought she would be one of them, he was wrong.

"I'm sure you can," he said, shooting her a sideways grin. "What time do you get out of here? What say you and I..."

"My shift ends at midnight," she said, cutting him off. "You got enough to buy me a glass of water, I'll meet you at the bar."

"Water. A purist." He winked. "My kind of girl. Done."

She laughed. There was no way he could afford a glass of water. He couldn't even afford a proper winter coat. Clean water was precious but synthetics were cheap and sanitary, so like most solid citizens, her only choice was to drink Nutri, a supposedly vitamin-and-nutrient-rich, sweet-tasting concoction that was spiked with faint traces of mood stabilizers, just the thing to keep the population obedient. The chemicals gave her a headache, and more than anything, she just wanted a taste of pure, clear water. Once a week she saved up enough for a glass, savoring every drop.

"Hey, man, either you're in or you're out. Holding up the game here," a young day-tripper snarled, interrupting. He was a flashy kind, the type of player who tried to flirt with the dealer or when that didn't work, complained loudly whenever someone made a move he didn't approve of—"That was my ace!" or "You're messing up the shuffle."

"Relax, relax," the new boy said, but he didn't take a step back.

"Sir, I'm really going to have to ask you to move," she told him, as she laid down her hand. Eighteen. She made to collect the players' chips.

"Twenty-one! Woot!" crowed the annoying player.

Nat stared at his cards. She could have sworn he'd held a ten and a six, but now his six of spades was an ace of clubs. How did that happen? Was he a lockhead? A hidden mage? Had he figured out a way to cheat the iron detectors as she had? She sucked in her breath as she calculated his bet, which meant a payout of— She shook her head. *No way. No one was that lucky. The house always wins.*

"What are you waiting for, girly? Pay out!" He slapped the table and the chips wobbled on the felt.

He was a cheat, she was sure of it, even as she began to count out four platinum chips on the green felt, and she hesitated before pushing them his way.

"I'm sorry, I'm going to have to ask for a rollback," she said, meaning she'd have to ask security to check the cameras, make sure nothing funny had happened. But when she looked around, Manny and the other supervisors were nowhere to be found. What was going on?

"Pay out, or else," the kid said in a low, menacing voice.

Now Nat saw that he was holding a gun underneath his jacket, and it was pointed right at her.

Before she could protest, there was a swift and sudden movement, as the handsome boy slammed the guy facedown on the table and pinned his arms behind his back, effectively disarming him in one go.

Nat watched with grudging admiration as he reached into the thief's pocket. "Beretta. Old-school, good taste," he said, laying the gun on the felt. He emptied the other one and a flurry of aces fell to the carpet. Nat understood now. The kid had used her interest in the good-looking boy to switch the cards and win the chips.

The chips…

Four platinum ones.

Equal to twenty thousand heat credits. Enough to pay a runner, enough to hire a ship. Enough to get her out of here…

She looked up and caught her newfound hero's eye

and they stared at each other for a heartbeat.

When she looked down at the table again, the chips were gone.

The handsome boy blinked, confused.

"Here," Nat said, slipping a few plastic chips into his hand. She thought of those warm gloves she'd been saving up for. "For your trouble."

"Save it for that glass of water," he said, giving her chips back and walking toward the exit.

SIX

Wes moved quickly through the casino, annoyed with himself. The platinum chips were *right there*. Four of them, equal to twenty thousand watts, his for the taking. So why didn't he have them?

It had gone down perfectly at first. He had hooked the dealer with his line, saw how she lit up when he smiled, and Daran had executed the play to the letter with that shady ace. Caused a commotion, and in the process allowed Wes ample time to take four of those platinum chips while the dealer's attention was focused elsewhere.

Except Wes hadn't taken them and he was going back to the rendezvous empty-handed. He frowned as he scissored his way through the slow-moving crowd on the way to Mark Antony's. All he'd had to do was slip those fancy chips into his pocket and they would have eaten like kings tonight. But he had hesitated, and then they were gone, vanished in the blink of an eye.

The walkway was full of hustlers peddling their wares, handing out cards and flyers, their good-time gals casting sultry looks at anyone who came by.

"What's wrong, handsome? I can make you feel better," the nearest one promised. "Or you can do the same for me…"

Wes found his crew assembled at the base of the Bacchus statue at the Forum Shops-in-the-Sky. They looked up at him eagerly. Daran wasn't there yet, but he would be okay. Carlos would take care of him.

"How'd it go, boss?" Shakes asked. The scruffy, goateed beanpole of a soldier was his right-hand man, and had been with Wes since their grunt days. They were like brothers. Shakes was solid, a rock, despite his name. He was a veteran like Wes, with a survivor's stoic determination. Shakes had been more than displeased the other night to hear that Wes had been back at the tracks. *I didn't save your butt in Santonio just so you could throw your life away as a death jockey*. He looked at Wes hopefully, but Wes shook his head.

"What happened?" Farouk whined. He was the youngest of the crew, all nose and elbows, a scrawny, twitchy kid with a bottomless appetite.

Wes was about to explain when Daran and Zedric came running up the walkway. The brothers were dressed identically, in the same tan windbreaker, the same dark slacks, the same shaggy dark hair and piercing black eyes. If Daran had been recognized by security, Zedric would have stepped in to play the part of the thief.

Unlike Shakes, the rest of the team were new hires.

Daran and Zedric Slaine and Farouk Jones. Farouk was thirteen going on thirty, a blabbermouth—he never stopped talking even when he didn't have the slightest idea what he was talking about—he was an expert on every topic with no experience to back it up. Dar and Zed were only a year apart, but Daran treated his younger brother like a kid. They'd been booted from the army before they could be eligible for full post-service benefits, which was routine military policy these days. Cut 'em loose before they get too expensive. Typical soldiers, they were brash, potty-mouthed, and hotheaded, but they were also dead shots who were handy in a firefight.

"How much?" Daran asked. "How'd we do?"

"Came up snake eyes, sorry," Wes told him.

Daran cursed long and creatively. He sneered at Wes. "You holding out on us?"

"I swear to god—I got nothing," Wes said, returning his gun.

Daran yanked it back furiously. "What d'you mean you don't have it? I had that golden. It was all there! All you had to do was reach out and take those chips!"

Wes looked around, people were beginning to notice, and while the sky patrols were giving them a wide berth, they would be moving in soon if the boys continued to make too much noise. "Keep your voices down. They were on to me. I couldn't blow Carlos's cover."

"No way! They knew nothing! I'm not buying it!"

Daran protested. "And Carlos is expecting his two thousand hot."

"Let me take care of Carlos."

"So there's nothing to eat?" Farouk asked again. "Nothing?"

"Not unless you like glop," Zedric intoned darkly, glaring at Wes. "I'm not going back to that food line— it's humiliating."

Shakes nodded. He didn't accuse, he didn't complain. He clapped Wes on the shoulder. "You can do this in your sleep. We've run that play a hundred times. What happened?"

Wes sighed. "I told you, I felt the eyes on us. I spooked."

He didn't want to tell them the truth, didn't even want to admit it to himself.

What *had* happened?

The blackjack dealer was beautiful, with long dark hair and luminous, fair skin. She had none of that bronzed hardness that was so popular now among the New Veg snow bunnies, with their dark-orange tans and bleached hair, a desperate attempt to look as if one could afford to travel to the enclosed cities where an artificial sun provided heat and light.

But it wasn't that she was pretty. It was that she was on to him.

Right at the moment, right when his hand was hovering over the platinum chips to take them away, she had caught his eye and stopped him with a look that said, *Don't even think about it*.

She hadn't been fooled by his theatrical heroics or distracted by his flirtatious banter. Not for a second. She *knew* what they were doing. What *he* was doing. That he was a fraud, and no hero.

Wes had backed off, startled. The moment was lost, and when he looked down the chips had disappeared. She must have put them back on the casino stack. It was cute how she tried to tip him, too, as if a few heat credits could make up for his loss.

"Come on," Daran said to his brother. "Let's go see if we can do better with the play at the Apple," he said. "I'll play the hero this time, get it done *right*," he said to Wes.

"Can I come?" Farouk asked.

"Sure—you can be lookout," Daran said. "Shakes—you in? We might need you for muscle; they don't know us as well at the Apple."

Shakes looked at Wes and sighed. "Nah, I'll catch up with you guys later."

"Suit yourself," Daran said.

"You're going to lose them if you can't feed them," Shakes said when the boys had left. "Then what? Without a crew we can't run any type of play."

Wes nodded. They would have to leave the city, or join up again, something. He hoped it wouldn't come to that. Then he wouldn't have the luxury of turning down his assignments.

"Something will come up," Wes said. "Want to try our luck at the lines?" It was humbling, but they had to eat.

"Yeah—why not," Shakes grumped. They walked through the casino, past the food courts, a myriad of treats available but not to the likes of them. Noodle shops, crepe stands, chic cafés serving coffees and tea sandwiches, five-star gourmet restaurants where reservations had to be booked months in advance. There were floor-to-ceiling tanks, brimming with exotic fish domestically farmed in saltwater pools—pick one and they'd slice it into sashimi while you waited.

Another restaurant boasted delicacies beyond imagination. Quail, pheasant, wild boar, everything organic, grass-fed, free-range. (*Where did they range?* Wes wondered. He'd heard that the heated enclosures were vast, but how vast could they be?) The tropical fruit display was the hardest to ignore. The colors alone made him stop and stare. He knew the bright reds and yellows were genetically modified for maximum saturation, but it was still a gorgeous sight. The fruit was stored under heavy glass, like diamonds of old, but the shops always left out a few trays to tease passersby with their flowery scent. They passed a chocolate shop selling handmade artisanal candy that cost more than the two of them put together (hired guns had nothing on small-batch truffles).

The food line was about to close, but they made it there in time. As they sat down with their bowls of cheap gruel, Shakes's pocket began to vibrate. He picked up his phone. "Valez," he answered. "Uh-huh? Yeah? Okay, I'll tell him." He flipped it closed.

"What was that all about?" Wes asked, slurping from his spoon and trying not to retch.

Shakes grinned. "Looks like we got us a job. Some chick's looking to hire a runner and they hear she's got credits to burn."

SEVEN

Nat stared at the four platinum chips in her locker. She tried to make them disappear and reappear in her pocket as she had the day before, when she'd nicked them from her table. Casino security was convinced the thief had somehow made off with them, although they didn't know how. There was nothing on the tapes. She focused on the chips, but nothing happened. They stayed on the metal shelf, unmoving. It was a shame that a mages' mark wasn't of much use to anyone, especially the marked themselves. While it had come in handy during a few tough situations, Nat had no idea how to use her power or how to control it; like the voice in her head, it came and went without warning, and if she tried to summon it directly, it was even more elusive. She could feel the monster inside her, feel its anger, impatience, and power; but it came and went like the wind and could abandon her at any moment. Days like today she almost agreed with the zealots on the nets. That the mark was a curse.

She had put feelers out for a runner yesterday, letting

people know that she could pay, that she had gotten lucky on a bet, but so far no one had bitten. She put the chips back in her pocket, feeling reassured by their weight next to the small blue stone. If she played her cards right, together they were her ticket out of the city.

At her table her predecessor, Angela, was in the middle of performing the ending ritual—clapping her hands and turning empty palms toward the ceiling to indicate to surveillance that her shift was over.

"You heard about the new ret scans?" Angela asked. She gathered her things and let Nat slide behind the table. "You know, to root out lockhead lenses?"

"Yeah," Nat said.

"Good thing, can't have any of that filth around," Angie sniffed. "You know what they're calling them now? Rotheads. Get it?"

"Right," Nat said, averting her eyes. She'd heard the rumors but she didn't believe them—had never seen any proof to the stories—and she should know. Just more lies and propaganda, just another way to keep the public fearful and submissive.

She dealt the cards but her players left one by one until there was only one guy at her table. It was Thursday, the day before payday, when everyone was poor. Tomorrow the casino would be filled with crowds angling to cash in their paychecks, some of them tossing down their stubs right on the gaming tables. Occasionally someone got lucky, betting it all on some hunch, riding the streak, beating the house at every turn. But that was like having your number come up for a visa to Xian. It hardly ever happened, and when it did, security was on the table so quickly your luck was gone before you knew it.

Nat shuffled the deck, letting the cards make a satisfying rippling sound as they moved from one hand to the other like an accordion, before dealing the next round.

The remaining player at her table was a sloe-eyed boy with a wisp of a beard on his chin, sporting scary-looking tats on his brown arms. A veteran for sure, a bruiser, a bodyguard on his day off, Nat thought. Then the boy smiled, and Nat was struck by how suddenly young he looked, how innocent, even with a malevolent hissing snake on his forearm.

She motioned for him to cut the cards.

The dark-haired boy squinted at her name tag as he did so. "Hi, Nat. I'm Vincent Valez. But everyone calls me Shakes. Oh and I forgot to give you this earlier." He handed over a worn-out food provision card, his fingers trembling a little, a telltale sign of frostblight. The human body wasn't meant to live in subzero weather. Most people ended up with a few tremors, while the unluckiest ones lost their eyesight.

"You know we're not supposed to take these anymore," she said as she swiped the card through a reader. Everyone in the country was given a Fo-Pro card, which entitled the bearer to the necessary sustenance—powdered soy milk, protein squares, the occasional sugar substitute—the government's one concession to public welfare, one step above the charity food lines. The cards weren't supposed to be valid anywhere but the Market Stations, but in New Vegas, anything could be traded for casino chips.

"But I'll make an exception," she told him, as his visible disability was hard to ignore.

A few more players took seats at her table and a waitress in a skimpy dress sailed by. "Cocktails?" she sang in a breathy voice.

While the rest of the table placed their order, Nat dealt the next hand, the cards flying off the deck to each spot on their own. She looked around, relieved no one had noticed, and wondered how long it would take them to realize she had no business working in a casino.

Somehow, the ace landed on Shakes's place, and she watched as he made a killing.

"Thanks." He winked.

"For what?" She shrugged. If only she could do that all the time.

Shakes leaned over, a little too closely.

Nat regarded him warily, worried that he read too much into his earlier win.

"Heard you're looking for transport. You serious about getting out?" he asked.

She looked around, then nodded imperceptibly. "Ryan Wesson?"

Ryan Wesson. It was the one name that had come up again and again when she'd asked if anyone knew a runner. *Well, if anyone can get you out of here, it's Wes. Wes has got the fastest ship in the Pacific. He'll get you where you need to go.*

Shakes took a sip from his mug. "Not by a long shot," he said, grinning. "But I do speak for him."

"Looking for Wesson?" asked a veteran at the table who had been eavesdropping on their conversation.

Nat nodded.

The toothless boy laughed a bitter laugh. "You know where you can find him, miss? Hell. After Santonio, that's where he should be."

"Hey, man, you don't know what you're talking about," Shakes retorted, his face turning red. "You weren't there, you don't know what went down."

Nat didn't have time for arguments. In a few minutes, Manny would move her to the next table as Shakes had won big on his next hand as well. She had to ask now before she got pulled out of there. Who knew if she would ever get another chance?

Waiting until the eavesdropper turned to the waitress to order a drink, Nat leaned in and whispered, "Look, I don't care what happened in Texas, I hear he's the only one who can get me past the fence and into the water." She pushed his winnings toward him. "So will he do it? I need to leave as soon as possible."

Shakes waved off the chips, gesturing instead for more

points on his Fo-Pro card. "It depends. How lucky have you been lately?"

EIGHT

"That her?" Wes asked, peering through night-vision 'ocs. The green screen on the binoculars showed a slim, dark-haired girl walking down the street. She wore a long dark coat and a wool cap pulled low on her forehead and a scarf that covered most of her face. He handed the glasses to Shakes, who stood next to him on the balcony.

"Yeah, that's her." Shakes nodded.

Wes frowned. Well, what did you know, it was the blackjack dealer from the Loss—the same one who had thrown him off his game, the reason his team had lost faith in him. "You think she's for real?"

"Pretty sure. Couldn't have been easy, letting me win with all those cameras around. Not really sure how she managed it in the first place."

"Maybe she was setting you up," Farouk called from inside the small apartment. The kid was always butting in where he wasn't invited.

"And maybe you talk too much," Shakes grumbled. "She's the reason you didn't eat goop tonight, you know."

Farouk put his feet up on the shabby couch. "So, she let you win a few credits, so what. So we got steak for dinner."

"Yeah, we don't owe her nothing," Daran agreed, taking the binoculars for a look. But he didn't seem to recognize her from the other night.

Farouk let out a large burp and Shakes grimaced. "She can pay, and god knows we need the work." He'd outlined her proposal to the team earlier: She needed a military escort, protection through Garbage Country, passage out to the sea as far as New Crete. She would pay them half now and the rest once they arrived at their destination.

"She's not marked, is she?" Zedric asked. "You know we don't mess with ice trash."

"What did they ever do to you, man?" Wes asked, annoyed.

Zedric shrugged. "They breathe. It's unnatural what they can do...they have no place in this world, and you've heard what they say happens to them..." He shivered and looked away.

"Relax, her eyes are gray," Shakes explained.

Zedric sneered. "Rets can be faked."

"Not easily," Shakes argued. "I'm telling you, she's legit."

"Why New Crete?" Wes wanted to know. "Nothing there but penguins and polar bears."

"You know why," Daran said. "Probably another

delusional pilgrim looking for the Blue, but she just won't admit it."

Wes sighed. He knew Daran had guessed correctly. There was no reason to go halfway around the world except in search of paradise. There's nothing out there, he wanted to tell her, and looking for something that didn't exist was a waste of time and heat credits.

Maybe he could sell her on the tent cities in Garbage Country instead. Try to talk her out of risking the black waters.

He thought of the last girl who'd asked for his help to the Blue. Juliet had also wanted out, but he'd turned her down. He wondered what happened to her; rumor had it she died during the bombing at the Loss. Jules did like her cards. He didn't want to think about what that meant, if she was truly gone. But what else was new. Everyone he loved was dead or lost. Mom. Dad. Eliza.

"We don't need this job, man. Remember there are *things* out there in the Pile. We barely made it out last time, and the water's even worse." Daran flexed his muscles, and the scars on his hands turned pink at the effort, souvenirs from the region's insurrections.

Wes agreed with him. He knew what was out there. And even if they made it through Garbage Country, the corsair ships would be circling the toxic oceans, ready for fresh meat, fresh cargo for the slave holds. It was getting harder and harder to evade them.

"What's your gut say?" Wes asked Shakes again. He

trusted Shakes with his life. They'd been through a lot together since they were rooks, especially that last deployment when they were sent down to what the government called a "routine police action" and what everyone else called the Second Civil War. Texas had been the last holdout to sign the new constitution and was punished for its insurrection. What was left of the state that wasn't covered in ice was covered in blood, its militia utterly decimated during the final battle at Santonio.

"She said she has the credits. I believe her," Shakes said.

They were in a standard-issue apartment, in one of the new developments off the Strip. Casino dorm. Much nicer than that hovel where they bunked. Wes looked west, where the shining lights of the casinos glowed in the gray sky. In a few minutes, as it did every night, *Kaboom!* would play on the main stage at the Acropolis, reenacting the huge blast that had torn a crater-size hole in the Loss the other week. "Excitainment" it was called.

Wes checked his watch and looked through the binoculars at the girl again. She'd pulled off her scarf, and he could see her face clearly now.

"How much did she say?"

"Told you—twenty thousand watts—half now, half when it's done," replied Shakes.

Twenty thousand watts. A king's ransom for safe passage through the Pacific. How could a lowly blackjack dealer have enough credit in her account to offer them a payday so big they wouldn't have to work the rest of the year?

Twenty thousand watts.

Wes inhaled sharply, remembering those glittering five-thousand-credit chips on the table.

There had been exactly four of them on the stack.

He hadn't swiped them, but somehow they had disappeared. Carlos told him that table had come up short exactly that amount, so where was his cut? Wes had told the security chief he had no idea what he was talking about, if he had it, he'd give it, and of course, Carlos hadn't believed him. Wes had been puzzled at first, but as the week wore on it became clear that Carlos was serious, that his old friend wouldn't cover for him. The credits were gone and he expected Wes to cough them up, favor or no. Wes would have to find a way to pay him off soon, or get out of the city if he knew what was good for him.

Wes hadn't been sure before, hadn't believed she had the audacity to pull it off, but now it was obvious he had underestimated the pretty dealer.

Nat hadn't returned those chips to the casino after all—she'd *taken* them. Somehow, she'd intuited that the blame wouldn't fall on her. Why not let him take the heat for it; what did she care? He was nothing to her.

Wes was impressed. He'd thought he was running a game, but he had been outplayed.

Natasha Kestal. Blackjack dealer. Pilgrim. Thief.

NINE

Wes was not one to take a job unprepared, and he'd had Farouk check out Nat, not that there was much to find. No school records, no military ones either; she hadn't been recruited for officer training and she hadn't volunteered. A civilian. With no record, no online profile. As far as they could tell, she'd only arrived in New Vegas a few weeks ago.

Those credits she was offering as payment were rightfully his, Wes thought, but now she was making him work for them. He had to hand it to her—that took style.

She'd let Shakes win a few big hands as an apology, and while it would be enough to feed them for a few more days, after that, they would be hungry again. Their Fo-Pro card was fake, and it would be deactivated soon, just like the others they'd forged. They weren't eligible for real ones, not with their records. Since he'd rejected Bradley and forsaken the death races, they were living on fumes.

"What's the holdup? We already agreed, we'll take the

bounty, that's a meal ticket for sure. And when we turn her in, if she's got the chips on her, we'll take them, too, along with whatever's left in her apartment," Daran argued. The military paid a reward of five hundred credits for each potential fence-hopper, and the plan was to turn her in so they could collect, as well as rob her in the process. "Pilgrims talk a big game; we've been taken for a ride before by people who can't pay."

Wes had to admit Daran was right, that was what they had agreed. It was even Wes's idea to turn her in, but that was before he had recognized her through the binoculars.

Down on the sidewalk, Nat crossed the street and disappeared from sight.

Wes studied the glittering landscape of New Vegas, the casinos, old, new, destroyed, and refurbished. Thank god for the Hoover Dam. The fossil fuels left were only available to the military or to those who stole from or bartered with the military, but hydroelectricity let Vegas pay its electric bill.

Wes had been an errand boy for several bookies before he was ten. He understood New Vegas was a cockroach; it would endure through greed and lust. It had shrugged its sequined shoulder at the Big Freeze. Wes respected the city that had shaped him into a survivor.

He had to make a decision. *Kaboom!* was about to climax with a massive explosion, and the noise would be loud enough to drown out their assault. Wes looked down at the floor that was rigged with bombs, enough to create a hole in the floor and drop them through the ceiling below, where they could snatch her, haul her in for the reward, and take whatever she had on her. It was getting harder and harder to disappear someone these days; the city had cameras on every corner, every bridge; otherwise he'd have just taken her off the street.

The team looked at him for orders. He had to decide.

Farouk knelt by the complicated mess of red and green wires. It would be easy enough to patch up the hole and leave no trace of their operation. When they were done, she'd be just another missing person, a flyer on the wall of a bus stop, a photo on the back of a Nutri carton. And they would be five hundred credits richer, more if they believed Shakes.

"'Rouk?" Wes asked.

"Say the word and we can blow the joint and be inside in fifteen seconds."

"Think she knows we're right above her?" Wes asked. Nat had crossed the street to enter the same building they were in; she lived in the apartment unit located directly below them.

Shakes grunted and spoke in a low tone so only Wes could hear him. "Don't take the blood money. Snitching on border jumpers is for cowards. We're no thieves. C'mon, boss, let's do the job. Think of what we could get with twenty thousand watts. A warm bath, and not just at the hostel either, but at a real hotel. The Bellagio even. The Sweet Suite."

"It's too risky," Wes argued. "We can't all die because she wants out." It wasn't just about the credits. He couldn't put their lives on the line. He knew what awaited them in the black waters, and he had no desire to see if Bradley had found someone else to do that job. If he took her out there, they would be targets, vulnerable to scavengers and opportunists, if they even made it that far, if the food didn't run out…"She seems like a nice kid, but…" He understood Shakes's desire to help out, he really did, but the journey was too uncertain, no matter how badly they needed the watts. "Farouk, on my count—"

"Wait! Boss, hold on, hold on, hear me out!" Shakes protested.

Farouk looked up at Wes questioningly. Wes waved off the assault for now. "What is it?"

"I heard she might have the map," Shakes whispered urgently.

Wes stared hard at Shakes. "And you're just telling me this *now*?"

His friend looked chagrined. "I know it sounds crazy, so I didn't want to mention it earlier, but…" He looked around to make sure the rest of the team couldn't hear him.

"Did she show it to you?" Wes asked. "Was it like some kind of stone or something? An opal or an emerald?"

"No. She didn't even mention it. I was talking to Manny the other day, and he asked me if I knew what the

71

police were looking for in Old Joe's place when they took him. Seemed real important since they tore the place apart. Whatever it was, Manny thinks maybe she has it. He saw Joe hand her something at the casino, right before he disappeared."

That got his attention. Like Shakes, Wes had heard that Josephus Chang had won Anaximander's Map in a legendary card game.

The map the whole world was looking for. *But there is no map, because there's no such thing as the Blue*, Wes thought. It was wishful thinking on everyone's part. Escape to another world. Anaximander's Map was the biggest scam in New Vegas if Wes had ever heard of one.

But Joe had insisted the map was real. The old shark was one of the best poker players in Vegas, and supposedly he'd won it from a guy who had given him a bushel of apples as proof. The genetic code for the fruit had been lost for years; there were no more apples since the Big Freeze. Wes always wondered why Joe had stuck around, why he didn't just up and leave immediately if he had it in his possession.

So they'd gotten to Old Joe but hadn't been able to retrieve the treasure he'd held. Now, that was something to think about. If Nat had it, she was worth much more than mere bounty money.

"How much do you think we'd get for it?" Shakes asked.

"Who knows," said Wes.

"What do they want it for anyway?"

"Isn't it obvious? This world is dead. If there is another world out there—with blue skies, fresh water, *food*—they're going to take it. They wouldn't even let Texas leave the union, and there's nothing there but frozen cow dung."

"Let's take the map," Shakes said. "Could solve all our problems. Keep the crew happy, keep the military off our backs."

"I thought we weren't thieves," Wes said with a crafty smile.

Shakes returned it with one of his own.

"So we play the long game," said Wes, nodding. He saw the truth in it. If he took the map, handed it to Bradley, they would have work, credits; he'd be able to run an even bigger crew, maybe set themselves up as a private security force, have a real future in Vegas. Enough begging for scraps, enough humiliation, enough of the food lines forever.

But he wasn't a thief. If he took the map, and if the Blue was real…it was Santonio all over again.

Maybe it didn't matter. Maybe he was damned either way already.

And even if this blackjack dealer did have the map, Wes didn't think she would simply hand it over. She was too smart for that…

The team looked to their leader.

Wes clasped his hands. Map or not, she was still asking

a lot of his men. When they joined his team, he'd promised to keep them alive as best as he could. "All right. Let's put it to a vote. We get in and take her out, collect the bounty, or we do what she wants, do the work, and get paid."

"Heard they've upped it to eight hundred a head for a jumper these days," Daran sniffed.

Zedric nodded. That made two votes for bounty.

"How d'you plan on getting across the ocean anyway?" Daran asked.

"I'll figure it out when we get there." Wes shrugged. He'd never been one to plan ahead. "Shakes?"

"You know what I think."

"Two for blood, one for life. 'Rouk?" Wes asked.

"Screw it. I wanna see the black water, why not." Farouk shrugged.

Kaboom! This was it. Sparks flew from the Acropolis stage. The sound was deafening; even the air vibrated from the force of the explosion.

"Your orders, sir," Farouk yelled.

"We do the deal," he said finally. "We take her where she wants to go and we all come back rich and alive." When it came down to it, Shakes was right, trading her in for bounty money was a coward's move. The trip would be dangerous, sure, but in the end, they needed to work, and she had the credits. And if she had the map…well…he would keep his cards close to the vest for now.

He stared Daran in the eye. "You in? Get out now if you're not."

Daran held his gaze, then looked away, shrugging.

Wes nodded. Daran would follow orders like a soldier. Wes had taken the brothers on his team when no one else would—he'd heard of their reputations as burnouts but he thought he could rehabilitate them into better stuff— and so far, as surly as they were, they hadn't failed him.

The team exhaled. Shakes smiled. Farouk began dismantling the bombs.

Wes took a comb from his back pocket and smoothed his hair. "Let's go knock on her door."

TEN

Nat didn't know what to make of Ryan Wesson—whether she wanted to slap him or kiss him. Slap him, definitely. He looked so smug, standing at her doorway, with his hair slicked back and his collar turned up, a gun belt strapped low on his hips, his beat-up vest shrugged off his shoulders like some kind of snow cowboy, grinning as if he'd won the fireball lottery.

She'd just left the casino that evening, only a few hours after closing the deal with Shakes, and while she had impressed upon him her need to leave immediately, she was still surprised at how quickly Wes had appeared.

"Hey there, remember me?" His voice was low and pleasantly hoarse, *sexy*, she thought, *just like all the rest of him*. Nat shoved the thought out of her mind. *He's a runner and a con man*, she reminded herself. *A liar.*

"How could I forget?" she asked.

"Ryan Wesson," he said, offering a hand.

"Like the gun or the cooking oil?"

His grin broadened. "What about you, Nat? Like

the insect or the princess?"

"Clever," she said. "Neither."

"Right. Just call me Wes, okay by you?"

"Fair enough." Nat nodded, and shook his hand.

"I believe you have something of mine," he said. "Four platinum chips, perhaps?"

"I have no idea what you're talking about," she retorted. Too bad for him. She'd taken her chance when Wes didn't.

Sucker.

"You're cute when you're lying." He smiled. "But since you have them and I don't, I guess the only way to get them back is to take you where you want to go. So hop to it, peaches."

"I'm ready," she said, showing him her packed bag.

He tried to hide his surprise. "Once we drop you off at New Crete, I'm taking my boys back to Vegas. You're on your own, no matter what we find there. We're not sticking around after that. Got it?"

"Who says I want you to stick around," she said tartly.

His dark eyes sparkled. "Careful, you might change your mind about that once you get to know me."

"Doubt it," she said, even as her cheeks flushed a little.

"Gotta say, you don't look like someone who believes in that hoodoo stuff about some door to nirvana in the ocean," he told her.

"Excuse me?"

"Come on, New Crete? You're looking for the Blue,

just like all the true believers."

"I'll keep my reasons to myself, won't I? I'm paying for passage, not therapy."

"All right, all right," he said. "No questions asked, that's our motto. Can't help but be a little curious is all. You got the deposit?"

Half the fee. Right. She handed him two of the platinum chips.

He smiled. "Let's go. Breaking curfew's not going to be easy."

She followed him out to an LTV parked in the alley behind her building. The truck was painted with a swirl of white arctic camouflage, and even its wheels were cut from a thick white rubber that rendered it almost invisible. It was a modified Hummer, with three rows of seats and a cargo hold in the back.

He opened the door and hustled her inside.

In the row behind her were a few guys dressed in thermals and gray-and-white snow camos outfitted with an impressive array of weapons. She wasn't surprised to find the guy who'd drawn a gun on her the other day was part of the team.

"You've met Daran," Wes said. "That's his brother, Zedric, and that's Farouk. Guys, this is Nat, our new client."

"Well, hello again," Daran said, as he shook her hand just a little too long. "Sorry about the thing at the Loss. All in a day's work, right?"

She regarded him coolly. "Where's Shakes?" she asked, looking for the boy with the friendly smile.

"Hey, Nat," Shakes said, turning around from the driver's seat.

She smiled, seemingly relieved Shakes was here, and Wes felt a hint of jealousy at that.

She was even prettier than he remembered, the kind of girl who could get anyone to do anything for her, he thought. A mouth on her, too, and she sure hadn't blinked when he accused her of stealing those chips. Still, he'd been sure she would fold; her room was warm and cozy. No palace, but a place to call home. Why not use those credits for something else? He wanted to tell her not to waste it on him and an impossible dream of freedom. There was nothing out in the ocean but trash and trouble.

She seemed like a cool chick. Not that he was looking for anything in that direction right now, even with that bit of harmless flirting earlier. Just wanted to see if he could charm her was all, to get on her good side if he was going to figure out if she had the map or not. He had no need for any kind of attachment, especially after the thing with Jules ended so badly.

He helped her into the backseat and Shakes gave her a thumbs-up from the wheel, then the truck sped off into the darkness, spitting sparks into the air as they brushed icy concrete on both sides.

"How does he know where he's going?" Nat yelled,

struggling to fasten her seat belt as the LTV careened through the empty streets.

Wes tapped the infrared goggles on Shakes's helmet. "Here, have a look," he said, throwing his own pair her way so she could see.

She put them on. The truck was barreling through a back road that ran parallel to the Strip, where the redevelopment efforts had carved a trench in the ice.

"What about the Willies?" she asked. It was after curfew, when the only vehicles allowed in the streets were the Willie Winkie patrols or those with the right after-hours licenses, and from her tone, it was clear she didn't think Wes had one of those.

"Let me worry about them," Wes said curtly. "Most patrols are around the eastern perimeter, and we're headed the other way."

"Boss!" Shakes yelled, as the red flare of a rocket flew overhead.

Wes cursed. He'd spoken too soon. One of the heavily armored tanks that usually lumbered around the ice desert, transporting grunts to the eastern base, just happened to be in the area. "YOU ARE IN VIOLATION OF ORDER 10123: EVERY CITIZEN MUST BE INDOORS. STOP YOUR VEHICLE AND PREPARE TO SURRENDER YOUR SECOND-LEVEL INDENTIFICATION PAPERS."

"I don't have any," she said worriedly.

"You and everyone else in here," he said. "Keep

going!" he urged Shakes.

A bullet shattered the rear window, the truck struck a wall of ice, and everyone was thrown forward.

"Gimme those!" Wes commanded, and Nat threw his goggles back to him as he barked orders at his team. "Farouk! See if you can track their signal and jam it. Slaine boys—take out their snipers! I'll take care of the behemoth." He reached for his gun even as he hoped it wouldn't come to that. Guns were antiquated weapons for a dying empire. Wes carried one because he had to, but he'd never killed anyone with it; he'd threatened many, of course, he'd waved it around, and shot drones and trucks and who knew what else, but his hands were clean, and so were his boys'. There was enough killing in the world. He turned to Nat. "Cover me—you know how to use one of these things?" he asked, motioning for her to pick up a rifle.

She shook her head, and he stared at her for a moment. Every child in the RSA was trained to shoot; "every citizen an armed citizen" was the country's unofficial motto…but there was no time to question. He called to Farouk and the boy shouldered the rifle, peered through the scope and set off a few rounds through the window. "Okay, go!" he yelled, backing down as Wes popped through the roof, rifle in hand.

Wes scanned the area, the goggles having turned the world green and black. He could see the tank coming after them a few blocks away. They were past the Strip

81

now, close to the edge of the city, not far from the border. If he could stall it, they would be home free. There had only been one rocket.

He fired and missed the first two shots. Steady, he ordered himself. Steady…

Two more bullets sailed through the cabin. One nicked Farouk's arm. "Snap out of it, boss!" the kid shrieked from the back. "Next one will be through our heads!"

"It's the sniper—take him out already!" Wes yelled back.

"He can't hide from me," Daran promised, peering through his scope for the elusive shooter.

"Over there!" Zedric yelled, pointing to the top of the nearest building. "I see him!" They let off a few rounds, but the bullets continued to whiz by their heads.

A shell exploded just aft of the LTV, rattling the vehicle and sending them spinning.

"This is some escape," Nat said, rolling her eyes. "You're going to get me to the water? You can't even get me out of the Strip."

"Hey now, a little confidence would be nice," Wes snapped. "Trying to keep us alive over here."

"Get that tank down!" Daran yelled, while Shakes fought to keep the truck upright.

"That's what I'm trying to do," Wes huffed. "Patience, everyone, patience." He wasn't planning on dying in a firefight.

Wes popped back up through the hatch and saw that

he had his first clear shot. He targeted the engine, so he could disable the vehicle without hurting any of the soldiers. He'd been in their shoes not so long ago.

But just as he was about to fire, the whole world went dark. He was blind. His finger jerked as he pulled the trigger. He missed again. He let out a string of expletives. Frostblight. He'd been ignoring it for some time now, the blurred vision, headaches, but lately it was getting harder to deny.

A bullet whizzed past his ear. A second shot blew off their truck's left-hand mirror.

"Hurry, man," Shakes said from the driver's seat, his voice calm but with an edge. His hands were gripping the wheel so hard it was vibrating.

"Let me," Farouk said, reloading his weapon.

"I got it, I got it, everyone relax," Wes said, with a slightly injured air. He lifted his gun again. The tank's sleek white hull glistened like a child's toy in the snowy air. He focused. The behemoth was an easy target; they were made that way so that their four-foot-tall wheels could grind up the snow. But there were half a dozen holes in the armor already. Typical. The white elephants looked intimidating, but they were vulnerable. Nobody knew how to fix anything anymore. The country was living off the past—all the technology dated back to the wars before the Flood. It was as if the toxic waters had washed away not only New York and California but all the knowledge of the world as well.

His hand steady and his vision clear, Wes pulled the trigger, and this time the bullet hit the target, piercing the armor and blasting the engine with a single round.

One more and the tank was dust, but the temporary blindness had dulled his reflexes, and before he could move, a fiery round hit him square in the chest. Where did that come from—?

"Sorry!" Daran yelled.

"Got him!" Zedric whooped, as his bullet shot the rifle out of the sniper's hand.

Wes's body shield held, but the pain was unbearable. The Kevlar jacket caught on fire, and he ripped it off, tossing it into the snow. A hole the size of a baseball was burnt through the fabric of his down vest. Black smoke drifted from the burn, bringing tears to his eyes.

"You'll be all right," Nat said, helping him down into his seat. "Surface wound."

He grunted.

Up front, Shakes swerved to avoid a second round of rocket fire. The convoy had arrived, more tanks, and soldiers on snowFAVs. But the fence was only a few blocks away and once they crossed, they were free. The army wouldn't risk a nighttime mission into the Trash Pile; at most they would send a seeker party in the morning, but by then Wes hoped to be well into the wastelands and impossible to track.

"Gimme a hand," Wes said, slinging an arm around

Nat's shoulder. His right arm was numb and he had to switch hands to shoot.

"But you don't have your armor," she warned.

"Doesn't matter, I need to get this done," he insisted.

Nat nodded, helped him back up, and steadied him.

They were so close that he could smell her hair, even as his head hurt and he knew he would pass out soon. He lifted the gun and peered through the sight, then jumped back, startled.

The tank's big gun was trained right at his head. He didn't have time to think, didn't have time to move; he fired, the gun an extension of his mind. The second shot destroyed enough of the engine to stop the tank. The big white heap of metal spun violently, its gunfire spraying a nearby building, rattling windows. There was a sharp cry from inside the beast, then silence.

Three more white elephants slammed into the faltering tank and the whole convoy came to a stop, just as Daran and Zedric took care of the snow bikes, sending them crashing into the ice walls.

The top of the tank opened suddenly, and its captain appeared, a boy his age, who'd wanted to get a look to see who had grounded their pursuit. He gave Wes the finger.

Wes saluted him with a smile as the LTV sped out of the city toward the fence, an invisible electric barrier that Farouk had just disabled with his handheld.

"Hit it, Shakes," Wes said, rapping on the roof of the truck. "Time to root through the trash."

PART THE SECOND

LILACS
OUT OF THE
DEAD LAND

Human society sustains itself by transforming nature into garbage.

—MASON COOLEY

ELEVEN

Nat had no idea how Wes had survived that hit. She was burning with adrenaline, fear, and excitement. His heroics were no joke, not like the show he'd conjured up at the casino. For the first time, she allowed herself to feel optimistic—maybe there was more to this cocky runner after all.

"Get someone to help you and choose wisely," Manny had advised grudgingly. "Runners will swear up and down they can take you to where you want to go, but instead most of them end up dumping their passengers or selling them to slavers. Or they're *overtaken* by slavers, which is almost the same thing. Or they give up when the food runs out. You want someone who can think on his feet, who's fast, who's brave."

She had chosen Wes, and while she still wouldn't put it past him to ditch her if a better opportunity came along—and she sure wasn't ready to trust him with the treasure she carried: the stone she wore on a chain around her neck—she was on her way now, and he had gotten her this far.

But still a long way to go, the monster in her head reminded. *Thankfully I am patient.*

Her happiness faded a little at that—to know each step led her closer to fulfilling the darkness of her dreams. For a moment, she saw the face of her former commander again. *You are not using the extent of your power*, he had told her. *You do not even try.* She wondered how much harder he would have tried to break her, if he had known what her dreams bore, if he knew about the monster in her head.

"You okay?" she asked Wes.

He gave her quick nod, but his face grimaced in pain. "It'll pass. It's just the shock. You?"

She shrugged. "How far to the fence?"

"Couple of blocks, we should be clear," he said, as the truck made its way far from the glittering lights of New Vegas and the snowy terrain became harder to navigate.

"Good."

Even though there was no physical barrier that kept the city from the borderlands, the fence was as real as the invisible electric volts that killed anyone who breached it. Nat noticed the group in the LTV hold their breath as they crossed silently into the darkness. But Farouk had done his job, and they made it through without incident.

Beyond the fence was a mountain of junk. A century of trash tossed over the border, forgotten and left to rot in the endless cold. "No wonder they call it the Trash

Pile," Nat said, a little awed by all the strange electronic equipment, rusted, burned-out cars, and mountains of plastic, cardboard, and glass.

"My family was from Cali," Wes said, peering out the window over her shoulder. "My dad said his dad's dad used to talk about it—how pretty it was, how you could go from the mountains to the desert to the beach. They'd moved after the Flood, of course, and did the March down the Ten. Vegas was the only city left standing. Family legend had it they went straight to the casinos." He leaned back and gave her a wry smile. She could see that he was still in pain, but trying to make light of it.

"What's that?" Farouk interrupted suddenly, pointing at the twinkling lights far in the darkness and what looked like distant figures moving through the frozen garbage landscape.

"Don't mind that," Wes said curtly. "There's nothing to see out there. Nothing we want to see, anyway."

Nat kept silent, staring at the moving lights, wondering how much Wes had told his crew about what they would face out here.

"How's that second fence coming along?" Wes asked.

The boy turned back to his device, working furiously. The LTV was barreling through the rocky roads and the next barrier was coming up soon. They had to disable it or they would fry.

"There's some code on it I can't figure out. It's got to

91

be one of the German ones—those are the hardest," grumbled Farouk.

"They must've changed it since the last time we did a run," Shakes said.

"German codes?" Nat asked with a frown.

"The army recycles codes from the old wars. No one can make up new ones. They were lucky to find these," said Wes.

Nat knew it was the same story for everything. The generation that had come up with the heat suits and discovered cold fusion were long gone: survivors from Before, who remembered a different time, when the world was still green and blue, and who'd marshaled their resources and knowledge to figuring out how to survive the cold. But there were very few scientists these days, and the only books that remained were the physical ones that dated back to the early twenty-first century.

"Can I try?" she asked Farouk.

He handed her the device, a small black phone with a tiny keyboard. "It's talking to an old Enigma machine, using radio signals. The fence is locked by a certain transmission, but I can't figure it out. I need to send a message to the machine that's holding the wall. But this is all it's giving me," he said, showing her the screen of numbers.

She stared at the sequence, at the pattern it made, and typed out an answer. "Try it now," she told Farouk.

He studied her work, then hit the send key. "Here

goes nothing," he muttered.

But a few minutes later, Shakes called excitedly from the driver's seat. "Fence is down!" he whooped, checking the electromagnetic sensor.

"How'd you do that?" Farouk asked.

"I just saw it." She shrugged. Numbers came easily to her. Patterns. She'd been able to break the code, and read its simple request. to open gate say hello. She'd simply typed the word "hello" in the code and the fence had opened for her.

"Good work," Wes said. "You're almost part of the team." He smiled. "Hey!" he said, noticing that Daran and Zedric had opened the food packs. "You boys better share."

Zedric threw him a foil-wrapped object and Wes caught it deftly. "Mmm. Curry pizza burroti." Wes grinned. "Want a bite?" he offered. "Best McRoti in Vegas. And looks like the boys picked up some McRamen, too."

"No, thanks." Nat shook her head. "I'm not hungry."

"I'll leave you a piece if you change your mind," he said. He offered her his chopsticks. "Pull for luck," he said.

She took one side and the sticks broke off, leaving her with the bigger half.

"You win." He grinned. He was such a Vegas boy, superstitious about everything, including the chopsticks-wishbone game. He began to unwrap his food, whistling a melody that sounded familiar.

"What is that?"

"Dunno. My mom used to sing it," he explained, and his face pinched a little.

"Listen, I know you from somewhere—don't I? I feel like we've met before," she asked him suddenly. She was certain of it, she just couldn't place him, but it would come to her soon enough. That tune he was whistling…if only she could remember, but her memory was gray like her lenses, cloudy; she could put together bits and pieces but not the whole thing, not her whole life.

"Nah, I don't gamble." He smiled, taking a big bite of his burroti.

"Only with his life," Shakes said, from the front. "Hey! What about me?" he said, holding up his hand, and Farouk tossed him his own multi-cuisine mash-up.

"I swear I've met you before, and I don't just mean from the casino the other day," she said to Wes. It was suddenly important that she remember why his face was so familiar to her. "But I guess not."

Wes regarded her thoughtfully as he ate. Nat became worried that maybe he would think she was flirting with him—even if she wasn't. Besides, she thought with a secret smile, if she was flirting with him, he would *know*. She was about to say something else when Shakes released a yelp from the front seat that startled everyone, including Nat.

"What is it?" demanded Wes.

"Drones in the sky; they sent a seeker team out," Shakes said, pulling out his scanner, which was beeping. He shook his head as he peered out the window at a small black plane circling the distant horizon.

"Where?" Wes asked, sticking his head out the window.

"Not sure. He's off the radar now."

"Fine, we'll take the back roads," Wes said. "Seekers stick to the main highway. We'll have to loop around, take us close to MacArthur, but it'll be okay. We should be able to shake them once we—" Wes never finished his sentence, as a blast of cold air hit and a cloud of silver flakes filled the cabin.

"What now!" Daran yelled, as the flakes flew up his nose. They were everywhere. A second gust of wind sent more snow pouring through the openings.

The boys yelped and Nat batted at the flakes, feeling them fall on her eyelids, her ears. "Burglar alarm," Wes said tightly. He explained the silver cloud wasn't smoke or snow. Crossing the fences had released nanos—machines no larger than a grain of dust that sensed and recorded human pheromones. Nanotechnology was old hardware, just like the fusion batteries; it was from the last global war before everything started breaking down. The military didn't know how to upgrade the system, only how to maintain it.

"They're like robo-bloodhounds," Farouk said

95

excitedly. "They catch your scent and then feed it into the defense network."

Wes cuffed him in the shoulder. "What are you so hopped up about?"

"I've never seen one before, is all," Farouk said. "A nano cloud, I mean."

Wes gestured out across the garbage-strewn landscape. "The locals call 'em pop-cans. The bombs are usually hidden inside old soda cans, and the Pile is littered with them."

"What do they do?" Farouk asked.

"They pop," Shakes said, cutting in. "You get close enough for one of them to sniff you, to make a match for one of the pheromones that just got transmitted into the system, and they blow, taking out whatever part of you is closest to it."

"We've never been in the system before," Daran complained. "I didn't sign up for this. I ain't losing an arm or a leg to a soda can."

Nat shuddered as Wes stared out at the snow-covered landscape. "Look, I wouldn't think less of you if you wanted to turn back," he said. "We snuck you out, we can sneak you back in. You can have your credits back, less a percentage for our trouble, of course."

"I'm not turning back," she said, annoyed. Was this his way of trying to scare her out of the trip? Get her to change her mind? Pop-cans didn't scare her like her nightmares did.

"You're sure about this?" he asked again, his voice gentle.

She realized then that he wasn't trying to wriggle out of the job, he was simply being decent; she felt another rush of affection for this impulsive, good-looking boy.

Nat gripped his forearm and nodded. "I'm not scared. I'd rather take my chances with what's out there than go back."

"All right then." Wes sighed. He put a hand on top of hers and held it tightly. "Nothing wrong with being scared, you know. I've seen a lot of things that have scared me on this side of the fence."

She nodded. His hand was warm on hers, and it lingered there for a while before he took it away. She wasn't sure which one of them was more embarrassed about that tender moment.

He cleared his throat and addressed his team. "I'll drive. We take the back roads. It'll be a five-day drive to the coast, but once we hit the Pacific we'll pick up speed and we're back by Christmas. Okay?" He waited for anyone to argue.

No one did, but then again, no one looked convinced either.

TWELVE

They drove straight through the night, moving deeper into the Pile, and as day came, the sky turned a lighter shade of gray. Underneath the snow and twisting through the garbage, Nat could see bursts of color—green vines, improbable tiny white flowers. She blinked and they were gone. She looked to the boys to see if anyone noticed, but half the team was asleep in the back and in front of her, Farouk was driving, while next to him Wes was studying his screen with a concerned look on his face.

He looked so serious that she felt a sudden impulse to reach over, sweep her fingers though his hair, and tell him everything was going to be okay. Feeling her gaze on him, he turned around and caught her eye. He smiled and she smiled back, and for a moment they were just an ordinary boy and girl in a car, neither runner and client, nor mercenary and thief, and Nat saw a glimpse of how normal things could be. The voice in her head was quiet, and for once in her life, she felt as if she were just like anyone else.

The truck hit a bump and the moment passed. Wes went back to what he was doing and Nat turned her attention out the window, unsure of what she was feeling. *He's handsome and brave, and any girl with a pulse would be attracted to him*, she thought, *but he's nothing to me, a flirtation, maybe, someone to pass the time with, to make the trip more interesting. Remember what the commander said*, she told herself. *Remember what you are.*

The trash was heaped on either side of the road, and it felt as if they were burrowing through a tunnel. The piles were skyscraper-high on either side, but it was a smoother ride, as if the road was newly plowed. "Wait a minute—if the snow's plowed it means there *are* people are living out here," Farouk said with a start.

"Of course there are," Nat said impatiently. What kind of crew had she hired that he didn't know that? Then she remembered that Farouk had mentioned he had never been past the fence before.

"Don't believe everything you hear, 'Rouk," Wes mocked from the passenger seat, grinning at her. No one was allowed in the wastelands. There was nothing out here but death and decay, or so they had been told. But they knew better. The government lied. They lied about everything.

The piles receded in size as they moved down the road, and they drove in tired silence for a few hours. "What's that?" Farouk asked suddenly, pointing to a monumental cliff that loomed over the area. "I thought Hoover Dam was the other way."

"And you thought right," Wes said.

Nat felt the voice in her head rumble awake, aware of the danger; she had known there was a chance the journey would take her past this place, but was unprepared to see it again so soon. There was an edge to her voice. "That's not Hoover Dam."

"No, it sure isn't," Wes said, raising an eyebrow. "You've been out here before?" he asked lightly.

She frowned and didn't answer, feeling goose bumps forming all over her body. Had she escaped only to be sent back here? She didn't know who he was or what his intentions were. *Most runners will sell you down the river as soon as you get out of New Vegas, toss their cargo, rob you of your credits.* Maybe Wes was one of the good guys, but then again, maybe he wasn't.

Farouk was right, it did look like the old photos she'd seen of the Hoover Dam, its massive concrete walls towering over the valley, holding back the immense pressure of the river beyond. As they moved closer to the sheer rock face, it became clear it wasn't stone at all but concrete painted to look like stone, several feet thick, and it wasn't a barrier, but a building, stretching to the sky, a row of windows at the very top, with one panel, Nat knew, that had recently been replaced. Tall fences topped by razor wire ringed the perimeter.

"Let's get out of here," Shakes said. "That place always

gives me the creeps. It's why I hate taking these back roads. Seekers can suck it."

She exhaled slowly, relieved to find out it was just a coincidence. The truck gained speed when a trail of black smoke flashed across their windshield.

"What was that?" Farouk asked nervously.

"I'll check it out," Wes said, and popped through the moon roof, goggles on. "Something's going down."

There was another black flash, and puffs of smoke, a crackling sound that rippled across the snow banks, and from afar he saw three figures running. Wes fell back to his seat. "Breakout. Looks like a few convicts are trying to escape tonight."

"Breakout? It's a jail?" Farouk asked.

"No, loser, it's a hospital," Daran sniggered. "You never heard of MacArthur Med?"

"You mean one of the treatment centers? For the marked?"

"Bingo," said Zedric with a cruel smile.

Wes stood back up through the open hatch and looked around. "Two patrols chasing, one on either side of us, running parallel. We're pinned in here."

Shakes called up to his friend, "Let's just run between them."

Wes nodded.

"What are you doing?" Nat asked, twisting her hands in her lap.

"Just pretending we're one of them. At this distance,

we look like another patrol. If they don't get too close, we'll be fine. Relax."

Gunfire rang in the distance, along with the sounds of shouting and screaming. The Slaine boys took their places by the window, guns trained on the horizon.

Wes slid back down and tapped Shakes on the shoulder. "Drive slowly—let them inch away from us."

The truck moved forward and the atmosphere inside was tense. Patrols still flanked them on both sides as they made their way past. Wes cursed suddenly and they all saw why.

In the distance, the fences along the perimeter narrowed on both sides toward a checkpoint; the path they were taking was leading them right to the guardhouse. "Double back, Shakes, double back," Wes said.

"It's a long way back," said Nat. "Won't it look suspicious?"

"It will, but we've got no choice." He pointed the way to Shakes. "Take us back."

Shakes turned the truck, which kicked up more snow, spinning its tires in a mush of icy, wet dirt. The sound of gunfire grew louder. They heard a scream and saw the sky turn black with smoke again—their only escape was taking them closer to the prisoners.

A hard thud shook the truck, followed by footsteps scrambling on the roof of their LTV. Through the windows Nat saw a trio of escapees headed for the cover of the nearest snowbank, all wearing the familiar gray pajamas. Then one of them fell, facedown, a bullet in his back.

"Don't shoot!" Wes ordered his boys.

"Wasn't us!" Zedric yelled.

"We've got to help them," Nat whispered urgently, catching Wes's eye. "Please."

Wes snorted. "Help them? Unless you've got a pimp roll full of heat credits, you're the only cargo I'm taking on." He looked at her closely. "What do you care?"

Nat turned away, willing the tears in her eyes to stop; she had revealed too much. She wouldn't make that mistake again. He didn't know anything about her, and she swore to keep it that way from now on.

Do not despair. They will find their own way, the voice murmured, but Nat felt her stomach twist: Here she was, in the safety of the truck, while outside, her friends—her friends were dying. People like her, hunted and killed.

"Shakes—just plow through the fence—look, there's a hole over there—we'll just rip it through," Wes ordered.

The truck barreled through the nearest fence, ripping through the metal with an ugly screech, but soon they were back on the road, and moving at a fast clip, taking them farther and farther away.

Nat didn't look back.

THIRTEEN

The back roads turned to out to be more of a challenge than Wes had expected. The smooth snow-covered landscape concealed many obstacles. The ice hid tree stumps and posts, guard rails and ditches. There was no way to prepare; he only figured it out when the wheels hit them or when the hidden junk crashed against a side panel. He'd made the offer to take her back so that the boys could know he was looking out for them, but also because he wanted her to know the exact nature of the dangers they would be facing. The night had brought another blizzard and they were traveling in complete darkness again, with only the headlights of the LTV to guide their way.

He wondered about the girl next to him. It was obvious she knew about MacArthur, as well as the people living in the wastelands, which meant this wasn't her first time at the rodeo. He guessed she'd probably tried to get out of the country before. She was a liar and a thief. Wes had pegged her correctly from the moment she had hired them and yet he couldn't help but admire her anyway.

Nah, you just think she's pretty, he chided himself. *But, really, she's nothing special. There are lots of pretty girls back in New Veg.* Jules had been one, for sure, but his memory of Jules—of her thick, brown, almost russet-colored hair and smoke-gray eyes—had faded a little. All he could think about was Nat. The way they had smiled at each other earlier, the way she had placed her hand on his arm…

Which got him thinking—if she did like him or at least liked the looks of him—he might have an opening there; maybe he could use it to his advantage. That stone she wore around her neck was awfully pretty. It was all so messed up: He liked her, and he *wanted* her to like him, but only so he could use it against her later. Definitely messed up. But what choice did he have?

She had taken the chips without caring what happened to him. Could he do the same to her? He would have to at some point.

"Hey, come on, let me take a shift," Nat offered. "You're still healing from that shot."

"Suit yourself," he said, switching places with her. He massaged his shoulder. "Thanks, by the way," he added, to be polite. He noted there was a distance between them again and was relieved at that.

Nat drove while Wes kept an eye out for drones in the sky or any sign of a seeker team. He was glad for the distraction; it kept him from thinking about her and he was already thinking about her too much. But as they drove, Wes found he wasn't cut out for silence either. The Slaine boys weren't talking to him, giving him the cold shoulder to make it clear they didn't care for the mess back at MacArthur and his decision to travel off-road. Shakes was asleep, and Farouk was resting.

"Hard to believe this was all desert once," he said, deciding a conversation would be harmless enough.

"Desert—what's that?" Nat joked. "I grew up in Ashes."

He grunted. The city was one of the coldest outposts in the country.

"Ever seen pictures of what it looked like Before? Rolling dunes, cacti?" she asked. "You know what it used to be called right?"

"Phoenix," he replied. "But the Phoenix is gone, and all that's left is Ashes."

"Poetic," she said.

"Told you, there's more to me than meets the eye." He smiled, flirting with her again, in spite of himself.

"Can't be much," she said slyly.

"Want to find out?" he said playfully.

"Maybe," she said, and his stomach flipped.

"Ever seen photos from Before? It's like another planet," she said, changing the subject. "Can you imagine what it's like to be that hot?"

"Nope, I surely can't. Can't imagine ever being warm outside," he said. "Supposedly deserts still exist somewhere." Seeing the look on her face, he quickly explained lest she think him a dolt. "Not here, obviously, but in the enclosures."

"Desert enclosures?" Her tone sarcastic.

"Yeah. Messed up, right? Fusion hogs, most like. I heard they have beaches in them, too. Man-made ones, of course," he said. "I've been to the beach once. When we were stationed in 'Tonio, there was a little bit of it left when we went over to Galveston. Couldn't swim in the water, though. Not unless you want your kids to have three legs."

"What was Texas like?" she asked.

"Freezing," Wes said tersely, suddenly unwilling to say any more. He didn't know why he'd mentioned it; he never wanted to talk about what happened in Texas. "Just like everywhere else."

"You've seen a lot, haven't you?" Her voice was warm, and sitting next to her in the truck, it felt as if they were alone, as if it were just the two of them left on earth.

This was his chance, he saw, to tell her about himself, to earn her trust. Maybe he didn't have to flirt with her. Maybe he could just trick her into being friends. Maybe then she would tell him why she was on her way to New Crete, tell him what Old Joe had handed her right before he disappeared. Tell him what he needed to know so he could figure out a way to take it from her.

"I've seen enough," he said. "When my parents died, I joined the service. They sent me everywhere. You

107

name it, I've patrolled it."

"What were your parents like?" she asked as the truck crunched over the ice-covered road.

"They were all right, you know, for parents," he said. He didn't say any more.

"Do you miss them?" Nat asked. "I'm sorry, it's a stupid question. Of course you miss them."

"It's okay. Yeah, I miss them, I try not to since it's too hard, but there you go. I had a sister, too," he said, almost as an afterthought.

"Younger? Older?"

After a while, he finally answered. "Younger."

"What happened to her?"

He shrugged. Outside, the blizzard had stopped, and the air was clear again. Wes fiddled with the music player, switching through songs until he found one he liked. "I'm not sure. They took her away." It was hard to talk about what happened to Eliza.

From the corner of his eye, he saw Nat gaze out at the endless mounds of garbage buried underneath another layer of snow. "Took her away?" she asked. "Who took her away?"

"Military family, higher-ups," he sighed. "They said it was better for her. My parents didn't have the license to have a second kid. So they came to collect." The memory of that horrible day was still seared in his memory. He wasn't ready to tell her the truth about Eliza. Not yet. He turned up the music a little and the cabin filled with the sound of jangling guitars and a thin, reedy voice singing over a harmonica.

Nat hummed along for a while then said, "Well, at least she's with a family; it's more than many of us get or can hope for."

"That what you were? Orphan?"

"You had me checked out," she said, narrowing her eyes.

He shrugged. "Standard procedure."

"Then you should know my story."

"Not much of it."

"What happened to 'no questions asked,'" she said.

"I did say that, didn't I? No big deal, just making conversation." He didn't push. One day at a time, he thought.

He would be patient.

The garbage-strewn border gave way to a graveyard of ships and trucks that had been washed inland by the floodwaters over a hundred years ago. Monstrous steel hulls, skeletons of cruise ships and navy carriers loomed over the snowy terrain; dark, thick vines sprouted from the dead machines, weaving through the carcasses. Winter branches, they were called, some sort of plant that thrived in the tundra. Wes stared at them. He could have sworn the branches were iridescent, almost glittering, sparkling. But he was just seeing things, wasn't he? When he looked again, the branches were the same dull color, reaching toward the heavens, weaving a tangled web of rusted metal, along with trailer homes and tumbled-over cars on the snow-covered desert floor. The Black Flood had carried the junk almost as far as Vegas before receding. As they moved closer to the coast, they could see the failed levees and makeshift dams that the military and a few desperate civilians had erected in an attempt to stop the rising waters.

It was their second day on the road and Shakes was back on driving duty, with Zedric acting as navigator. Wes and Nat shared the middle seat, and each clung to the opposite corner, as far away from the other as possible. In the back, the boys were awake, jostling and teasing; an annoyed Daran had pushed Farouk's cap down low over his eyes.

"They'd lock that door once they saw you coming—" Farouk was laughing and hiccupping. "A year's share of marital-day passes in a week! That must have been a record!"

"Daran likes the ladies," Wes explained to Nat, as Daran looked smug and made a rude gesture with his hands.

"No doubt the ladies like him," she said with a smirk. Daran was pretty hot, with his sharp cheekbones and glossy dark hair.

Wes laughed, although for a moment his face twisted at her words. There were two kinds of marriages these days—day passes for temporary unions—so that you could rent a room at one of the love hotels—and real ones from chapel. Day passes kept the population clean of disease. No sexual activity without a license. There was a license for everything. In his experience, it took a lot of the romance out of the equation, standing in line at the bureau, checking the little boxes, waiting for the result of the blood test before you could do so much as kiss a girl.

"So you like Daran, eh?" he asked.

"I didn't say that," she huffed.

"You ever filled 'em out?" he asked, looking at her sideways.

"What—forms for a marital pass?" She looked offended.

"Sure, why not? What's the problem, no offers?" he teased.

"Exactly the opposite, my friend," she said archly. "Too many to mention."

"That's what worries me." He grinned wickedly and she tossed a wadded paper napkin at his face.

"You should be so lucky," she huffed.

"I should," he said, still smiling as he batted it away.

"Don't worry, I turned them all down," she told him.

"All of them?"

"Shut up!" She laughed. "I don't have to answer to you."

She wasn't the only one being teased about it. Farouk was giving Daran a hard time in the back.

"It's a miracle you passed the STD monitors—not with those girls from Ho Ho City!" he said, while Zedric chimed in from the front, "Yeah, bro, you're so twisted I swear the last one was a freaking drau!" Daran pummeled Farouk and threatened his brother, and finally Wes yelled at the three of them to shut up, they were giving him a headache.

"Hold up! Hold up! What's that?" Farouk suddenly yelled, underneath Daran's fists.

"What's what?" Wes asked, studying the black metal forest, looking through the tangle of vines. Then he saw it. There were shapes moving through the devastated landscape, and even the vines seemed to be moving. The figures multiplied in the distance.

"Thrillers," he cursed. "Let's hope we don't come closer to any." He took the binoculars for a closer look. The creatures were dressed in ragged clothing, stumbling and staggering with jerky, strange movements, some of them as small as children, and a few tall, wraith-like apparitions with hair the color of straw. And he wasn't losing his mind—the vines were moving, swaying of their own volition.

"Thrillers?" asked Farouk.

Shakes began to hum a tune. "You know, that old song… 'Thriller, thriller night.'" He began shaking his head and waving his arms while he sang. The Slaine brothers watched and laughed.

"All right, knock it off," Wes grumbled.

"The lights that glow at night—are they from them?" Farouk asked.

Wes didn't answer for a long time. "No one knows. Maybe."

"But what made them that way?" Farouk asked, as the team stared at the strange, frightening creatures in the distance.

After a long silence, Wes finally answered. "Military does a bunch of chemical testing out here, could be they're victims of the fallout, but the government won't say or confirm any of the theories. I know one thing, though, they scare the hell out of anyone unlucky enough to run into them. Word is that's why the army sent out nanobots in the first place; the thrillers were freaking out too many men. That's why there're very few seekers out here."

He explained that the official explanation for the retreat from Garbage Country was toxin-induced schizophrenia. The chemicals that remained from the toxic floods were said to have driven the men to insanity. But there was no official mention of the shambling, horrific creatures roaming in the garbage. A few years later, the army developed the bot-based defense system. Exploding bombs and robots didn't get nightmares and didn't scream at the sight of a thriller.

"Bad news, boss," Shakes said, looking up from the dashboard. "Looks like we've got a gas leak. Bullet must have grazed the tank. We're not going to make it to the coast with what we've got left in the cans."

They had been lucky to even get this far with what they had, Wes knew. "How much we got left?"

"A few miles at most."

Wes sighed. "All right, I wasn't planning to, but we'll have to make a detour to one of the tent cities for supplies. K-Town isn't too far, we'll go there."

"Whoop, whoop! K-Town!" Zedric yelled, throwing up his gun and catching it.

"What's in K-Town?" Nat asked.

Wes smiled. So there were some places she hadn't been. "You'll see. You think New Vegas is the bomb, wait till you see the fireworks in K-Town."

FOURTEEN

To get to K-Town they would have to cut through what was once Los Angeles. The formerly sun-drenched city had been one of the hardest hit by the Flood, the waters submerging it almost completely. The truck had to make its way through the hilly, snowy terrain above the waterline. Zedric cranked up the stereo hooked to Daran's player, and a loud dub-reggae hybrid, the Bob Marley Death-Metal Experience, throbbed inside the truck.

The music was angry and violent, in contrast to the gentle lyrics. *Could you be loved?*

It was a good question, Nat thought. Could you? Could *she*? Her gaze landed on Wes and she looked away. For a moment she had seen the two of them filling out day-pass forms, giggling, teasing each other, anticipating a night alone together. She shook the image from her head, annoyed that her thoughts kept turning back to him. Besides, she felt nothing for him, and never could. She'd only been flirting with him because maybe if he liked her he would think twice before tossing her overboard.

As the truck sped through the tundra, Nat looked out the window, relieving her anxiety by marveling at the relentless nature of the frozen environment: snow and more snow for miles around. In one of her old books she'd read that the Eskimos had a hundred words for it. She thought it was a shame they weren't around to see this: so many different kinds. The white virgin powder on the rooftops contrasted with the hard ice on the ground. The snow rolled over roofs and cars with no interruption, just a white expanse, a visible blankness. Once in a while, she saw footprints, animal trails maybe, although there were some too big, their patterns too deliberate, to be anything but human. She thought of the thrillers they'd left back in the snow-covered desert and shuddered. Wes was right to hope they wouldn't run into any.

When she was still in school, she'd learned about a town in Ukraine called Chernobyl, where a nuclear reactor had exploded. The place was so radioactive that it wouldn't be fit for humans for hundreds of years and it was still off-limits now. The whole area was declared an exclusion zone, an evacuated land where no one was allowed to live. In reality, though, the Chernobyl exclusion zone teemed with life. With the absence of humanity, wildlife flourished and the toxic landscape became a kind of animal preserve. Looking at the trails in the snow, she wondered whether Garbage Country was the same. She wondered what kind of life was flourishing here.

Nat didn't have to wonder for long, as a polar bear materialized from the snow, its burly white body moving with lightning speed. She gasped in surprise—she had never seen an animal up close before.

"What is it?" Wes asked, just as the truck swerved to a stop.

Shakes muttered curses as he turned off the engine, and he and Wes hopped out to see what had happened. Nat followed, watching as Shakes kicked away a mound of snow from the left front wheel to reveal a thick fork of rebar wedged into the front tire.

"'Rouk! Zed! Dar!" Wes called. "C'mon, we need help out here."

As the boys pulled shovels from the trunk and began working to free the trapped tire, Nat stepped away. Where was the bear?

She scanned the horizon, but saw nothing.

Behind her, she heard curses mixed with the whine of crushing metal. She looked back at the tire. The entire crew had gathered around the trapped wheel. Farouk, Daran, and Zedric were shoveling snow while Shakes worked to free the metal rod that had ground its way into the tire.

Nat took the binoculars to scan for the bear. There it was! She smiled in delight as the polar bear bounded over a mountain of snow. It paused, looked around—twitched nervously. From behind, she heard Wes warn, "Best to stay in the truck." Nat ignored him.

"Just a moment, I've never seen one this close." She walked closer to the bear.

Without warning, the mighty white animal turned and bounded forward. She stood stock-still, wide-eyed, staring at the creature until too late—she realized the bear was coming directly at her. Pushing a pile of snow ahead of it, the bear leapt forward, its mouth open, tongue out, and teeth bared. It roared. She stood transfixed, unable to move, staring death in the face.

"Nat!" Wes called, but it was too late. She heard a pop, like thunder, echo across the snow. The bear skidded toward her, it warm red nose colliding with her foot, a steady stream of red fluid pouring from its head, mottling its once pristine coat with thick clumps of blood.

Dead.

She was safe.

She turned to Wes, but saw that his gun was holstered; the rest of the crew were still working on the tire. None of them had fired the shot.

A pair of white hooded figures appeared in the far distance. They wore thick goggles—military grade, heat and low-light lenses. They were at least a quarter mile away. She saw one drop his rifle and wave his fist in the air. Was he cheering? What was going on?

She turned to Wes. "Seekers?"

"Nope, caravan hunters." He knelt down to hide, and

she did the same. "You're lucky you didn't get hit in the crossfire. We need to go; they'll be coming for it." He called out to Shakes, "Get that wheel free, now! We need to move." The rebar had not moved from the tire.

She turned back to the hunters.

A second pop rang out in the distance. They'd shot a second bear, closer to them, nearly at their feet. The hunters ran eagerly to the fallen polar bear while a third began taking photos.

"Are they hunters or tourists?" she gaped.

"A little of both—a company runs garbage safaris here. It's illegal, but you know how it is—some things are more illegal than others."

He patted her shoulder. "I think you should get back in the truck now."

The hunters finished dragging the second bear to their snow jeep. Nat went back to the LTV. She watched Shakes dig the shaft of a shovel beneath the rebar and heave. The rusted metal bent and sprang from the tire. The hunters turned toward the first fallen bear, the one that had nearly crashed into Nat. She saw those thick goggles trained on her.

She slid back into the truck, the boys followed. "Wes, they saw me—we should go."

"What do you think we're trying to do? Shakes, hit it!"

With the door still open, Shakes stepped on the gas as he flung himself into the driver's seat. Wes had barely slammed his door when the LTV started moving. The big truck lurched forward, then ground to a stop.

Her head slammed into the back of the seat. Shakes swung sideways, nearly flew out of the truck, as the truck swung in a semicircle. "The tire's still wedged." Wes cursed. He was out of the truck before it stopped moving.

She looked for the hunters; the caravan hunters' jeep was headed their way. What would they do? Would they report them to the seekers? Three shots rang through the air and she felt the truck lurch. Out front, Wes was firing down at the wheel. "It's just some old wood; I'll blast it out." His voice was distant, barely audible through the truck's armored exterior.

She heard two more pops and Wes was back in the truck. They lurched forward again. Shakes shook his head. "Still not free, boss."

They wouldn't be able to get away. The caravan had made its way to their first kill, and hunters were getting out of the jeeps and walking toward them.

Wes hung his head in frustration. "I was hoping I wouldn't have to do this," he muttered. "Everyone out. Boys, try to look angry. Nat"—he turned to her—"don't say a word, look annoyed."

The caravan hunters were gathered around the bear; the tourists had pulled off their goggles and were posing alongside their fallen prey, taking more pictures. Wes walked up to the first and pushed him back hard. "What do you think you're doing? That was her bear! We've been out here all day trying to get her a decent shot and you douche bags take it out right when she's about to make her kill." He looked back at Nat and smiled before turning back to the tourists. "I don't get paid unless she gets a kill!"

The safari guide leapt out of the jeep, rifle in hand. Wes turned to face him. "This is the last bear in twenty clicks. What were you thinking? This one was ours! I've checked heat and satellite. There's nothing else out here and you already shot one!"

She nearly laughed. Wes was so convincing, more of a con artist than she guessed. Would he pull it off? Would he convince the hunters they were just another safari out here looking for souvenirs? She watched as he poked his finger in the guide's face. The guide was built like the truck, wide and stout, and there were several more, blank-faced, carrying nasty-looking guns, but Wes wouldn't back down even if they were outnumbered.

"You've got your skin; take it, and get out of here! This one's mine. She can hang the head on her wall and tell all her friends she popped a big white. You want this one, you've got to pay my fee, 'cause she sure won't!" The guides studied Wes's crew. The boys smiled broad grins. The tourists howled as their guides herded them back into the jeeps.

Wes turned. "You want the bear?"

She feigned a laugh, but the sight was too horrid. The

121

creature had been truly beautiful. "You think they bought it?" she asked.

He shook his head. "Who knows, I've run these cons so many times I've just quit worrying." The boys shoveled snow over the fallen bear, a burial of sorts, then loaded back into the truck. Tire free and hunters gone, they started forward once more.

FIFTEEN

Shakes had to park the truck again to try to patch the hole in the gas tank. They weren't far from what used to be called Korea-Town, a formerly jumbled neighborhood of barbecue restaurants and foreign embassies, but they might have to walk the rest of the way if he couldn't coax out a few more miles. The team disbanded, and the boys wandered around snow-covered houses while Nat stayed close to the vehicle. It looked as if it would take awhile, so she took a book from her pack.

"You can read," said Wes, noticing.

"Yes," Nat replied with an embarrassed smile. "Mrs. A—the lady who raised me—taught me." The book was one of the few possessions she had left, a poetry collection from the archives.

"Lucky duck," he said.

"It passes the time," she said, trying not to make a big deal out of it. Literacy was the lowest it had ever been. Truly, there was hardly any reason to read anymore—information was relayed through the net in videos and images, and if written communication was necessary, most people used an amalgam of symbols and acronyms that had replaced formal language instruction in schools. Supposedly textlish—which had been compared to Egyptian hieroglyphics by bygone intellectuals and academics—had been invented by a couple of kids with their handhelds before the Big Freeze. The latest RBEs, or "Reading-Based Entertainment," were all composed in textlish, but Nat couldn't quite get excited by a story called XLNT <3 LULZ.

The RBEs on the top download lists were all imports from Xian anyway—dull "work" novels about how to move up in the world, capitalist tracts about jerking the corporate chain. All the books Nat preferred to read were written by people who had lived long ago. No new songs, either—the current crop of pop stars were all cover bands, rehashing music from another era. It was as if even imagination had died when the ice came.

Wes peered over her shoulder at the cover. "Who's William Morris?"

"He was a poet."

"Read me something," he said. Nat didn't think he was the poetry type, but she flipped through the pages and cleared her throat before deciding on a passage.

"It's a story—about a dragon—and a hero," she told him.

"What happens in it?" he asked.

"The usual." She shrugged. "The hero slays the dragon."

Wes smiled and left to help Shakes with the engine. All around the white snow, Nat swore she could see small white flowers popping up everywhere. It had to be some kind of illusion. Flowers couldn't grow in the snow and the garbage. She walked closer to a snowbank, sure that the illusion would disperse, but it didn't. She reached down to pick a few flowers.

"Look," she said to Wes, who was standing nearby. She handed him one.

"How is that possible?" he said, marveling at the delicate bloom in his hand.

She shook her head and once again, they shared a quick, shy smile.

The sound of thunder booming across the valley caused them to drop the flowers they held and forget about it for the time being. In a flash, they were crouched behind the truck.

"What is it?" Nat asked. Had the patrols finally caught up to them somehow? She'd heard too many bombs in her lifetime and could immediately recognize the sound of an exploding shell when she heard one. "Think the seekers found us?"

"Let's hope not," he said as a second explosion rocked the truck. "Shakes would have picked up their signal on our scanner."

They were parked on top of a winding road—MULHOLLAND DRIVE, an ancient street sign read. The houses were still intact here, except they were buried to the roofline in snow. At least they were away from the black vines now, and the air was fresher up here and a new coat of pristine white powder covered the ground.

A third thunderous blast rocked the hillside, loud as a cannon.

"Wait a minute," said Wes. "That sounds like one of ours—"

"What are you doing?" Nat asked as Wes crept along the side of the truck, muttering Zedric's name as another blast echoed across the hilltop.

She ducked as a shower of snow rained down from the trees.

"Put it down! What do you think you're doing?" Wes yelled, walking out from behind the truck.

She stood from her place and saw where Wes was headed. Zedric was perched on top of an old black Bentley. Its tires were flat and all the windows were missing. Someone had pulled out the seats and the engine was gone. Zedric laughed as he tried to steady himself on the hood of the car that was slowly collapsing under his weight.

"Watch this!" Zedric yelled, as he aimed his RPG at a pair of thin steel-and-wood beams that supported a big house across the hill. The long glass façade must have been beautiful once, but its windows were all smashed now and its roofline as wavy as a noodle. The neighboring houses were similarly perched out over the hill on tiny thin posts.

A loud smack interrupted her thoughts.

Wes had knocked the rifle from Zedric's hand, which hit the boy's nose as the gun fell to the snow. "What the hell!" Wes demanded.

Zedric glared at him. "I was just having a little fun!"

For a moment, Nat thought he was going to hit Wes, but the smaller boy seemed to think better of it.

There was a pop—another explosion—but different this time, and all of them turned around to see the long white house slide down the hillside and crash into the trash pile below.

"You shot out the supports, didn't you?" asked Wes.

"It was fun," Zedric repeated, reaching for his gun as he wiped a trickle of blood from his nose.

"Thanks a lot. You just let the seeker team out there know exactly where we are. Where's your brother? We need to get out of here before they come."

Zedric shrugged, but they all knew where to look.

"Once a scavenger, always a scavenger," Wes muttered and Nat understood the temptation had been too great for Daran. Zedric's hyena laugh echoed through the canyon as a second house disappeared down the cliff side.

"I'm assuming you weren't dumb enough to shoot at the house your brother's in?" Wes demanded.

Zedric glared at Wes as blood streamed out of his nose. "What's your problem, man?" he whined. "Ain't hurting no one."

"Just get him already."

"Daran!" Zedric called.

"Daran!" Shakes took up the call and Farouk did, too. Nat did the same.

After a few minutes Daran lumbered out of the house, his arms filled with a collection of junk: toasters, an electric fan, what looked like part of a blender. He ran, breathless, back to the truck.

"Shakes—we good to go?" Wes asked.

"Ready when you are."

Wes barked his orders. "Everyone in the truck! Now!"

"What's the rush?" Farouk asked, as they watched Daran hustle toward them, wading through the snow.

"These houses are packed with pop-cans, every single one of them. It's common knowledge. Daran should have known better, he does know better," Wes said, frustrated. "C'MON!" he yelled.

"He's stuck," Nat said, as they watched Daran flail in the deep snow. But as she moved to help, Wes pulled her back.

There was another explosion. This one wasn't from the big gun or the sound of a house skiing down the hillside. The two of them were blown backward to the ground as the air filled with a mix of white powder and black smoke.

"Pop-can," Wes said, kicking away a rusted can that Nat had accidentally stepped on. "An old one; that's why it didn't immediately explode when you hit it."

Nat just stared at him, too shaken up to speak.

"You can thank me later," he said. "DARAN, COME ON, MAN! Zedric—go help your brother."

Zedric stood his ground, staring at Wes, his eyes wide with fear.

"We're not going to leave you boys—you hear me? Go get your dimwit brother out of that trench! Now!"

Zedric didn't move.

"Pop-cans have a proximity detonation feature," he explained to Nat. "When one of those things go off, it sends a signal to the rest. This whole valley could collapse. All this so Daran can buy a hit of oxy in K-Town."

On cue, another explosion atomized the house behind them. Wes cursed—the explosion had sent Daran flying, and he was wedged facedown in the black snow. "Mask!" Wes yelled, and Shakes threw him a gas mask. "If you hear another pop, hit the gas—I'll meet you in K-Town!" He put on the mask and waded through the snow and smoke toward the fallen soldier.

"C'mon," Zedric said, pushing Nat into the LTV. "Every pop-can within a mile is going to explode in a few minutes!"

But Nat held her ground. "We can't go without them. Shakes, we can't leave him here!" she said wildly.

"Don't worry, haven't lost him yet," Shakes promised.

A third explosion triggered a fourth. Nat knew they would have to go soon—otherwise they would all end up dead.

But after a few minutes Wes finally emerged from the

smoke, Daran slung over his shoulder. She caught her breath and raced out of the truck to help him drag the unconscious kid through the snow. Shakes jumped out of the cabin and opened the back door. They slid Daran into the cargo area, then sped off down the hillside, the valley echoing with bombs.

SIXTEEN

The canyon walls collapsed behind them, and as the snow fell, crushing the blanket of flowers, the petals released their seeds, filling the air with a glittering cloud of specks. Even as they were making their escape, Wes thought it was one of the prettiest sights he had ever seen.

"Nanos!" Farouk yelled.

"No! They're not nanos!" Wes said. "They're something else."

"Seeds—they're seeds!" Nat said excitedly. "Look!" The team watched as the seeds were swept high by the wind and spread over the snowy landscape, twinkling and swirling, a cloud of life, instead of death.

Wes caught her eye and he knew she was thinking the same thing. So this was how the flowers came to cover the area. Somehow, some way, something was growing in the wastelands. Was the earth healing? Was there such a thing as hope for the future? A way beyond this frozen hellhole?

For now, the hillside had liquefied under the stress of the many explosions and was cascading down into a waterfall of wet snow and debris. Wes shook his head. It was all such a waste, and frightening how easily everything had been destroyed—as if the houses were made of straw—all it took was one puff and they were gone. It was a miracle they had survived this long.

When they were halfway down what was left of the 101, Daran woke up, annoyed at having dropped his loot. He had little left to show for his pains: a gold watch and a silver spoon stuffed into his pants pockets. Metal had some value in K-Town but not much. He would have been better off if he'd held on to the kerosene lantern he'd found in the garage. He was still complaining as they hit the streets of the phantom, snow-covered city, mumbling under his breath and cursing his trigger-happy little brother for his prank.

"Ah, shut up already," Shakes said, uncharacteristically edgy.

Wes shook his head at Daran; he was too tired to be angry. He turned to Nat. "You're bleeding," he said, motioning to the side of her head.

Nat put a hand to her scalp, surprised to find her hair covered with blood. "Funny, I didn't feel anything."

"Shakes—stop the truck. Zedric—get your brother bandaged up, that cut might get infected, and bring me some of the antibio when you're done," Wes ordered.

They stopped at an abandoned parking lot of what used to be a shopping mall. Nat leaned against the hood while Wes cleaned her wounds with a sponge. "Pop-can must've got you after all," he said. "Huh." He stared at her.

"What?" she asked.

"I guess it wasn't as bad as I thought—I was ready to stitch you up, but it looks like it's almost healed."

"I told you, I didn't feel anything," she said. "I'm okay."

Wes could have sworn he had seen a deep, ugly gash, but when he pushed her hair away, it was nothing—a surface wound—the blood had slowed to a trickle. He didn't want to think about what that meant and decided to ignore it for now. Maybe she hadn't been hit that badly. Yeah, right.

"Nice crew you got there," she said, rolling her eyes toward the Slaine boys. Daran was yelling as Farouk and Shakes held him down while Zedric rolled a canvas cloth around his middle.

Wes shook his head, his jaw hardened. Now why did she have to go and say something like that? He didn't like it when anyone insulted his boys. "They're all right. Not my first choice, but it's a dirty job, taking people through the Pile. Not many would want to do it," he said, looking at her pointedly, as if to say, *If they weren't here, you wouldn't be, either.* "Dropouts are all I could get."

"Right," she said, chastened. "I'm sorry."

He sighed. "You know how it goes." He wasn't sure if she did, but she had to have been in Vegas long enough to know that dropping out of the military was like dropping out of society. The army was the only game in town for the likes of them. Without an honorable discharge, there was a slim chance of being hired for any decent work.

"Leaving the military's no joke," he told her. "So when they end up with me, I try and teach them to be better soldiers. There's no room for heroes or horseplay in this line of work. When it comes down to it, a soldier's only goal is to stay alive, nothing more, nothing less." He frowned and continued to clean her wound, trying and failing to ignore the spark between them as his fingers touched her forehead. "A guy goes off and starts shooting randomly, it's my duty to take him down a notch, put him back in line. I did Zed a favor when I busted his nose. It might save his life one day, the next time he thinks of doing something that stupid."

"So why'd you leave, then?" she asked. "Shakes said you won a Purple Heart and a Medal of Honor. He said you could have been a general one day, maybe."

He sighed, placing a bandage on her head, pressing it down so it would stick. "I didn't have it in me to be a career man, I guess, let's leave it at that. How about you, where'd you serve?" he asked innocently.

"I didn't," she said.

"Oh, right, you got an upper school pass?"

"No…" But she didn't elaborate. "I thought you said you had me checked out?" She smiled, but her tone was guarded.

He gave her a long look. "No questions."

"Thanks for this," she said, pointing to his work.

"Don't mention it."

"Boss, we gotta move," Shakes said, coming up to them. "Farouk picked up a seeker signal on the radar. They're two clicks north."

Wes nodded, hiding the wave of nausea he felt from the news. "Let's go, maybe we can lose them."

They climbed back on board the LTV and Wes took the wheel again. He stuck to the back roads, plowing the truck through front yards and rough earth, forcing the truck to go as fast as it could. The team was quiet, tense, and even the Slaines were subdued. They knew Wes was angry with them for giving away their position.

"What happens if the seekers find us?" Nat wanted to know.

"Let's hope they don't," Wes said.

"You keep saying that. Will they kill us?"

"There are worse things than being shot and dying quickly," he said tightly. There was no use frightening everyone. Either they would be caught or they would be able to evade them. Life or death, but wasn't it always? Military prisons were notorious for their brutal treatment of captives, and Wes sure hoped they wouldn't end up in one. He'd been lucky so far; maybe his luck would hold.

"If it looks like they'll be able to take us into custody, just shoot me, okay, boss?" Shakes whispered next to him. "Promise. I'd rather die at your hand than theirs."

"It won't come to that," Wes said testily. "Cut that self-defeating chatter."

"Go faster," Nat whispered from behind him. Her breath was almost at his ear, and he felt his skin tingle.

"I'm giving it all she's got," Wes said.

"I think we lost them," Farouk said, looking up from his scanner.

Nat exhaled, but it appeared the young soldier had spoken too soon. She looked up just as Wes hit the brakes and the truck screeched to a halt.

A pair of white-camouflaged Humvees were blocking the road.

The seekers had found their prey.

SEVENTEEN

There are worse things than getting shot and dying quickly, Wes had said just moments ago. Even he had to admire his own bravado. That was a good line. He willed his fear away. Maybe there was hope yet, since the Humvees hadn't shot them on sight.

"It's fine, leave it to me," he told Nat as he turned off the engine.

Zedric's fun with explosives in the hills had brought the seekers directly their way, just as Wes had warned, and running into the rebar and the caravan hunters hadn't helped. They were trapped now. There was no use running; the trucks were too close to them and heavily armed. Even if he tried, there was a pair of drones circling above that would fire on command.

A soldier wearing officer stripes on his jumpsuit got out of the nearest Humvee, followed by a team of his men. They all had rifles slung over their shoulders, but no one made a move to attack.

Daran gripped the top hatch and drew his weapon.

Shakes moved to follow, but Wes stopped him. "Sit tight, boys, I've got this one." He kicked open his door and jumped down onto the muddy, snow-covered road.

"What are you doing?" Shakes wanted to know. "Those aren't some fool tour guides you can bullshit, those are RSA boys, you know."

"Yeah, well, and so was I once," Wes said. He got out of the truck, his heart beating in his chest, but his walk as smooth and languid as ever. He kept a lazy grin on his face as he approached.

The officer was leaning against one of the Humvees' front grilles, its engine rumbling behind him, making clouds of steam rise from the truck's warm hood.

"Morning, sir," Wes said.

There was no reply. The soldier just stared up at the cloudy white sky and waited for Wes to come closer.

I hope I'm right about this. Wes kept his cool as he walked toward the seekers. He saw that both of the Humvees had their long guns trained at his head, the massive barrels rotating slowly to follow his progress. He noticed that the group of soldiers hanging back had a marked one with them, a boy his age, his red eyes gleaming with hatred, the mark on his forehead like a third eye. Wes had heard those who bore the third eye could read minds. The seeker team had probably used him to sense them. That program was supposed to have been shut down after Santonio, but knowing how things worked,

Wes should not have been surprised to find it up and running.

He deliberately kept his thoughts blank.

"Explosions that size are pretty hard to miss around here," the officer drawled, breaking his silence at last. "Next time just radio us your location. It'll make all of our lives a little easier."

"Sorry about that." Wes smiled. "I hate to inconvenience you."

"Don't your guys know better than to play around in the hills?"

"They're just kids," he replied.

"All the more need to keep them safe." The officer stared him down.

Here it comes, thought Wes.

"I hear you runners make a good living hauling illegals through the Trash Pile. What's a trip fetching these days? Five, ten thousand watts?"

Wes stared at the red-eyed soldier. "Five." It was a lie, but Wes made himself believe it was true.

The boy did not argue.

Wes was relieved; maybe it had worked somehow, since he'd kept his poker face on, his mind clear.

The officer smirked. "Well? Hand it over. I'm cold and my men want to get out of this godforsaken junkyard. Then you can be on your way."

Wes just shook his head as he reluctantly gave the officer one of the platinum chips from his pocket. "You guys are making it hard out here for an honest smuggler."

The officer grinned broadly as he took the chip from Wes. "Next time, just wait for us at the border and I might cut you a better deal. Rather not dig for gold if we can help it."

Wes tried to laugh, but the whole thing stunk. He needed those credits and so did his guys. He thought about clocking the smug bastard on the chin, but then he remembered those t-guns. Both barrels were still trained on his head, and the marked boy never took his eyes off him. He didn't put it past them to shoot them still, or drag them away to one of their prisons.

He turned and jogged back to his truck and slipped into the driver's seat. "What did I tell you guys, we're fine," he said, revving up the engine.

"They're just going to let us go? Just like that? What did they want, then?" Nat asked as the boys exhaled.

"Entrance fee at the toll booth," Wes quipped. "Look, we're finally in K-Town."

EIGHTEEN

There was nothing across the line—that's what the government said—what they wanted you to believe, anyway. As the LTV drove down battered Wilshire Boulevard, Nat saw signs of life everywhere—buildings dug out from the snow, with flashing signs in Korean and textlish, the symbols almost interchangeable. The streets were teeming with people of all kinds, a cacophony of noises and a variety of smells. This was more than a tent city; if there was such a thing as the capital of Garbage Country, this was it.

Wes put a hand on her arm as she stepped out of the truck. "Watch your step," he said, and she nodded to let him know she understood; he meant not just her footing but to be mindful as she moved around the area. This was a lawless place, populated by all manner of criminals—scavengers, slavers, vets, refugees, and illegals.

The Slaine brothers and Farouk disappeared into a nearby building with a pharmacist's symbol painted on its door. Oxygen addicts. The clean-air craze.

"Lunch?" Shakes suggested.

"Is food the only thing you think about?" Wes chided him.

"What else is there?" Shakes asked, and it was a good question.

Nat realized she was starving; she hadn't eaten much since the night Wes knocked on her door. She wondered now when anyone would notice she was gone. What would happen to her apartment, to the books she'd shoved underneath her bed? She had thrown her lot in with Wes and his crew without looking back for a moment; there was only the way forward.

But what if Wes—and everyone else—was right? What if there was no such thing as the Blue? She waited to hear the voice in her head protest—but there was nothing. Maybe because it knew it was too late for her to turn back now. They weren't very far from the coast, and with enough gas, they could probably get to the pier tonight. She fingered the stone around her neck, thinking it wouldn't be long now.

Shakes led them into a dark building, down the stairs, into a bustling turo-turo restaurant in the basement. At a turo-turo (Nat knew it meant "point point" in a forgotten language), all a customer had to do was point at the food they wanted to eat since hardly anyone could read a menu. There was a big lunch counter with steam tables featuring an array of dishes of varying ethnic origins. But unlike the corporate mash-ups,

142

the food was singular and unlike anything she had encountered before.

There was a vat of fish ball soup, a doughy concoction that didn't look like fish at all, but tasted delicious; charred meat skewers—pork from the smugglers who worked in the heated enclosures—almost impossible to find and incredibly expensive in New Vegas, but available here; fragrant rice dishes stuffed with real vegetables; and slippery noodles filled with slivers of real garlic and ginger, steaming and tempting.

"Does it all come from the runners?" she asked, as they pointed to their choices and accepted heaping plates of rice, noodles, and meat.

"Most of it." Wes nodded. "But some are military rations that the cronies unload here, trading food stock for weapons."

"Military rations! But that would mean—"

"K-Town wouldn't exist without the military's permission," Wes said. "They need to keep an eye out in Garbage Country and have a place where they can conduct business with slavers without anyone knowing."

"So the food shortages aren't real either," she said. The lack of resources was the reason every citizen was given a Fo-Pro card. Unless you were rich and could eat from the tiny but luxurious private sector, every aspect of the food supply was rationed, given out piecemeal.

"Who knows, but there's food here," Wes said.

"While we starve on slop." Shakes shook his head.

"Five centavos," said the cashier behind the counter.

Nat was surprised to find the girl had bright burgundy eyes, and the girl stared back at her with a languid, almost bored expression.

Wes paid for their lunch with a real silver coin. "They don't take watts here—only the old currency from Before."

But Nat was still staring at the girl. She couldn't wrap her mind around the fact that the marked girl was moving about so freely, without anyone noticing or caring.

"A lot of marked refugees get stuck in K-Town," said Wes, bumping her elbow to move her along. "They save enough watts to get past the border, but have nothing left to go anywhere else. So they work, hoping to earn enough to pay for transport out of here. But most of them never do."

"And no one cares?" she said, looking at a few military personnel scattered around the place.

"Not here at least."

They settled down to eat their meal. Nat marveled at the texture—she'd never had vegetables like this before, never had meat that hadn't been processed or wasn't just tofu made to taste like meat. It was a revelation. Still— just as in New Vegas—everyone drank Nutri. Clean water was rare, even in K-Town.

Wes took a swig from his cup and motioned to a bearded man seated at the next table. "Howie, you know if Rat still runs the table? Is that game still going on? Slob happen to be around? Or any other of Jolly's boys?" he asked, wiping his lips with a napkin.

"Should be. Doesn't change. You in?"

Nat pushed away her plate. She felt ill after eating such a huge meal. "There's a casino?" she asked, feeling a gambler's excitement at the prospect.

"Better yet—there's a high-stakes poker match," Wes replied.

She raised her eyebrows. Things were starting to get interesting. "What've you got in mind?" she asked.

"For one thing, I need to get my ship back."

She stared at him. Did he just say what she thought he'd said? "What do you mean, get your ship *back*? You don't have a ship? How are we going to get across the ocean?"

"Relax, relax—I have a ship—just not right now. But that can be rectified." He shrugged.

She goggled at him and turned to Shakes. "Did you know he doesn't have a ship? And you guys took this job anyway?"

To his credit, Shakes managed to look sheepish.

"I thought you didn't gamble," she accused Wes.

He shot her a Cheshire cat smile. "What can I say? Easy come, easy go."

Shakes guffawed. "How? Once the Slob sees you, he'll leave the table. He knows you'll be after it. He's not going to risk having to give it back after you won it from him in the first place."

"I'm not going to win it," Wes said, pointing at Nat. "She is."

NINETEEN

The place wasn't a casino exactly. It was just another crowded subterranean basement room with a few roulette tables, card tables, a craps table, and a bar. Nat found the noise and the smell of sweat and smoke overwhelming as she walked into the room, a little unsteady on her high heels. She was dressed as a tai tai, a rich Xian trophy wife, slumming in K-Town on her way to Macau.

With the help of a video blog and a few silver coins from Wes's stash, she'd managed to find an appropriate costume. She was wearing a tight red cheongsam, her long dark hair was held back in a bun with two sparkling chopsticks, and the blue stone remained looped on a chain around her neck, masquerading as a decorative bauble. Farouk had outfitted the dress with a fake fusion battery, which blinked red at her collar. She'd protested she would freeze before she got inside the door, but Wes had been adamant. The tai tais did not wear bulky layers of any kind; they slithered around the city flashing their bare legs as a sign of wealth and ease.

"You look good," Wes had allowed before she left the shelter. "You think you can do this?"

"Watch me," she'd told him. Even if she was nervous, it was too late to back out now, and he knew it, too. Besides, of all the things she could do in the world, she could play poker.

The Slaine brothers, dressed in chauffeur uniforms, would act as her bodyguards. If anything happened, they would make sure to get her out of there alive. She didn't know if she trusted Zedric and Daran with her life, but, once again, she didn't have a choice. Without a ship, she might as well go home.

"VIP room?" she asked the bouncer guarding a door near the bar.

"Fingerprint," he grunted, pointing to a reader. "And no muscle inside," he said, shaking his head at her companions. He held up a flashlight to check her pupils.

Wes had warned her there was a chance she would have to run the play alone, but if she had entered the hall without any protection, no one would believe she was who she pretended to be.

Daran winked and whispered, "Don't worry, I'll be close by."

She dismissed them with a wave of her manicured fingers and smiled at the bouncer as she put her designer sunglasses back on her nose. She pressed her hand against the print reader. Farouk had entered her photo and fake background into the system. She was Lila Casey-Liu, the sixteen-year-old wife of a molecular phone magnate.

Nat would have to do much more than convince a bouncer; she'd have to deceive the Slob, one of the most feared slavers in the Pacific. His real name was Slavomir Hubik, but everyone called him Slav, or the Slav, or SLB, his handle in textlish, which had turned into Slob. The Slob was far from one. He was a trim nineteen-year-old pirate from somewhere in New Thrace, the most notorious of the outlaw territories. He was one of the top men in a fearsome scavenger armada that trolled the black waters, supplying garment slaves to Xian factories, drugs to New Vegas, and pleasure girls and boys to anyone who would pay the bride price. There were even rumors that the slavers weren't just trading animal meat either; to desperate buyers, they were willing to sell the human cargo that wouldn't sell otherwise.

The Slob had a scar above his right eyebrow, dyed white-blond hair "drau style" in a military fade, and tonight wore a vintage velour tracksuit—a real synthetic, not the cheap animal furs that the other slavers preferred. His face was all sharp angles, handsome but with an edge. He didn't look up when Nat joined the table.

"Deal me in," Nat said, taking a seat next to the dealer, traditionally the luckiest draw in the table. "One hundred large," she said, with a brilliant smile as she slipped him a doctored heat-credit card. Farouk assured her it would pass the scanner in the room, but once it was out of range it would read zero.

"Feeling lucky tonight?" she asked her fellow gamblers. The Slob wasn't the only slaver at the table; she could tell by the tattoos on their faces. There was a girl, about her age, similarly bejeweled and bedecked, who nodded when she approached. "Love your shoes," the girl cooed.

Nat played conservatively at first, allowed herself to win a few hands, but not so much that she attracted attention. Wes had cautioned her to reel him in slowly. *He's a wise guy—he won't expect you to be a hustler—the tai tais like to gamble for the thrill—the slavers let them in because they bring big money to the table. He'll like a challenge. Beat him up a little.*

It was time. Nat won the next hand and the next, by the third, she had quintupled her money.

"Big win for a little lady," the slaver said in his clipped accent.

"Eh," Nat said dismissively.

"Too boring for you?"

"Let's make it exciting," she said with a gleam in her eye.

He shrugged. "Sure. What do you want?"

"I hear you have a fast boat," she said.

The slaver seemed amused. "You can't have *Alby*. Out of the question."

"Too scared you'll lose, Slob?"

For a moment, Nat saw the rage in the slaver's eyes. No one called him Slob to his face. But Nat knew she would get away with it. She had seen the way he looked at her legs. She giggled, letting him know she was flirting, playing her role.

The slaver gave her a thin smile. "Please, call me Avo."

"Avo, then," she said.

"If I put the bird in play, what will you give me?" he said, leaning over with a wolflike grin. "That gem around your neck?" he asked.

"This? A mere trifle," she said, slipping the stone underneath her collar and wishing he hadn't noticed it at all, irritated with herself that she had worn it. "This is the real treasure." Nat placed a small velvet pouch on the table. She pulled the string and showed him what was inside: tiny crystals that sparkled in the light, bright as diamonds.

It was fleur de sel. Sea salt. Real salt, not the synthetic kind—which was at once too salty and not salty enough—but the real thing, from before the floods, when the world was still whole. The last in the world, harvested before the oceans were poisoned. It was one of the souvenirs she had taken from the treatment center, nicked from the commander's kitchen, and she had been saving it for just the right moment. Wes didn't ask her where she got it, only told her it wasn't enough to buy a ship, but it might be enough to win one back if she was clever enough.

Avo Hubik eyed her. "Do you know how valuable that is?"

"Yes," she said evenly.

"I doubt it; if you did, you would not wager it so

easily," he said, picking up his cards.

"In New Kong we bathe in it," she said, and waved her cards like a fan. The rest of the table folded, watching the two circle each other—like a mating dance—one before a kill.

"Why do you want *Alby* so bad?" he asked.

"I have a hobby. I like taking what matters most to people. It keeps life interesting." She yawned.

"You can't have the boat."

"We'll see," she said sweetly.

"Fine. Let me see the salt."

He held it to his eye and then tossed it to the beautiful girl with bright orange hair and gold eyes who was standing behind his chair. A sylph, maybe? Nat couldn't be sure. The mages' mark on her cheek shaped like a serpent meant she was a healer, Nat knew. "Check this," he said.

"It's real," the girl said, tasting a little of it with her finger. Her eyes shone greedily.

Nat flicked her eyes away, disturbed. "Show me your cards," she said, laying down hers: a straight flush.

This time, the slaver smiled broadly. "Full house." He took the velvet bag of salt off the table.

"My husband will kill me," she mumbled.

"I'll make it easy; you win this next one, you can have the bird," he said with a smile now that he could afford to be generous. He threw the keys to the boat in the middle of the table. "I'm a gentleman."

152

Nat nodded. She was prepared. Wes's words rang in her ears. *He'll get arrogant, he'll want to show off...and when he does...*

Now was her chance. She had been watching the game closely, counting cards. The dealer put down the first cards. King of clubs. Queen of diamonds.

Avo Hubik smirked.

The next one: two of hearts.

The slaver studied his cards with a frown.

An image came to her unbidden: Avo taking another card and drawing a king, which would give him a high pair, which would win him the game, as she held nothing but garbage in her hand. The image faded. It was a premonition. A warning. She understood that she couldn't let that happen, and she began to panic. She had to do something! But what? She couldn't control her power, she couldn't do anything...she was paralyzed, cold—

A sudden gust of wind blew the cards from the deck, which scattered across the table.

"What the...?" the dealer cursed.

The gold-eyed girl stared at Nat, her eyes blazing.

Nat didn't dare look up and scrunched her forehead, pretending to concentrate on her cards.

Was that her? How did that happen? It didn't matter; what mattered was that the deck had been shuffled.

Avo didn't seem to think anything of it. He tossed a card and picked up a new one.

She picked up the next card, and somehow, before she

153

had even looked at it, she knew she held the winning hand. Two of clubs. With the two of hearts on the table, it made a pair.

The dealer threw down the river card. Nine of clubs.

Nat felt her skin tingle with anticipation.

The slaver showed his hand with a grin. Ace high.

Nat showed hers.

She had won with the lowest cards in the deck. A pair of twos.

The slaver's face paled.

She took the keys off the table. "I believe this is mine."

TWENTY

"*This* is what I won? This is your legendary ship? I say we give it back to the Slob!"

Wes ignored her and jumped onto his boat, which was moored to a rotting pier at the far end of the city. A skeleton of a roller coaster and a Ferris wheel stood not far from them, and a handful of boats bobbed in the water, all of them half-flooded derelicts, their hulls blasted full of holes, engines missing. The rest of the team followed him on board, but Nat remained on the pier, her arms crossed in front of her, an angry, frustrated look on her face.

"Are you going to stand there all day or are you going to get in?" he said finally, as he helped Shakes pull off the tarp.

"I'm not getting in *that*...it looks like it's about to sink!"

"Suit yourself," he said, whistling as his crew found their places and hauled in the supplies for the journey. He unrolled the canvas, feeling a glow of pleasure from being back on board. Wes had missed his ship, and its loss had been a harder blow than he would care to admit. He wasn't one of those sentimental fools, overly attached to their vehicles. A car was just a car, a truck was just a truck. But he did have a soft spot for this one, although he was more amused than annoyed by Nat's insults. The boat was an old Coast Guard ship, a converted fishing trawler, more than a century old, and built to last, fifty feet long, with a battered hull, a deck pocked with holes and a Jolly Roger painted crudely on the starboard side, alb-187 etched on the transom. The steel rails had rusted, and the paint was chipped, sure, giving the boat a saggy, dilapidated air, but there was more to *Alby* than looks alone. Nat might not know it, but he and Shakes had done major work on its engines, and the old girl practically had rocket boosters for propellers, that's how fast it could go.

"Seriously, we traded one of the most valuable things left on this planet—salt—for this?" Nat was saying. "This isn't funny!"

Wes looked up from his task, trying not to roll his eyes. He had to hand it to her—she was as tough as they came, she hadn't blinked once. Without her, he'd never have gotten his ship back. But enough of the princess act already. "We're not laughing," he said. "I'm sorry *Alby* isn't one of those sleek white whales the navy uses. If I'd known you were such a snob, I'd have turned you in as a border jumper."

He went back to his task, but she remained on the pier.

"Are you getting in or what?" he snapped. Then he saw the look on her face.

"Behind you," she whispered.

Wes sniffed the air and sighed. He knew the stench well, knew immediately what was standing behind him. With one graceful motion, he unholstered his sidearm and fired before he'd even turned around. The first bullet struck the deck of the boat and the second flew past the creature's ear, tearing a chunk of flesh from the earlobe. The thriller, a rotting corpse of a boy that had most likely huddled in the shadow of the canvas, staggered backward, away from him. It was human in shape, but its skin reflected no light and his eyes were a blind, glassy white. Wes emptied the rest of the clip into the air, and the creature dove into the black water.

He exhaled in relief until he saw it wasn't his only problem. "Nat! Get in the damn boat!" he yelled, firing his weapon once more.

Nat turned to look behind her and screamed. A rotten corpse was reaching for her. It was a girl once, but no more; the face hung from its ear, the flesh had decayed to a turgid, swollen mass, and it was grasping for her with its cold, dead hands. It slumped to the ground, as Wes shot out its knees. "COME ON!" He extended his hand and she finally took it.

They were everywhere—swarming the boardwalk, shambling out of the shadows, out of the rotting carnival booths and the broken carousel. There were so many of them, some of them fell through the rotted wood planks of the pier into the black water. The thrillers were far from mindless, moving with intent, their hands and feet grasping for holds.

"They're not dead!" Nat said shakily, as he pulled her into the boat.

"Tell me something new," he muttered. But he knew what she meant. Saw the horror on her face as she processed the information. The thrillers weren't dead at all. They were very much alive—*conscious*—their distress and desperation unnerving in its intensity.

"SHAKES! CUT THE ROPE!" he ordered, sliding his key into the ignition and jamming the engine out of neutral. The boat was still moored to the pier, and as he pulled forward, the two aft ropes snapped, their long lines whipping through the air. A third line, wrapped over the bow, pressed against the front of the craft, slowly sawing at the hull. The sound was excruciating.

Nat pulled a knife from Wes's belt and severed the rope. Her hands on his waist unnerved him for a moment, but he quickly recovered and nodded. "Good call."

The gray cord went flying across the deck and slapped Daran hard in the back. "Watch it!" The soldier glared in their direction.

"Sorry!" she called.

When he saw it was she who had caused it, he grimaced and tried to smile. "It's all right!"

But the boat was free, and they shot away from the pier, out of danger finally—when from belowdecks came the sound of a gunshot. He cursed the slaver and his lazy crew. Wes and his boys knew how to secure a ship from a thriller infestation, but obviously the slavers didn't care to take the same precautions.

"Take the wheel," Wes ordered, giving Shakes command of the ship.

"I'll come with you," Nat said.

He didn't argue, and Daran followed them down the stairs as backup.

Down below, Zedric had a gun pointed at one of the creatures. The thriller had a gunshot wound in its shoulder where the soldier had shot it. Under the bright lights of the cabin, Nat could see the thriller's face. It was a girl. Her skin was mottled and gray, and her purple eyes were lifeless as the rest. And she was wearing a familiar-looking pair of light-gray pajamas.

"Help me," she whispered. "Please." Her hair—Nat saw that underneath the mud and the dirt and the filth, the girl had hair the color of light, a bright, dazzling yellow. She was a sylph, or had been once, and Nat felt her blood run cold at the discovery. What was happening to them? Why were they like this?

Daran raised his gun to fire, but Wes grabbed the barrel. "Give it a rest, man, we'll let this one swim," he said, twisting the weapon from the soldier's grip.

The creature saw her chance and dashed away, out onto the deck, and there was a splash as she fell into the ocean.

Zedric kicked the wall but Daran hustled him out of the cabin. "Come on! She didn't touch you? You're sure?" he said, yelling at his brother.

"Why'd you do that?" Nat asked Wes, staring at him. "Why'd you let her go?" He never shot to kill, she had noticed.

He put away his gun and led them back upstairs. "She's not our first stowaway. They all want to come with us, hitch a ride out to the water."

"The thrillers?"

"Yeah."

Nat looked out at the pier, where hundreds of them had gathered, shuffling and groaning, their arms reaching out toward them, begging, asking for something. There were a few more bright-haired sylphs underneath the grime, and white-eyed ones with silver hair. Drau. They had to be, but these weren't frightening at all, just incredibly sad. It was why Wes didn't shoot them. Because the thrillers weren't attacking them, they were asking for help.

She had never been close enough to see them before. When she had escaped, she had seen them from a distance, and had managed to keep away from them, but now she saw all too clearly the truth.

So there was one thing the government hadn't lied about.

Those who were marked by magic were marked for death.

The thrillers weren't the victims of chemical testing or nuclear mutation. They were people. Marked people. Magic people whose mages' marks rotted them out from the inside, melting their flesh, their bodies decaying while their minds remained tragically alert. The military herded them into the safe zones and centers to keep them away from the rest of the population, kept the borders tight for that same reason.

It was why the military personnel in K-Town didn't care to arrest the marked girl working as a cashier. As far as they were concerned, she was already where she belonged. She was already refuse, already part of the garbage. The thrillers were escapees from MacArthur, refugees who could not find passage, left to roam the Trash Pile, unable to die.

Looking for refuge, hoping for the Blue.

Just like her.

If she stayed, the magic inside her would kill her slowly, draining her of life, but keeping her alive. She would be trapped in a decaying physical shell, while her mind was alert to the full breadth of the horror happening to her.

She watched the marked masses flailing on the pier, their terror and their desperation at their inability to escape. *Take us with you. Take us home.*

Wes looked at her. "Ready to go?"

They were out of the shallows and in the open sea.

Nat gave him the same answer she'd given just a few days ago. "Ready."

If she stayed, she would rot. But if she went...

She closed her eyes. There was a monster in her, a monster that was part of her, and the closer she drew to it, the closer the dark voice in her head sounded to her own.

There would be fire and smoke and devastation in her future. She would be the catalyst for something terrible. She could feel the power within her, the wild, savage, and uncontrollable force that had the ability to destroy entire worlds.

I am the monster, she thought. *The voice is mine.*

PART THE THIRD

THE
VOYAGE
BETWEEN

"God save thee, ancient Mariner!
From the fiends that plague thee thus!—
Why look'st thou so?"—"With my crossbow
I shot the Albatross."

—SAMUEL TAYLOR COLERIDGE,
"THE RIME OF THE ANCIENT MARINER"

TWENTY-ONE

She shouldn't have been so hard on him about his boat—Nat felt a little bad about that—because even with her inexperienced eye, she noticed that, like the LTV, Wes had improved upon its structure to fit its new environment. He had upgraded the hull, attaching layers of steel and carbon fiber paneling over the old aluminum shell, and every inch of the craft was painted—splattered, really—with shades of gray and black paint, a camouflage meant to mimic the dull sludge of the ocean.

The crew cabin was outfitted with bunks, the beds nothing more than metal mesh hammocks strapped to the walls, each with a blanket. The room next to it had a big plastic picnic table bolted to the floor, near a black charcoal grill. The ceiling above the grill was open to the sky, so the smoke could escape, and piled next to it were a few wood crates filled with food stores they had brought on board for the journey.

The ship offered little privacy and no amenities, but what else was new. Unless she was tossed in solitary, back at the center she had had a cot in the middle of a room the size of a gymnasium. She found a corner bunk that looked unclaimed and threw her pack on the rough blanket. She peeked through the dirty porthole. Outside, the gray sky was nearly indistinguishable from the gray waters of the Pacific. The toxic sea never froze but seethed with poison, occasionally glistening in the dim light of day, glowing in iridescent colors. It could be beautiful if it wasn't so deadly, its shimmering waves swirling with clouds of orange and green, the waves dancing on occasion with slim wisps of fire, yet another product of the ocean's unknown chemical cocktail.

She heaved herself up on the hammock and rested her head against the wire mesh. But after a while, she felt claustrophobic in the cabin and wandered out to the upper deck. She found Wes leaning against the rail, staring out at the dark water.

"Find something?"

He pointed to a distant spot in the middle of the ocean surrounded by large black ink dots.

"What are those? Island groupings?" she asked.

"No—those are trashbergs."

"Trash—oh, like icebergs?"

"Made of trash, yeah." Wes smiled. "The ocean's full of them."

Nat had seen it on the nets, how the pre-Flood oceans had once been flat and blue and empty. Now the Pacific was packed with junk, clouded with chemicals, dense and cluttered with trash, a floating Garbage Country. It was a briar patch, the perfect place to hide, the perfect place for slavers to loot and prey on pilgrims and refugees.

"Think we'll make it?" she asked, almost as a challenge.

"Sure hope so," he said, with that signature grin of his. "I need those credits."

She smiled at that. "Sorry about freaking out about the boat earlier…I was just…anyway, it was rude of me," she said.

"No harm done." He smiled and scratched the scar on his face. She hadn't noticed it before, the thin white line above his right eyebrow.

He must have noticed her staring. "Souvenir from Texas. I fell in the avalanche, and Shakes accidentally hit me with the ice pick while digging me out. I thought he was going to kill me instead of save me." He laughed.

"Nice one." She smiled, liking the way the scar made him look at once more dangerous and more vulnerable. "Sounds like that happens to you a lot. Bet your girlfriend wasn't thrilled, though." She wasn't sure why she said it, but it came out before she could think.

"Who said I had a girlfriend?" he said, raising his scarred eyebrow. His dark eyes crinkled.

"No one," she said.

"Well, I don't anymore, if anyone's interested."

"Who's interested?"

"Are you?" He looked her straight in the eye.

"I could ask the same of you," she scoffed.

"So what if I was? Interested, I mean." He shrugged.

"It wouldn't be a surprise," she said. "I'm sure half the crew has a crush on me." She rolled her eyes. She wasn't sure what she was doing, but it was fun to rile him up a little. So he was interested, was he? About time he admitted it.

"Only half?"

"Well, I don't like to brag," she said coyly.

They stared at each other and Nat felt the pull of those warm brown eyes of his, the color of honey and amber, playful and glinting. She faced him so that they were inches away from each other, their bodies almost touching. They were outside in subzero weather, yet she had never felt so warm.

"What are you doing?" he asked finally.

"Same thing you are," she replied.

He shook his head. "Don't start something you can't stop," he warned.

"Who says I want to stop?"

He stared at her and there was a long, fraught silence between them, and for a second she was scared to breathe. Wes turned to her, leaning down, his face so close to hers, it looked as if he was going to kiss her, but instead he changed his mind at the last minute. He wasn't looking at her anymore; he was staring at the stone she wore around her neck.

He pulled away and looked back at the churning

waters, tossed a pebble from his pocket into the ocean. "What do you want, Nat?" he asked.

"I could ask the same of you," she said, trying to keep the hurt from her voice. Did he know about the stone? Why had he stared at it like that? *You can't trust a runner. They'll sell you up the river for a dim watt.*

He frowned. "Listen, let's start over, can we do that?" he asked. "Why don't you tell me something about yourself, something that's not in the official records, something Farouk couldn't dig up about you."

"So you can get to know me, you mean? Why?"

"Why not? Like I said, it's a long road ahead of us."

Maybe he was lying and he did have a girl back in New Vegas. Maybe he had more than one. Or maybe he really only wanted to be friends. Nat couldn't figure out which possibility bothered her more.

"Go on, tell me something," he said. "Tell me about the first time you were in the Pile."

"How did you...okay, fine." She inhaled. "You're right. I've tried to get out before. This isn't my first trip through the G.C. I was an orphan, just like you'd guessed. I was living with Mrs. Allen then—the lady who raised me. It was her idea to try and get us out of the country when I was six years old. She wanted a better life for both of us, lost her faith in the RSA."

Wes leaned his chin against his hands. "What happened?"

"The runner who'd taken all our money didn't pay the

right bribe at the first checkpoint, so after the guard waved us through, he called in the border police and we got hauled in for not having visas."

"In our business, we call those donkey men," said Wes. "Clueless guys who don't know the deal."

"They took her away, and I never saw her again," Nat said softly. Mrs. Allen wasn't her mother, but she was the only mother she'd ever known. Her eyes misted a little. "Mrs. A found me when I was a baby. She says I was a DFD," she said, hugging herself tightly. Dumped for Deployment.

"Your folks were soldiers then." Wes nodded.

"That's what she told me." Mrs. Allen had explained to Nat that it happened a lot, people leaving their kids, not wanting to take them wherever they were stationed, thinking it was kinder to leave them than to bring them to the front lines; abandonment as a form of love. "I guess they were army. I don't know. I have no idea who they were."

"So what happened to you?" Wes asked.

She shrugged. "The usual. Ward of the state. I grew up in a group home." She didn't mention the real reason her mother had abandoned her. The reason Mrs. A had tried to hustle her out of the country.

"And I thought Shakes had a sob story." Wes smiled.

"Worse than mine?" she asked.

"Ask him to tell you later, it's a doozy," he promised. "Must have sucked, growing up like that," he said.

"Group homes are no joke." He shot her a sympathetic glance.

"Yeah, well." She nodded. "At least it's over now." She was touched by his concern, even though she was sure there was an ulterior motive behind it, especially with the way he ran hot and cold toward her. She was a card player, she knew the deal. "Now it's your turn. Tell me, Wes, why'd you take this job? I'm not paying you enough—not for the risks that are out there. What's in it for you?"

"Maybe I want to see what's out here, too," he protested. "If there's such a thing as paradise—I don't want to be left behind."

But Nat knew there was something behind his smile. Something he wasn't being honest about. She tucked the blue stone underneath her shirt.

That made two of them.

TWENTY-TWO

Wes watched her walk away from the railing, then went back to staring out at the water. He wondered how much of her story was true. Who was she, anyway? She said she recognized him from somewhere, and Wes wondered whether she was right and he had just forgotten. But he was certain that he'd remember meeting Nat. He scratched the scar on his forehead. Funny how she'd wondered about it, just like Jules. That story about Shakes and the pickax was a lie. But maybe one day he would tell her the truth. The one he'd never even told Jules.

On his first date with Juliet Marie Devincenzi, she'd laughed when he'd told her the story of the avalanche, all that rigmarole about how he'd made Shakes feel guilty about the scar.

Wes was still on deck by the rail when Shakes found him, staring at a photo he'd pulled from his wallet.

"Put that away," Shakes said with a grimace. "Let sleeping dogs lie."

"I know, I know," Wes agreed.

"Look, boss, Jules was all right, but..." Shakes shrugged.

"But?" Wes asked.

"You know why," his friend reminded him. Shakes had never liked Jules very much and blamed her for some of their trouble.

Wes put away the photo. "You think she really died at the Loss?"

"It's what I heard. What's the problem, boss? She left us high and dry after that Dreamworks hit. I mean, rest in peace and all, I don't like to speak ill of the dead, but she messed you up good."

"No, man." Wes shook his head. "That's not how it went down."

He'd met Jules right when he'd gotten out of the service. She was already running the cards then, a real pro, and she needed some muscle, a driver, a getaway car, and she'd picked him for the job, having heard that he'd made his name as a death jockey and knew his way around New Vegas. Jules had been a few years older. They hit it off immediately.

Wes had never been in love until Jules, didn't even know that's what he'd been feeling, until he was in over his head. She loved him, too—he would never forget that. He would have done anything for her at one point, but she'd asked for something he couldn't give.

"I never told you, but she wanted to get married, get the license, the whole deal," Wes told Shakes. "She wanted to get out, too. She always talked about escaping to the Blue. She believed in it. But she was willing to make a go of it anywhere, in K-Town, or Xian maybe, she had some friends who lived in Shangjing."

"And you didn't?"

"No." Wes shook his head. "K-Town's not any place to live, and since we wouldn't merit visas, I didn't think we'd be able to hack it as illegals in Xian." But there was more. His sister Eliza was out there somewhere, and he couldn't leave without finding out what had happened to her, whether she was even still alive.

Juliet had said she understood, she hadn't pushed it. So they stayed in New Vegas, and slowly, imperceptibly, whatever love had existed between them began to fade, and they fell apart. Jules had wanted out—and he'd let her down. Wes found he couldn't live with her disappointment. It stared at him in the face every day. He couldn't choose between them. Jules or Eliza. It ate at him, destroyed the love he felt, left him furious and stymied. Shakes got it wrong; Wes had broken up with her, not the other way around, right before the Dreamworks casino gig. After that, they stopped speaking and never ran a job together again.

He pulled out his wallet and stared at her photo again. He hadn't wanted to feel close to anyone else after that. The crew began to call him a priest and joke he was celibate. He didn't care. He began to think that maybe the boys were right about him, that he'd given up on that sort of thing, that he was no longer interested. But something in him sparked to life when he'd met Nat, and he felt the beginnings of something familiar…not just an attraction, but the embers of an emotion he had suppressed for so long. She wasn't his girl anymore.

Natasha Kestal.

He couldn't be with another girl who needed so much from him. He had nothing to give. His heart was as patched together as his ship.

Nat.

Jules.

When he heard that Juliet had died at the bombing, he didn't want to believe it, but it had been at least a year since he'd seen her. A long, lonely year.

He wondered what would have happened if he'd kissed Nat, if he had risen to the dare—he'd seen the look in her eye, the invitation—and more than anything, had wanted to accept. He was glad he had restrained himself, had not let her win; she was playing with him somehow, and he wouldn't give in to that game. He was playing one of his own, as Shakes reminded him.

"So, boss, you ask her about that stone yet?" his friend said. "Ask her where she got it? What it is?"

"In time, my friend," he said, thinking of the sparkly blue sapphire Nat wore. "In time."

Maybe he should have kissed her. Wasn't that what he was after? For her to fall for him so he could take what he wanted? So why hadn't he?

TWENTY-THREE

After their conversation the other day, they avoided being alone together. Wes kept himself scarce, eating his meals by himself and hardly leaving the captain's quarters. Nat tried not think too much about it, or why she had instigated that almost-kiss in the first place. She had hoped he would take a shine to her so that he would think twice before messing with her. That was all it was, so why did she feel so strange? He was nothing to her...and yet... she had wanted him to kiss her because she had wanted *him*...If only they were already at New Crete, so she would be rid of Wes and his ship and her confusion.

She took to reading her book up by the transom in the afternoons, and for the next few hours she was engrossed in the story. Daran and Zedric came up as well and sat away from her, at the bow of the ship, their legs dangling over the edge. Daran gave her his usual smarmy smile, and asked if she wanted to join them, but she shook her head and went back to her book.

After her eyes tired, she put it away and looked

down at the ocean. It was black and oily as usual but underneath...she saw a glimmer...a flash of color? What was that?

A fin?

A fish?

But there were no more fish in the seas, everyone knew that.

But it was a fish. It had to be. She saw its brilliant red flash flit through the water. "Did you see that?" she asked, pointing.

Daran squinted at it. "A redback!" he said. "It's got to be! I've seen photos of 'em from before. That's crazy—nothing's supposed to live in this water!"

"Nah, it's not a redback. It's one of those eels," Zedric said.

"No, it's a redback, jackass, that's not an eel; that's a fish, or you've got frostblight."

Daran was right, it was a fish. It looked like pictures she had seen of salmon in facsimisushi restaurants.

Nat marveled at it. "How did they get that coloring?"

"Got me," Daran grunted.

"It's *camouflage*," Zedric informed him. "When the water was green-blue the fish were, too, to blend in, but now that the waters aren't blue, neither are the fish. They're changing along with the water."

Daran chuckled. "I don't know where you get this stuff, bro."

The three of them sat in companionable silence. Nat

was glad; the Slaine boys gave her the creeps, Daran especially. She was about to return belowdecks when she heard Zedric yelp suddenly. She turned and saw that there was a white bird perched on the ship's antenna.

"What is it?" Zedric asked.

"It's a bird," Nat explained, wondering how he knew the name of an obscure fish and yet had no idea what a bird was.

"He's never seen one," Daran explained, a bit embarrassed for his brother.

"Neither have I," Nat breathed. Aside from the polar bears, the only animals she'd ever seen were from the old newsreels on the nets, or in surviving picture books. Pets were an indulgence, a rarity, and zoos were nonexistent in New Vegas. Supposedly the government kept animal and nature preserves in the enclosures, costing hundreds of thousands of heat credits while the rest of the population froze, but she'd never been to one.

The small white bird was beautiful, its feathers fine and lustrous, its black eyes bright with curiosity. As it spread its wings, it suddenly changed color, turning pink, yellow, and turquoise, the swirl of colors bright against the gray fog. Magical. It jumped onto Zedric's arm and began to dance on his shoulders. Nat smiled.

It was a miracle to find such vibrant life in the refuse and swill of the dark, polluted ocean. The bird hopped from Zedric's palm to Nat's and greeted her with a friendly peck. Then it unfolded its wings, puffed up its chest, and began to sing a wondrous song, echoing across the water.

A beautiful song, and Nat was enchanted. But the boys heard the song differently. They held their hands to their ears and howled in pain. Zedric was doubled up and Daran's face was red.

"STOP IT! STOP THAT THING!" Daran cried angrily. "It'll call the wailer!" He reached into his cargo pocket and pulled out his pistol, aiming for the bird.

"NO!" Nat cried, trying to protect the creature. But it was too late. Daran's bullet met its mark, and the bird let out a plaintive cry as it fell to the deck, blood flowing from its white breast.

Nat knelt to revive it, but its small lifeless body was already cold. Dead. It had been so beautiful, and now it was gone. She looked up and glared at the soldier. "You killed it!"

"Hey—" Daran said, stepping back.

But Nat was upon him. She had only meant to push him a little, but without her laying a hand on him, he flew across the deck, nearly tumbling over the edge.

"Daran!" Zedric yelled, and he pulled his brother back to safety. He dragged Daran onto his feet, breathing heavily. "What happened?"

"She did it," Daran said, pointing to the girl in their midst.

The two soldiers stared at Nat, who was still holding the dead bird in her hands. She was cooing to it. *Come back to me, come back to me, my little friend.*

"Downstairs, now," Daran said. Nat looked up and saw that the two of them had their guns pointed her way.

"Move it!" Zedric yelled.

As gently as she could, Nat dropped the bird into the ocean and marched downstairs, wondering how she would get out of this one.

"Don't touch her!" Daran warned as they hustled Nat into the crew cabin and shut the door.

"Everyone, calm down," Nat said, thinking fast. "That was an accident—it wasn't me—the ship lurched." She'd never been alone with them before, and Wes was nowhere to be found. Where was he? And where were Shakes and Farouk? In the engine room, she realized, where they would never hear her.

"I didn't do anything!"

"Yes, you did!" Daran said, waving his pistol, his face menacing. "I felt it. You pushed me—but with your mind. I should've known."

"We never should have taken up with this crew; everyone said Wes was crazy—soft—and now we know for sure!" Zedric was close to hysterics. "What are we going to do? We're all going to die!"

"Shut up!" Daran urged his brother. "Calm down, no one's going to die. But we have to make sure."

"Make sure what?"

"That she's marked."

"I don't—I swear—I'm not marked," Nat said,

horrified. "Look at my eyes!"

"You could be wearing lenses," Zedric said. "I heard about those, they cover up the colors, turn marked eyes gray."

"I'm not!"

"Prove it," Daran said. "Show us you're not marked." He leered.

"What do you mean?" Nat asked, feeling shivers up her spine. She'd noticed Daran had locked the door behind him; she was alone with them, and Wes was all the way at the other end of the ship. She was so freaking stupid. It was true what she'd said—she hadn't meant to push Daran—she didn't know how to control her power. She wasn't even sure if she could summon it now—the voice in her head was silent; it had abandoned her once again.

Daran glowered. "I said, prove it."

"No. No. No way." Nat shook her head. "Are you serious? Is this a joke?"

"Go on now…show us you don't have it," he grunted menacingly, ripping her jacket off her shoulders, and his brother actually grinned.

"No!" She tried to appeal to them in a different way. "You guys don't want to do this. You know what they say about what happens when you come in contact with—"

"Hold on. My, my, what is this?" asked Daran, zeroing in on the stone around her neck that had come into view when her jacket was torn. "What do we have here?"

"You heard what Shakes said," Zedric said.

"Oh yes, we did. Old Shakes talks too loudly, and we heard him ask Wesson about the stone. You can hear everything they say by that railing. Wind carries sound up to the helm, don't it, Zed? What did Old Shakes say? 'Did you ask her about the stone, boss?'" he said, mimicking Shakes's voice in a cruel fashion. "And we all know what stone it is, don't we?"

Daran was so close she could feel his breath on her cheek, and she shuddered in revulsion. "Oh, I get it, you don't like me, but you'd hand out the lot to him, wouldn't you? Hand yourself on a platter, most like, to our fearless leader," he said, and stepped even closer, peering at the stone. "Just like Wesson to hold out on us again, right, Zed? Not much of a boss, is he? Keeping this from his boys? When we could be back in Vegas now, rich as kings—"

"I don't know what you're talking about," Nat said, covering the stone protectively, taking a step backward.

"Give it here," Daran growled. He reached for the stone—

"DON'T TOUCH IT!" she screamed, and in an instant, she was fire and flame, and her eyes blazed green and gold, burning away her gray lenses, and Zedric was screaming and Daran was holding out his hand, which was on fire.

Someone kicked the door open and Wes stood at the

182

entryway. "What's going on in here?" he asked, and when he saw what was happening, with one powerful move, he slammed Daran hard against the wall.

"What the hell do you think you're doing?" Wes growled, his voice soft and dangerous.

"Taking what's rightfully ours," Daran sneered, his hand smoking and red. "Look what she did! LOOK WHAT SHE DID TO ME!"

"She's marked! She's a monster!" Zedric cried, cowering from the corner.

Daran grunted and Wes stared him down, his dark eyes flashing with a piercing anger. He slammed Daran against the wall again, so angry he couldn't speak.

"You *knew* what she was and you brought her anyway," Daran accused. "She got a treasure greater than god and you let her keep it!" he seethed. "You didn't even try to take it away from her! What kind of runner are you?"

Wes punched him in the face and Daran crumpled to the ground.

"SHE'S ROTTING!" Zedric screamed.

"SHUT YOUR MOUTH!" Wes ordered. He turned to Nat, who was back on her feet and had put her jacket back on. "You okay?"

She nodded. Wes moved to help just as the boat began to heave sideways. Boxes slid across the metal floor; the hammocks and lamps swung wildly.

"Trashbergs that weren't on the map, has to be," Daran

croaked from the floor.

"Shakes can't hold the wheel alone," Zedric said nervously, eyeing his brother, who shrugged.

Wes glared at his soldiers. "LEAVE! But we are not done here," he promised, as the boys brushed past Nat on their way back up the stairs.

TWENTY-FOUR

"You all right?" Wes asked, walking slowly toward Nat, keeping his balance as the ship lurched starboard. "He didn't—hurt you—did he?"

"No," she said bitterly. "Don't worry, I'd never let him touch me."

"The boys only know what they've seen on the nets. I could toss them overboard now, but they're the only crew I've got," he said. "I'm sorry I can't do more than promise I'll make damn certain they keep away from you for the rest of the trip."

She shook her head. "How long have you known about me?" she asked, her fingers shaking a little as she zipped up her jacket, making sure the stone was hidden underneath many layers once more.

Wes gazed to the ceiling. "I didn't know, but I suspected."

"You didn't care? You don't think you'll—catch it? And rot?" She pulled her jacket closed, zipped it to her neck.

"No," he said softly. "That whole thing is bunk anyway. You can't catch the mark. Either you're born with it or you're not, right? It's not a disease."

She was still shaking from the heat and the fire—she could have *killed* Daran. Worse, she *wanted* to kill him, wanted nothing more than to set him ablaze, and she felt the shame then, of being who she was, a monster. She didn't say anything about the stone, although Wes knew about it, that was clear. So why hadn't he tried to take it from her like Daran had?

"That's why your friend—Mrs. A—tried to get you out of the country, wasn't it? Because you were marked."

Nat raised her green-gold eyes to his dark ones. "I was three years old when I understood people were afraid of me." She told Wes about playing in the neighbor's apartment that day; Mrs. Allen sometimes left her there when she went to work. Nat didn't like the boy she was meant to play with—he was older and mean, pinching her when no one was looking, making sure she never got the cookie she wanted, telling her she had to stand in the corner for a myriad of trivial infractions. She was scared of him, and one day he told his mother a bald-faced lie, that she had been the one who had thrown the ball through the window and let the cold in. Then when his mother left the room Nat pushed him. She hadn't laid a hand on him, but she had pushed him with her mind—slammed him across the room, so that he hit his head on the wall and he crumpled to the carpet, wailing.

"She did it! She did it!" he'd screamed.

"I didn't touch him!" she'd yelled in her defense.

"Did she push you?" his mother demanded.

"No," David had said. "But she did it." He'd looked at her with those mean black eyes. "She's one of *them*."

After that, Nat was no longer welcome in their home, and when Mrs. Allen found out what had happened, the old lady began planning their escape.

"They sent you to MacArthur, didn't they? When they caught you at the border?" Wes asked, lifting her chin with his fingers and softly wiping away the tear on her cheek. His skin was rough against her smooth face, but she found comfort in his gentleness. "That's where you're from. You broke out."

"Yeah."

He whistled. "I'm sorry."

"It wasn't your fault. You didn't put me in there."

"So that's why we couldn't find anything on you," he said. "Farouk's pretty good on the nets; I thought it was strange you didn't have an online profile."

"They keep us off it. It's easier to disappear someone if they've never existed," she said.

"MacArthur's a military hospital. You were part of the gifted program?"

She looked up at him, startled. "You knew about that?"

He grimaced. "Yeah. I ran one of the first teams."

"We might have worked together, then," she said.

"Is that why I look familiar?" he asked.

"Maybe." She hesitated. "I was under Bradley. My commander."

Now it was Wes's turn to look unnerved. "He was mine, too." He knitted his brows. "What kind of work did you do for him?"

"If only I could remember," she said. "They mess us up, you know, to keep things confidential, to make us forget…they used to put us in ice baths, to freeze our memories somehow. I don't even know who I am, what my real name is," she said bitterly.

"I like 'Nat,'" he said with a smile. "It's as good a name as any."

"So, now you know what I am for sure, what are you going to do about it?" she asked.

"Take you where you want to go. You're headed for the Blue, aren't you? You can admit it now."

She exhaled. "Yes."

"Well then, that's where we're headed. I'll take you there or die trying. Okay?"

"Okay. I'm fine, you can go now."

"You're sure?"

"I can take care of myself."

"So you keep reminding me." He sighed. "Listen, maybe it's best if you get out of the crew cabin—you can bunk with me in the captain's if you'd like."

"Thank you," she said, and she found herself giving

him an awkward hug, surprising them both. She pressed her cheek against his chest. This was not like the other day, when she was toying with him. She wanted to hug him because being close to him made her feel better. She never realized how tall he was; she only came up to his chin, and she could hear his heart beating underneath the many layers he wore.

"You don't need to thank me," he said, patting her back somewhat stiffly. "I'm taking your credits," he joked.

"So you keep reminding me," she said quietly.

They stood in the middle of the room, simply holding on to each other, and she found solace in the warmth of his embrace. "You knew from the beginning, didn't you?" she whispered. "That I was marked?"

"If I did, does it matter?" he asked. "You don't have to hide anymore. Not on my ship, at least. Besides, it would be a shame to cover up your eyes."

She felt his breath on her cheek. "Why?"

"Because they're beautiful," he said. Their faces were inches apart, and she trembled in his arms. He leaned in and she closed her eyes…

Then the ship lurched to the port side again, throwing them against the far wall. They heard an unbearable sound—like a scratch on a chalkboard—a high-pitched whine of discord and then a grinding crash, as they parted from each other.

"Go," she said, pushing him away. "*Go!*"

Wes shook his head and cursed as he ran out of the room to see what had happened to his ship.

TWENTY-FIVE

The sound grew louder and more unbearable. Wes held his hands to his ears as he ran up the deck toward the bridge. He hesitated for a moment, paralyzed, when he saw what had happened. It was worse than he'd thought. Towering above him were two floating mountains of junk, twin trashbergs composed of rusted machinery. Souvenirs from a dead civilization and a different way of life—leather luggage with gold lettering, chromed espresso machines with complex levers and dials, soap bottles with French labels, and designer sunglasses— things Wes had heard about, but never seen. It was all junk now. The metal rusted, the leather faded, the paper rotted with mildew, even the plastic that was meant to never degrade had now cracked and melted. It all blended to make a new kind of landscape, a mountain of floating refuse.

First Daran and now this—could his day get any worse? Or was he just irritated that he'd lost another opportunity to kiss her? He'd meant what he said, but he was surprised at the depth of his feelings for her. He'd been worried when he hadn't seen her reading on the upper deck—and the lack of the Slaine boys disturbed him as well—and when he'd heard the screams he feared the worst—and to see her like that, her jacket torn off her shoulders...he could have pounded Daran's head against the floor until he was still. Wes felt sick and ashamed of his crew, and wondered if he'd made the right call to take on those boys.

Farouk stood by the navigation system and looked up nervously as Wes approached. "They weren't on the radar—I swear it—they came out of nowhere," he said.

"How bad is it?" Wes asked, directing his question to Shakes, who was at the helm.

Shakes couldn't answer, as he was throwing his full weight to pull the wheel starboard with the help of Daran and Zedric on either side, the three of them fighting to steer the ship as the trashbergs squeezed *Alby* between them, the piles of broken steel and shattered glass digging a long ugly gash along the ship's hull, biting into the thick metal.

"Move!" Wes yelled as he took the helm. "You can't steer your way out of this!" He pulled on the gearshift levers. The two engines and their propellers were side by side, and he figured if he threw one into reverse and the other forward, they would force the boat to pivot.

But the hull continued to tear. Wes powered both engines as high as he dared.

"She'll hold!" Wes said. "STEADY NOW!" The bow was starting to turn, forcing half the ship to push through a mound of trash. He scrambled to keep his balance as the trashberg pushed from below, lifting the front of the boat precariously out of the water.

"We're losing her!" Shakes warned.

Wes glared at the wheel. "Not on my watch! HOLD ON!" He jammed both engines into reverse, and the hull vibrated as he fought for control of his ship; the screeching grew louder as the boat pushed against the behemoth. The water behind them began to bubble as the propellers spun wildly, captured in their own wake. It looked as though the trash mountains would claim their ship for their own.

Shakes yelped as a wave of debris tumbled over the deck, but that was the worst of it. Since the engines were both taken from ex–military tankers, they would tear the boat apart before they stopped turning. But Wes understood he could make use of their power by jamming the starboard engine back into forward while he let the other rev in neutral for a moment. He was using the two engines to pull them out of the trashbergs by force alone.

They watched as broken refrigerators, rusted toasters, waterlogged couches, and a coffee table missing two legs fell from the sky, crashed onto the floorboards. The furniture slid together, forming grotesque living room sets before washing back into the ocean as the ship tilted to the other side. A moldy Barcalounger remained on the deck, its leather pocked with holes.

Wes kept a firm grip on the wheel, wrestling with the breakers, and steering away from the trashbergs until they were in relatively calm waters.

Farouk slapped him on the back. "We did it."

He nodded and relaxed his hold. "Take it," he told Shakes. "I'll check out the damage."

Once on the deck, he saw Nat there, helping the boys clean up. The Slaine brothers were smart enough to keep their distance, he noticed sourly. He would have to deal with them later. Put the fear of god into them if they thought they could get away that kind of crap on his watch.

"How bad is it?" Nat asked, pulling a scarf around her neck.

"We got stuck in the middle of a trashfield." Wes sighed. "We'll need to go around; it's dangerous running too close to them. We could end up stuck on a pile of junk, or worse, buried underneath one."

Shakes came out to help and pushed a lounge chair off the deck and into the churning waters. "Guess your trip just got extended," he said.

"Wonderful." She sighed.

Wes wiped his forehead with his glove and peered over the railing to study the long ugly gash on the side of his boat. "Luckily it didn't hit the inner hull."

"Otherwise?"

"We'd be sunk, literally," Shakes said cheerfully. "But don't worry, that hasn't happened yet."

"Good thing I don't charge by the mile or you'd be in trouble," Wes said, a smile twitching at the corner of his mouth.

Nat started to laugh, but her laughter quickly turned into a cough. She buried her face in the crook of her arm. "Well, it's not a perfume store, that's for sure."

Wes sighed. The trashbergs smelled even worse than the ocean, and the thought of extending the trip even farther would be a challenge for everyone, but he couldn't let it sink their spirits. "Looks bad, but we can patch it up, can't we, Shakes?" Wes asked.

"Not like we haven't before." Shakes nodded. "We'll get right on it." He stared at Nat. "Hey—you look different," he said. "What is it?" He squinted at her face.

"My eyes," she said shyly. "You can't see the difference? Really?"

"Our friend Shakes is colorblind." Wes winked. "It's all right, Farouk will fill him in," he said, as the youngest boy openly gaped at Nat, but said nothing.

"Come on, don't stare," Shakes said, pulling Farouk away so they could return to the bridge, leaving Wes and Nat on the deck. As the boat drifted out of the trashberg's shadow, they were able to see the full extent of the garbage mountain.

"It's endless," Nat whispered, fascinated by the

immense ziggurat of rot and decay and discards in front of her.

"Continents of junk," Wes said.

Nat shook her head, troubled by the sight of all that waste. The world was irretrievably broken, filled with refuse, from Garbage Country to the poisoned oceans, and the rest was an uninhabitable frozen nether land; what kind of place was this to grow up in? What kind of world had they been born into? "Is it like this— everywhere—in all the waters? Surely in some places the waters are clear?" she asked hopefully.

Wes narrowed his eyes. "Maybe. If the Blue is real." He removed the locator from his pocket and began to punch in a new course on the blinking green screen. He had nabbed the satellite phone from an abandoned LTV a few years back in garbage land. It was military-grade and had the ability to track and plot a course from live satellite data. If he was caught using or trying to sell the thing, it would mean his head, but he kept it for emergencies. "We'll have to go way out of our way to dodge 'em. Some are ten or fifteen miles across and there're bigger ones swirling all around."

As the boat plowed slowly through the churning waters, the surf was wilder on the far side of the junk mountain, and dark, filthy water rose in waves and washed over the deck again.

"Come on, let's get out of here," Wes said, holding out his hand to help her avoid stepping in the toxic wash.

She took his hand and they picked their way down to the lower cabins. "I'll take you up on your offer, if you don't mind," she said, as they walked down the stairs and he let go of her hand. "To move, I mean."

Wes nodded. "Sure."

Nat watched him silently, wondering what would have happened if the ship hadn't hit that trashberg...if they had been able to...if he had...what difference did it make? At least he hadn't tossed her overboard when he found out the truth about her. Wasn't that enough? What did she want with him anyway? She couldn't be feeling what she was feeling, if she was even feeling anything for him.

Even so, she moved her meager possessions over to his cabin. Instead of hammocks, the captain's quarters had a real bed. One bed. One small bed. "Um, Wes?" she asked.

"Yeah?" he asked, pulling off his boots and sweater, so that his T-shirt pulled up above his belt and for a brief moment she saw the hard muscles on his stomach.

"Never mind." She put her stuff away in the hold and climbed into the bed, making sure to stay all the way to the right side so that she was almost falling off.

"I'm not going to try anything, if that's what you're worried about," he said, sounding amused.

"Who said I'm worried?" she said, as he scooted in next to her. Their bodies were only inches away from each other, and when she turned to him, their faces were so close on the pillow they were almost touching.

"Good night," he whispered.

"Sleep well." She smiled and closed her eyes. They were sheltered from the toxic wash, but down below, the rocking of the ship was worse. She leaned over the edge of the bed and dry-heaved. If there was any thought of romance right now, it just went out the porthole.

"Here," Wes said, handing her a metal bracelet. "Strap it on. Helps with seasickness."

Nat wiped her mouth and accepted it with a grateful smile. Her stomach fluttered, which had nothing to do with the sea. "Thanks."

"It's not as pretty as that good-luck charm you're wearing, but it should do the trick," he said.

Good-luck charm?

He meant the stone she was wearing. She didn't say a word, but she was troubled. Wes was not Daran. But she couldn't be certain…did he want to keep her safe? Or did he just want the stone?

TWENTY-SIX

Inching along through the murky water was like wading through tar, sticky and scummy, while the smell of rotting garbage permeated the air. The days felt like weeks. Each day was the same as the one before it: gray skies, dark water, along with the rhythmic drone of the waves lapping against the sides of the boat.

The crew spent the time playing with their handhelds, drinking too much moonshine, blasting their metal reggae, bored and listless. Nat gave the brothers a wide berth and they kept to themselves anyhow, hanging around the isolated areas of the ship, whispering to each other. Once in a while she would hear them whoop and wondered what they were doing. She noticed Zedric shooting her apologetic glances every now and then, while Daran was a ghost; whatever Wes had said to him had worked. He couldn't even glance in her direction. She was glad to see his hand was still bandaged. *Burnt.*

She assumed Wes told Shakes and Farouk about her since they didn't ask her any questions, or maybe, like

Wes, they didn't care that she was marked, at least that's what she hoped; she gathered they were too busy trying to keep the ship together to pay attention. Wes didn't say anything more about the stone she wore, and she didn't bring it up. The boys filled their days repairing the hull, patching the hole by welding a few layers of steel plate that Wes kept in the storage room just for this type of eventuality.

Nat found there was little respite to be had; when she was down in the sleeping holds the rocking of the ship made her ill, and when she was up on deck the smell was worse. The crew took to wearing bandannas over their noses like bandits, and Nat was glad she had remembered to bring her silk scarf from home. It still smelled like the bottle of perfume she'd left on her dresser, although she didn't know if that even helped, since after a while she began to associate the sweet smell of jasmine with the putrid stink of decrepitude.

The mood among the soldiers was grim, after the adrenaline rush of saving the ship and their skins had subsided. The crew was touchy and grouchy: Daran and Zedric were resentful on top of it, and even Shakes, who seemed a cheerful soul, was often jumpy and irritable. Since the voyage was going to take twice as long as they'd planned, their rations were even more meager than they had expected. Everyone was seasick and hungry, and after a few days Nat learned to live with a throbbing headache and light-headedness.

That morning, she found Shakes at the galley kitchen, munching on a piece of bark.

"Can I have a piece?" she asked.

Shakes nodded, handing her a twig. "It helps with the cravings," he said.

Earlier, Wes had allowed everyone one quarter of a steak-and-egg-pancake breakfast wrap. He cut the thing in sixths and let it warm on the engine cover for half an hour before doling it out. That was it. While they ate, Nat told them that back before the floods, fat was a sign of poverty, and the rich flashed their status by going on extreme diets—juice "cleanses" and spa vacations where they paid for the privilege of not eating. None of them believed her.

She crunched the piece of wood in her mouth and spit it out. "How can you eat this?" She coughed.

Shakes smiled. "You'll do anything to survive." He took the bark back, his hands trembling a little.

Nat opened a can of Nutri. There was enough in the storeroom for centuries. She took a sip, tasting the flat, lukewarm liquid.

She watched as Shakes's hand jittered holding the bark, fluttering nervously like a hummingbird's wings.

"Do you take anything for that?" she asked. "I heard they've got a new drug now that helps with the shaking from frostblight."

"Oh, this?" Shakes asked, lifting his hand up and watching it tremble. "I don't have FB like the boss. I've

201

had this since I was a baby."

"Wait—Wes has frostblight?" she asked.

"Yeah, you haven't noticed? His eyes bother him sometimes," Shakes said.

"I hadn't." She felt an ache for Wes, now that she knew. It's not a disease, he'd said, about being marked. No, not like his. "I'm sorry for thinking you have it." Nat was embarrassed.

"No, don't be. It's an easy mistake." Shakes smiled.

"What happened? Wes told me your story was a doozy."

"It is. He tell you I have a brother?"

"No."

"I do. An older one. Patrick. Our 'rents were good people. Rule-following civilians, not like us," he said, smiling. "They got a license for both of their kids. They wanted more than one. Expensive, but they could afford it. They wanted Pat to have a sibling, a playmate. One day there was a knock on the door.

"It turns out Mom filled out part of the license application wrong. Secondary offspring license denied. I was illegal, and not a citizen. You know how it goes, the country gets low on a quota and they start looking for excuses to collect. Who knows if Mom ever actually made that error. But it didn't matter, Population Control was on the case. I was three, four months old? I'm not sure. Anyway, the repo man grabbed me and made for the door, while Mom grabbed my other leg and the two of them get into tug of war right there on the balcony.

202

They're pushing and pulling and somehow the guy drops me, and I hit my head right on the concrete. *Bam!*"

She covered her mouth in horror, but Shakes only grinned, clearly enjoying the story.

"I start to convulse, right, and the repo man freaks out; they can sell babies on the black markets for good money, just another way to keep the war machine going, but no one wants a defective one. They don't want me anymore, they tell Mom and Dad. They don't even apologize, and they stick them with the hospital bill, too."

"Ouch."

"My parents didn't care—they got to keep me." Shakes smiled. "Course it bankrupted them, which is why I had to volunteer."

"That's horrible," Nat said quietly.

"That's life." He didn't seem too perturbed. "I get blackouts, too, sometimes seizures; everyone thinks it's just frostblight, so I get to pass as normal."

"Not sure 'normal' is the right word." Nat smiled.

He chuckled. "Many won't disagree with you there."

"So are your folks still around?" she asked.

"Just my dad," Shakes said.

"Are you guys close?" she asked. She knew she was prodding, but she was always curious about the people who still had parents.

"Not really." Shakes grimaced and tossed the twig into the bin. "We never were, I guess, since he never forgave my mom."

"For dropping you?"

"For *having* me," he said. "He's not a bad guy, but you know how it is."

She didn't, but she nodded sympathetically "So they tried to take you away—like they did Wes's sister."

"Wes's sister?"

"He said they took her away because his parents hadn't applied for the second-child license."

"That what he told you about Eliza?"

"Yeah."

Shakes didn't say anything. He only looked confused. "But I thought…"

"Thought what?"

"That they got a pass on it. You know, the law makes an exception in their case. Because Eliza and Wes…they were twins."

"Huh." She didn't know what to say to that.

"He always told me that…"

"That what?"

Shakes tossed the twig away. "Nothing. Forget I said anything," he said, looking nervous.

She saw his discomfort and changed the subject. "So what are you guys going to do after this?"

"After we drop you off? Go back to working casino security I guess. Maybe by then, they'll have forgiven old Wesson."

Nat smiled. "Thanks for the bark."

"Anytime," Shakes said, giving her a salute.

TWENTY-SEVEN

Daran was trying to take the stone, and she was struggling, but this time, there was no escape, and he was jeering at her, and laughing, and she was so cold, so cold, and there was nothing she could do, the fire would not start, and the little white bird was dead, and there was no one to help, no one to break down the door, she was all alone, and he would take it away from her and then he would toss her overboard to die, and she was angry, so angry, but there was nothing, she could do nothing, and she was weak and helpless, furious and frightened and she was calling…calling out…and there was a terrible noise, screeching…

Wailing…

She awoke to the sound of loud shrieking echoing through the cabin walls. Nat fought through the haze of sleep and saw Wes standing, paralyzed in the middle of the room, shirtless in his pajama bottoms, listening.

"What is it?" she whispered. It was a long, high screech, a ghostly howling, unearthly, like the sound in her dream.

She was cold, so cold, like in her dream, so cold.

Wes shook his head and pulled on a sweater, and she followed him as they walked out of the room to find the rest of the crew standing stock-still outside their quarters, listening to that strange, horrible sound.

"Wailer," said Zedric, his voice cracking.

The shrieking continued, and Nat thought Zedric was right, there was something about the sound that felt like grief, the sound of keening—later, she would liken it to the moans of a mother who had lost her child—it was a whining, a doubled-down sort of pain.

"Wailer. Like funeral wailers," Nat said, thinking of the elaborate funeral rites that had become the norm for those who could afford it, where professional mourners were hired to wail and cry and pull their hair to show the level of wealth and the depth of bereavement of the family. The more elaborate the show of grief, the more expensive. Like everything nowadays, it was a tradition that started in the Xian and trickled out to the rest of the remaining world.

Nat had worked as a mourner once, walking in front of the funeral casket of a high-level casino boss; she'd learned the tricks to faking a good cry—a few drops of Nutri to start the tears flowing, then a little imagination—and she was soon sobbing away. It wasn't that hard to tap into the sadness she carried inside. The pit boss who'd hired her was impressed, offered her a steady gig as a griever, but she was done. She'd been emotionally exhausted after the experience, had wrung her soul dry for some exec who didn't care that his staff had to pay the cost of their own uniforms and housing from their tiny paychecks.

"It's out there," Zedric repeated, then crossed himself. "Coming to get us—"

Daran smacked his brother on the head. "Get a hold of yourself, man!" He turned angrily to Nat. "I told you— I told you that bird would call it! That bird was a bad omen!"

Even Shakes and Farouk looked nervous, but Wes scrunched up his face with disdain. "Wailer's just another bogeyman story. To keep people out of the waters."

"Just because no one's seen it doesn't mean it don't exist," Zedric said sullenly.

"You're right, people have only heard the cries." Wes nodded. "The wailer is a myth as old as this dead sea."

"What is it?" Nat asked.

"Some kind of animal, they say, like a dinosaur, a Loch Ness thing, although it would be a miracle if there's anything that's survived in this ocean." Wes mimicked drinking a glass of water. "If you swallowed a pint of that poisoned water every day, you'd screech like that, too."

The sound continued to grow louder, and Nat thought she could make out words in the awful noise, that the wailing made sense somehow, that it was communicating, sending a message across the ocean. Then it was silent, and Nat held her breath, hoping it would go away.

The sound was so familiar...

"And if it's not an animal, what is it then?" she asked.

"People. Dead people," Wes explained. "Some say the wailer's a phantom of all the spirits of those that have been taken by the black waters. The pilgrims the slavers deceived and dumped, or the souls of the slaves that were tossed overboard when they were of no use to their masters anymore, or they didn't fetch a good price at the flesh markets. They're trapped together, cursed to haunt the dead oceans forever."

Nat shuddered at the thought. So the wailer was just another type of thriller—except one that could swim. So why did she feel as if she could understand it then—almost as if she felt its pain? She began to shiver violently, her teeth began to chatter, and she felt as if she might faint.

"Nat—what's wrong?" Wes asked, and he held her, rubbing her arms with his, enveloping her in his embrace. "You're shaking...you should go back to sleep."

They stiffened as the air filled with long, low moans, echoing off the cold water. The screams grew in volume, and the sounds were no longer far away, but louder, closer and closer.

"It's here!" hissed Zedric, just as a large boom resounded from the ceiling.

"Something's hit the ship!" Farouk yelped.

"What now," Wes muttered, releasing Nat and running toward the steps heading to the upper deck to see what had happened, but he was thrown backward as another boom echoed through the cabin, and now there was the sound of tearing—a ripping, horrible noise, loud and angry—as if the ship were being torn apart piece by piece.

"WHAT THE..."

The boat lurched as the first engine died, and started to spin in a broad arc, rolling hard to one side as the remaining engine drove them in an out-of-control circle. A moment later the second engine failed abruptly and the ship coasted to a stop.

"The engines!" Shakes cried as Wes leapt to run upstairs, but Farouk pulled him back. "Stop! We don't know what's out there!"

"Let me go!" Wes said, as he pushed Farouk away.

Nat followed him up the stairs.

"Stay back!" he yelled.

"No—if there's something out there—I might be able to help!"

He shook his head but didn't argue.

They ran up to the deck together and looked down. There was a massive steel engine hatch on the aft deck, tossed upside down like a tortoise shell. The other hatch was sinking quickly into the dark waters. Only bolt holes remained where the hatches had been torn from their mountings. In the bilge, the starboard engine was nothing but a smoking black void—a broken hose leaked gas and water into the pit. There was a hole in the bottom of the ship where the propeller had been torn free and water was pouring into the cavity. The port engine was still in place, but impossibly damaged. Its thick steel housing had fused together, melted, as if it had been run through a blast furnace. Shards from the motor were strewn all over the deck. One engine had been torn deliberately from the ship, and the other one completely burned.

"There!" Nat said, pointing out to the distance, where the darkness coalesced into a massive, horned shape above the water.

"Where?"

"I thought I saw something—" But when she looked again, a faint light shone through the clouds, and whatever it was vanished. She blinked her eyes—was it merely a trick of the light?

The rest of the crew crept up on board. Daran kicked at the remnants of the motor while Zedric muttered voodoo prayers under his breath. "The wailer did this... we're cursed," he whispered.

Shakes sighed. "So much for the trashbergs." The massive trash mountains were the least of their concerns now.

"We're stuck!" Farouk groaned. "Without an engine we're dead in the water."

"Looks like it." Wes nodded, frowning.

Nat was silent as the crew contemplated the latest disaster.

They were adrift in a vast poisonous arctic sea.

TWENTY-EIGHT

No one slept. When morning finally came, Nat found the crew gathered on the deck. Wes had ordered them all back to bed the night before, the Slaine brothers grumbling and peeved, Farouk whimpering a little, at the latest setback with the loss of their engines. Only Shakes and Wes appeared untroubled.

"This is nothing." Shakes smiled. "When we were in Texas, we went for a month without eating, right, boss?"

Wes shook his head. "Not now, Shakes."

"Right."

The boys were rigging a sail and Nat watched as Wes drove a bent crowbar underneath a plate in the center of the deck and heaved the square of steel upward. Zedric raised two more panels in the same manner.

"Secret compartments?" Nat smiled.

"It's a runner's boat," Wes said with a grin.

Nat looked down through a crisscross of metal braces into the hold and saw a water-stained cloth wrapped around a steel mast.

A sail.

She was impressed. "You knew this was going to happen?" she asked.

"No, but I prepare for everything. You can't sail the oceans without one." Wes shrugged. "Never thought I'd need it, though. I never thought *Alby* would turn into a fifteenth-century ship. All right, pull it up, boys," he ordered.

Shakes smiled. "See? I told you, we've got options."

"Yeah, we're not dead in the water just yet," Farouk said. "C'mon, Nat, you know we got game."

"Farouk, stop flirting with the lady and help me with this," Wes grunted, and the boys struggled to erect the makeshift sail.

"Nice work," Nat said, walking over to put a hand on his arm—an affectionate gesture that was not lost on him. Or the crew. She felt Wes stiffen under her touch, as if a jolt of lightning had sparked between them.

"Who's flirting with the lady now?" Shakes laughed.

Nat blushed and Wes's smile deepened.

There was a moment of solidarity and Nat felt that after the ugliness of what happened earlier, things had settled. The sail caught wind, and for now, everything would be all right.

That evening, Nat retired to her bunk in Wes's cabin. Wes was already sleeping in the bed, an arm thrown over his eyes. He slept like a kid, she thought, looking at him fondly. The ship was moving silently through the ocean, the rocking had stopped for a moment, and Nat was glad. She turned her back to him, quickly changed into a T-shirt and climbed in next to him.

"Good night," Wes whispered.

Nat smiled to herself. So he wasn't as out of it as she had thought. She wondered whether he had watched her change, whether he had seen her out of her clothes, and she realized she didn't mind—she was more than a little intrigued by the idea...all she had to do was turn around and put her arms around him... Instead, she fiddled with the stone around her neck, and the moonlight caught its glow, sending a rainbow of colors around the small cabin.

"What is that?" Wes asked, his voice low in the darkness.

Nat took a deep breath. "I think you know... it was Joe's."

"He gave it to you."

"I asked for it," she said. She could sense him stirring in the dark, next to her, and now he was sitting up, staring at the stone.

"Do you know what it is?" he asked.

Nat felt a reckless inhibition take hold, and the voice in her head was seething—telling her to keep silent—but she did not. "Yes," she said finally. "It's Anaximander's Map."

The smugglers and traders named it after the ancient Greek philosopher who charted the first seas. But on the streets they just called it the Map to the Blue. The pilgrims believed that the Blue was not only real, but that it had always existed as part of this world, merely hidden from sight and called different names throughout history—Atlantis and Avalon among them. They swore that the stories that had filtered down through the ages—dismissed as myth and fairy tale—were real.

She watched him absorb the news. She had always assumed he knew she had it, and that it was the real reason he had taken the job. Runners like Wes knew everything there was to know about everything in New Vegas. He might be a good guy, but he wasn't stupid.

"You know the story, don't you?" Wes asked. "How Joe won it in a card game."

"I don't, actually."

"They said the guy he won it from was shot dead on the Strip the next day."

Nat was silent.

"Why do you think he kept it for so long?" Wes asked.

"Without using it, you mean?"

"Yeah."

"I don't know."

"Do you think it's real?" he asked.

"He did live an awful long time; you know what they say, it's supposed to be...well, keep you young or something. Anyway, look for yourself," she told him, taking it off and handing it to him.

Wes took the stone and held it gently between his

thumb and his forefinger. "What do you mean?"

"Hold it up, look through the circle. Do you see it?"

He did, and exhaled, and Nat knew he saw. "Joe didn't see it. He looked through it and saw nothing. Maybe the map wouldn't reveal itself to him somehow. That's why he never used it, because he didn't know how."

"This is incredible," Wes said.

"How long till we get there?" she asked.

"I'm guessing ten days," Wes said, studying the route. "More or less." He told her that, as many runners had guessed, New Crete was the closest port, but many ships had crashed or beached or gotten lost in the dangerous waters of the Hellespont. This route sketched a hidden, winding passage through the uncharted waters, to an island in the middle of an archipelago. There were a hundred tiny islands in that grouping; no one knew which was the one that led to the Blue. Except for this map.

He gave it back to her to hold.

"Don't you want it?" she asked, almost daring him.

"What would I do with it?" he asked her, his voice soft.

"Are you sure?" she asked.

For a long time, Wes did not answer. Nat thought maybe he had fallen asleep. Finally, she heard his voice. "I wanted it once," he said. "But not anymore. Now I just want to get you where you need to go. But do me a favor, okay?"

"Anything," she said, feeling that warm tingle all over

again. He was so close to her, she could reach out and touch him if she wanted, and she wanted, so very badly...

"If Shakes ever asks you about it—tell him you got it a five-and-dime store."

She joined him in laughter, but they both froze, as the sound of the wailer broke over the waves again—that awful, horrible scream—the sound of a broken grief—a keening—echoing over the water—filling the air with its mournful cries...

That thing, whatever it was, was still out there. They were not alone.

PART THE FOURTH

COMRADES AND CORSAIRS

Fifteen men on a dead man's chest
Yo ho ho and a bottle of rum
Drink and the devil had done for the rest
Yo ho ho and a bottle of rum

—Traditional Pirate Song

TWENTY-NINE

With the sails in place, the trip moved in small, quick bursts, gaining speed and putting miles behind them, or none at all, as the ship moved at the mercy of the wind. Wes was on deck, in the crow's nest at the top of the mast. He squinted. A small light emerged from the fog. It grew brighter and closer, and Wes could hear voices from the craft.

A ship!

Rescue!

Wes was not the type to believe in miracles but, against his better nature, he began to hope. If it was a mercenary ship, he might be able to make some sort of a trade—he just hoped it wasn't a naval boat or a slaver. Then they were sunk. But if it was a fellow merc... Wes believed there was honor among thieves, among traders and vets and runners like him who worked on the fringes. Sure, they were scavengers and sellouts, losers and gamblers, but they had to work together, or they would be picked off one by one by the RSA, who would either throw them all in the pen or shoot them on sight, or by the slavers, who were far more dangerous and answered to no authority but their own.

He hadn't told Shakes that Nat had told him about the stone, that she had confirmed it to be what they had suspected all along, and had even offered it to him. Why had he turned it down? He was supposed to take it—*steal it* from her—it was just a game to see who would win, who would give in first. Could he trick her into trusting him? He had won at last. So why did he feel as if he had lost?

She trusted him, so why was he so melancholy? Because Shakes would be disappointed, and didn't he owe the guy his life? And more? Nah. It wasn't that. Because if he'd accepted the stone and sold it to Bradley, they would be set up, rewarded, hailed as kings of New Vegas? Nah. It wasn't that, either. Bradley could jump off a cliff as far as Wes was concerned, and as far as riches went, all he needed was a decent meal and a place to sleep and he was happy. He was in a bad mood because now they were closer to their destination than ever before. Only ten days away, and once they arrived there, he would never see her again.

That was what was bothering him.

There was nothing he could do to change that, nothing he could do to make her stay. He hadn't planned on feeling this way, but there it was. Oh well, maybe he could make it up to Shakes somehow. Maybe today was their lucky day. There was a ship on the horizon.

"You see it?" he asked, climbing down to where Shakes was already at the rails with binoculars.

"Yeah. A boat."

"What kind?"

"Hard to say." Shakes handed over the binoculars and scratched the scruff on his chin. "Take a look."

Wes did and his heart sank. It was a mercenary ship all right, but it was much worse off than theirs, without motor or sail. Just another unlucky crew like his, maybe even unluckier. The hull had a huge hole in it, but unlike their boat, it wasn't patched, and the deck was quickly filling with dark water. It was sinking and was likely going to capsize at any moment. It was the ship's luck to run into them, not the other way around.

He zeroed in on the crowd huddled on the deck. Through the green lenses, he could see a family with small children. They were waving frantically. Wes handed the binoculars back to Shakes, calculating the risks, the odds. Five more mouths to feed, he counted. Two of them children. They had so little already, they couldn't possibly stretch their supplies any more; the soldiers were already eating bark. What could he offer this family?

His boys were massed on the deck, awaiting orders. The broken ship had drifted nearer, and now all of them could see who was on board and what was at stake. Wes knew how the Slaine brothers would vote, and Farouk would probably agree, although the adventure he had expected wasn't turning out quite as he had hoped. They were all cold, hungry, and lost. But Shakes was ready with the rope, and Nat looked at him expectantly.

"We can't just stand here and do nothing," she said, almost daring him to argue with her.

"When you save someone's life, you're responsible for it." Wes sighed. But even with his misgivings, he took the rope and threw it overboard, and someone on the other boat caught it. Better to let them drown, he thought; it was probably more merciful. But if he were that kind of guy, they would be heading to Bradley with Anaximander's Map in hand and Nat in the brig.

With Shakes's help, they pulled the sinking boat closer, and one by one the soldiers helped the family climb up on deck. The first to board was a young woman, draped in heavy black robes, her entire body and face covered in the black fabric so that only her eyes were visible.

"Thank you," she croaked, taking Shakes's outstretched hand. "We thought no one would ever find us out here." Then she noticed his fatigues and shuddered. "Oh god…"

"Relax, we're just a bunch of vets," Shakes assured her.

Following behind her were a mother, father, and two children. The group of them huddled in a blanket. The parents were deathly ill, with pale and gaunt faces, profoundly malnourished, and Wes guessed they had been out here for several weeks with little water or food, and whatever there was to eat or drink had been given to the children.

"Where's the captain?" he asked, taking the rope. The girl and the family must have been cargo; they looked like pilgrims searching for the Blue. This had to be a mercenary ship, but where was the crew?

He took the rope and climbed down to the sinking ship. Since he'd opted to do the right thing, he had to see it all through.

"Don't—" the girl in black warned. "It's—"

But it was too late, Wes was already on board and had headed down to the lower decks to see if he could find the crew. Down below, the empty cabins were filled waist high with water. He walked back up to the upper deck to the bridge, and there he found the answer to his question. Two deckhands, both dead—shot in the head, it looked like. The captain was at the helm, slumped over, cold and dead, another bullet in the middle of his forehead. The bridge was enclosed in glass on all sides. Wes could see the holes where the shots had entered and exited. The bullets had come from another vessel, and the clean shots to the head told the rest of the story. If the ship had been attacked by slavers, the men would have seen them coming and hid from their fire. But the crew never saw these shots coming. Only a trained sniper could take out a mark from nearly a click. The dead men never even knew they were targets.

Whoever did this hadn't even bothered to board the ship to look for passengers. With the crew dead and the hull leaking, the ocean would claim anyone left on the boat. Only the RSA would let its citizens drown and starve as punishment for crossing the forbidden ocean.

So, the naval carriers were out on patrol. They would have to be even more careful now, make sure none of the boys or Nat stayed up on deck during the daylight hours; the crew would hate it, no one liked being trapped down in the cabins, but if the snipers were out there...

The ship lurched to the side and Wes climbed quickly down the narrow stairs that led back to the deck. He nearly tripped on the last step. Something had changed, the walls were moving, the ship was taking on more water. The sinking ship had three open ports and maybe even a few blast holes that were allowing additional water to enter the craft, increasing her rate of descent as she sank quickly now into the sea. Wes reached the deck, but it was too late; one side of the craft had caught on the tip of a trashberg and the other was submerged below the water. The ship's metal hull ripped and the ocean flooded in all around him.

Wes ran back to the bridge where the dead men rested. Their blank eyes stared at him from all sides. The black water was following him up the stairs. In a moment the ship would be entirely under water. He pulled the captain's chair from its mount and rammed it through the broken glass. The shattered pane collapsed and the chair flew into the ocean. Wes climbed out, cutting himself as he struggled to reach the roof of the bridge.

He leapt from the wreckage toward the rope that was

dangling from his ship, but the distance was too far, and he flailed, falling to the water.

He locked eyes with Daran—who held the rope, his eyes flat and cold. Where was Shakes? "THROW IT BACK!" Wes yelled. Daran remained impassive, and Wes knew what he was thinking. Without Wes, Daran would only have Shakes to deal with, and that wouldn't be too hard; he would be able to take care of Shakes and Nat, throw them overboard with the stupid starving family as soon as Wes drowned, then take control of the ship and head back home.

"THROW IT BACK, I SAID!"

But Daran merely shrugged. He watched without remorse as the water rose.

Wes screamed as he plunged below the surface. He tried to close his eyes and mouth, but it all happened too fast. The black fluid burnt like alcohol in his mouth. He pressed his eyelids closed in an attempt to push back the black water. His arms flailed in the smooth alien liquid. But his legs kicked hard, and he was able to pull himself up, and break through, gasping for air. He squinted, looking around, but his blurred vision saw only gray sky and water. The rope was gone.

*Nat…*he cried in his mind, *can you hear me?*

Cold waves crashed over his head. He closed his eyes as he sank below again. Something crashed into his spine. Maybe it was a rail from the ship or just some random piece of junk; either way, it stung, and he opened his

225

mouth involuntarily. Black water filled his lungs. He was drowning. He would die.

But just as he took his last breath, he felt a warm, powerful force lift him up from the water and toward the rope, and he lunged out and grabbed it, as Shakes and Nat pulled him to safety. He fell onto the deck on all fours, and they helped him up, Nat putting her arms around him.

"All right, boss?" Shakes said, patting his back. "I'll get you a Nutri, be right back."

"Thank you," he said, taking Nat's hand. He felt the lovely warmth of her skin, so like the warmth that had saved him from sure death. He should have kissed her the other day. He wanted to kiss her now.

"Nat...look at me," he said. "What's wrong?"

She bowed her head.

"Don't cry."

"It's nothing," she said, pulling out of his grasp.

Wes let her go, feeling his emotions roil within him. She'd heard him call for her. There was something between them they couldn't deny anymore. It scared her—and it scared him, too. But another part of him was happy, happier than he'd ever felt in his life. He wished she hadn't run away like that. He felt a sudden emptiness, as if she had answered his question without him asking it, and the answer, alas, was no. This was not meant to be.

"What was that all about?" Farouk asked.

"She pulled him from the ocean," Daran spat.

"How'd she do that?"

"She can do that sort of thing because she's marked, dumb-ass. Or are you as blind as Shakes?"

"She's marked...right... I forgot..."

"And she's not the only one." Zedric nodded, pointing to the girl draped in black.

THIRTY

Nat stumbled as she walked away from the group gathered around the rail. She had heard Wes call for her—had seen his distress so clearly—the black water around his face, his open mouth in a silent scream. Before she knew what she was doing, she had been able to focus her power like never before, to send her strength to save him. He unlocked something in her that she'd never been able to do before, and it frightened her. She could sense the voice in her head was silent, disapproving. Wes was falling for her, too, and it was wrong of her to encourage it. It had been a flirtation, nothing more, but now…now it was different. The way he looked at her! He couldn't feel that way about her. He would only get hurt. She could only hurt him. That's what she did. She *hurt* people.

Fire and pain.

Rage and ruin.

Daran with his bloody, burnt hand.

She would push him away, she decided. She would make him forget her. It was wrong of her to have led him on…to have made him think that he could ever be anything to her but a runner she had hired.

When she'd recovered, she looked back to see what the crew was staring at—the girl wearing long black robes, a cowl over her head, a scarf around her neck and mouth, long black gloves on her hands. Her bright violet eyes and golden hair glittered from the darkness of her hood.

"I know what you are," Daran sneered, pointing his gun at her menacingly.

"Leave her alone," Shakes warned, coming up next to him and unlocking his gun.

But Daran wouldn't stop or he couldn't help himself. He'd gone unhinged, Nat realized. He was on the edge before, but now he was well and truly lost. Nat feared for the girl. Daran had shown his hand—had revealed his tell—he'd already tried to hurt Nat and, just moments before, he'd even tried to get rid of Wes. He was dangerous, a powder keg ready to explode.

"What do you look like under that curtain you wear? Like a candy-colored corpse? Or a painted skeleton?"

Zedric backed away nervously.

"She's a guest," Wes warned, his tone commanding. "And this is still my boat. Put the gun down, Daran. I won't ask you again."

There was an ugly silence, and no one moved; Nat felt as if she had forgotten to breathe. Daran shifted, and Wes preempted his strike, but Daran had already cocked his gun. He was raving. "I don't want no dirty sylph around—"

"PUT IT DOWN!" Wes yelled, holding up his own weapon. He fired, the bullet clipping Daran's elbow, but it was too late.

Daran had fired, shooting the dark-robed girl point-blank.

"NO!" Nat screamed as Shakes dove in front of the hooded pilgrim. But there was no need. The bullet had disappeared. In an instant, the sky darkened and thunder rumbled. Then the clouds parted and the strange light that had appeared the night before returned.

From out of the darkness came the screech of the wailer. One moment Daran was standing on the deck, and in the next, he was torn from the ship by an unseen hand.

"WHAT HAPPENED? WHERE IS HE?" Zedric yelled, spinning around, pointing his gun every which way.

A cry echoed across the water, angry and victorious. It wanted blood and had gotten it. Nat felt its exultation as if it were part of her. It was furious and excited, just like in her dreams. Fire and pain, rage and ruin, a dark uncontrollable force, waiting to lash out—murderous with revenge and hatred, it had taken Daran in an instant, had swept him off the deck as if he were a toy. Nat stepped back, unsure of what had happened—had she done that? Had she made that thing—that wailer—do what she wanted to do? No. It couldn't be. The wailer wasn't real, was it? What happened to the voice—to the monster in her head? She couldn't reach it. She couldn't hear it. She began to panic. What was happening?

"There he is!" Farouk said excitedly. "In the water—over there!"

Wes came up to the rails with binoculars in hand. He saw the small figure of Daran bobbing above the waves, waving his arms. Whatever had taken Daran had thrown him half a mile away in a few seconds.

"Bring him back!" Zedric screamed, cocking a gun and aiming it at the girl. But he wouldn't get a chance.

There was a blow, and Zedric fell to the ground unconscious. Shakes stood behind him, holding his rifle aloft, trembling a little, but with a smile on his face.

"Sorry about that. I need to teach the boys some manners," he said.

The girl smiled. "I am Liannan of the White Mountain," she said.

"Vincent Valez," Shakes said, smiling bashfully.

"Can you bring him back?" Wes asked impatiently, motioning to where Daran was flailing. They could hear his screams of fury echoing across the water.

Liannan shook her head. "No. The drakon took him and only the drakon can decide his fate now."

"Well—we'll have to get him out—he's a jackass, but he's still part of my crew." With Shakes's and Farouk's help, Wes moved to push a lifeboat into the water, but a

231

powerful gust of wind knocked them back on the deck. The sickly wailing sound returned, and Wes felt something hot and sharp rake across his back, tearing through the layers he wore and ripping into his skin.

He turned around, but there was nothing. Shakes returned his confusion with a dazed look on his face.

"What was that?" Farouk asked anxiously, holding his head.

"The drakon does not suffer him to live," Liannan said placidly. "Do not cross it or fear its wrath."

"We're risking our own lives to help that jerk," Farouk argued. "C'mon, boss, let him drown."

Wes shook his head. "No—help me get this boat in. I'm not leaving anyone behind."

"He killed the messenger, he assaulted its familiar, and so the drakon demands a life for a life," Liannan murmured. "I must advise you not to go against his wishes."

They tried again, and this time the wind stopped them, so that the ship teetered wildly and tipped to the starboard edge.

"Hold on!" Wes screamed, as Nat tumbled forward, Wes catching her just in time. As everyone scrambled for purchase, Zedric slipped, rolling toward the edge, but Farouk caught him and he was able to hold on to the mast.

"Shakes!" Nat yelled, as they watched Shakes tumble into the dark water.

"Get him!" Wes yelled to Farouk, but it was no use.

"Pull me out!" Shakes sputtered, his head appearing above the waves, his arms waving wildly. "Help me!"

But the wind kept everyone back, kept them clinging to the rails, unable to help. Shakes would drown. They were going to lose him, Nat knew. *Spare him. Please*, she prayed, not knowing whom she was entreating with her cry. *Not him. Not Shakes. He is my friend.*

Nat looked up to find the dark-robed girl staring at her. Liannan's eyes glowed in a rainbow of shockingly brilliant colors. She was staring at Nat, holding her gaze, studying her.

"SHAKES!" Wes tossed a rope to the castoff, but it snapped in the air, torn by an invisible force.

Please, let us save him. He's just a boy, Nat begged. Somehow, she understood that thing out there was punishing them because Daran had killed the little white bird. That thing out there was angry, and its fury would not be abated.

Please.

"HELP ME!" Shakes screamed.

Liannan shed her robe. "Drakon! The boy saved me! Let him live!" She pulled her hood and mask from her face. Underneath the dark drapery she wore a long, slim white tunic. Her long hair was the color of sunlight from long ago, dazzling and golden. The cold night air began to soften, the temperature growing warm as a light pierced the night. The light was strong and powerful, and the darkness faded and the wailing subsided.

Nat clutched her forehead, trembling as a wave of frustration and anger washed over her. It felt as if someone—or something—was pushing her to do something, but what? What could she do? She was angry, so angry at Daran and confused that Shakes had fallen into the middle of the entire thing. She took calm, steady breaths. She could hear the sylph. *The boy saved me. Let him live*. The danger had passed. That's what the sylph was trying to say, trying to make her understand.

The darkness dissipated as quickly as it came.

Wes grabbed the torn rope and lowered it to Shakes. With the crew's help, everyone pulling together, they heaved the soldier back on deck.

Shakes appeared, frantically rubbing his eyes and spitting. His skin and face were red, raw, his eyes wild and confused. Farouk ran up and dumped a liter of Nutri on his head.

Shakes yelped.

Wes knelt down and grabbed his friend by the shoulders. "*Shakes!*"

The shivering boy paused. "What?"

"You're fine! You're not poisoned, you're fine!"

Shakes looked down at himself, not quite sure what to look for. Then he smiled. "Right." He turned to the ocean. "But what about Daran?"

Wes threw a life preserver overboard, knowing it was a waste. "There's no wind, no way for us to reach him. At least this gives him a chance—it's all we can do," he said, not liking it, but not having a choice either.

Daran's screams began to fade; soon they mixed with the familiar sound of the wailer's mourning, and it became harder and harder to differentiate the two.

THIRTY-ONE

When Zedric awoke to find his brother still missing, he became violent. If they didn't subdue him, he would hurt himself or the crew. They put him in the brig; it was cruel, but they had no other option. "Go on—I'll take it from here," Shakes told Nat, as he handcuffed the boy to the nearest pipe.

She walked out of the room and saw the sylph approaching. The girl had put her dark cloak back on, but her hood was down. Her eyes were pure violet, the color of asters and twilight. Her pale blond hair was fragile and delicate like cobwebs, like fairies' wings. The mark on her cheek was a six-pointed star. She was lovely, far lovelier than Nat had expected, like an exotic, rare creature, like the extinct and legendary butterflies from the world that no longer was.

Liannan smiled at her. "You've seen my kind before, haven't you?"

"Yes."

"A prisoner, no doubt, or a token, a performing monkey."

Nat thought of the golden-eyed girl with the orange hair, the Slob's favorite pet, and understood now. "You spoke about something called the drakon—what is it?" Nat asked.

Liannan studied her before answering. "The drakons are protectors of Vallonis. They have been lost since the breaking, but now one has returned." Her voice was like the sound of falling water, it had a lovely lilt, like a melody.

"Vallonis...do you mean the Blue...is that what you call it?"

"Yes." Liannan nodded. "That is what I call my home."

Farouk came stomping down the stairs into the hallway, and when he saw the two of them, his face blanched and he crossed himself as if to ward them away. It pained Nat to see him—she'd thought Farouk was a friend, like Shakes—but now the young boy was gaping at them, pressing himself against the wall so that no part of his body would come into contact with either of them.

Liannan laid a hand on his shoulder and he visibly flinched.

"You have nothing to fear from me. I am not infectious. I can no more turn you into one of us than I can turn into one of you," she said.

Farouk did not look convinced and shook her hand off him. "Don't *touch* me."

There was the sound of footsteps on the stairs. "What's going on here?" Wes asked, looking at the troubled faces in front of him.

"She touched my shoulder," Farouk accused. "And she killed Daran."

"I did no such thing," Liannan said. "It was the drakon who decided his fate," she said, turning to Nat.

"Leave her alone," Shakes said, as he walked out of the room where they had imprisoned Zedric. "She didn't do anything to him. He asked for it, he was looking for trouble. Things happen out here in the water—you haven't been, you don't know."

"Or it could be nothing. Coincidence," Wes said, his gaze falling on Nat as well.

"What brings you to this part of the world, Ryan Wesson?" Liannan asked.

"You know my name," he said, and Nat felt a stab of jealousy to see him give Liannan the same smirk he'd given her the first time they'd met. She knew she had no claim to him, and that she had already decided to all but cut him loose, but somehow she couldn't help but feel as if he were hers and hers alone.

Liannan cast her cool gaze upon him. "I know everyone on board this ship. Ryan Wesson, the mercenary. Vincent Valez, second in command, more commonly addressed as 'Shakes.' Farouk Jones, navigator. Daran Slaine, currently in the water. Zedric Slaine, his brother. And... Natasha Kestal." Liannan turned to her and stared. "Who asked about the drakon…"

Wes raised an eyebrow and regarded Nat with a questioning gaze.

"You are marked," Liannan said.

Nat nodded.

"So you are one of us." The sylph nodded. "Do not worry," she told the others. "Our powers are not malicious in nature, no matter what you have been led to believe. Do you know why they cast us out? Why we are hunted and killed, or confined to prisons? Why they spread lies about our people? Because their world is broken, their world is ending, and so they fear us, they fear what is coming. The world that is returning, that is growing in the ruins of this one. A drakon flies again, and we are renewed in its presence." Liannan's voice had grown lower, and her eyes were kaleidoscopes.

Farouk was shaking. "She's…cursing us, I swear… stop her…"

Nat sucked in her breath, and Wes was frowning now. He turned to the golden-haired girl. "Okay, enough. You're scaring my crew, and you've cost me a soldier," he growled.

"And you have gained a guide. I believe our journeys are the same. You are ostensibly on your way to New Crete, yet in truth you seek the Blue. You are headed to the doorway at Arem. Natasha wears the Anaximander stone."

"The stone!" Shakes said. "I knew it!"

Nat's hand flew to her neck as she stared at the sylph. "How did you...?"

For his part, Wes did not answer, but remained wary.

"I can help you reach your destination," she said.

Wes sighed. "Listen, I hate to break it to you, but you're no better off on my ship than you were on your own. We lost our engines to the same thing that took Daran. There's been no wind for days, and we're down to eating twigs. You want to join us? Be my guest."

THIRTY-TWO

The sylph had no answer to that other than a cold gratitude, and Wes went with Shakes to check on the sail—they could hear it flapping, which meant a wind had finally kicked up.

They circled back again to look for Daran, but there was no sign of him; either the water or that thing in the water had claimed him. With Zedric in the hold, Wes ordered the family placed in his cabin, which was more comfortable. He went to check on their progress and found the parents lying on the bed, covered with a thin woolen blanket. Nat was sitting by their bedside, next to the two little ones.

"How are they doing?" he asked.

She cast him a stricken look that told him everything. They were dead. There was a cry of pain from the younger boy, and his brother soothed him.

"I'm so sorry," Nat whispered, and only when the child turned to her did Wes realize his mistake. He had been wrong about the new passengers. The little ones were not children. They only looked like they were. The boys were smallmen.

Wes faced the group, taking a knee.

"This is Brendon and this is Roark," Nat said, introducing them. Brendon had curly red hair and tears in his eyes. Roark was dark and stocky. They were the size of toddlers—three feet tall, but proportioned and fully grown; Wes had never met any before, but they struck him as being about his age. The smallfolk were said to be wily and malicious; they could see in the blackest dark and hide where no hiding place could be found, giving rise to their reputations as thieves and assassins. But the two in front of him looked nothing like the sort. They had ordinary, pleasant faces, and their clothing was rough-hewn and handmade.

It was Brendon who spoke. "Thank you for taking us on board."

"I'm sorry about your friends," said Wes, shaking his hand.

Brendon nodded, blinking back tears; he looked as if he were about to collapse. "They sheltered us from the raids when we were separated from our families. With their help, we found Liannan and the boat. We would not be here without them."

The smallmen told them their story. They were refugees from Upper Pangaea, where the RSA had just taken over. The smallkind had lived in the open there, along with a few tribes of sylphs. It was peaceful for a

242

time, but things started to change. Many of them were suffering, dying from the rot, the strange plague on the marked and magical that no medicine could cure. As part of the cleansing, they had been rounded up with the rest of the marked and others like them, herded and made to live in confined areas until they were moved somewhere else. So Brendon and Roark had hidden with their friends on their farm and survived for a time, hiding in the attic, in the recesses of the walls, but it became too dangerous. The neighbors had become suspicious, so they looked for passage and decided to undertake the dangerous voyage to the Blue, where they heard there was a cure.

For a while they had been lucky; their captain was savvy and the ship was fast, and they had made good time. Then they had hit a trashberg, and their ship began taking in water, which slowed them down. Supplies began to run out, then they were ambushed and drifted for weeks, with nothing to eat...and being human, the young couple had taken the worst of it. They had died of starvation.

Roark put his face in his hands and sobbed. They were great, terrible sobs, and Wes felt helpless around such grief. He wondered at the depth of feeling and was envious of it, in a perverse way. He hadn't cried like that since his parents died, since he and Eliza had been separated. Wes had seen so many of his soldiers die before him, and felt nothing but an abstract, removed sadness. Perhaps if Shakes had perished, he would feel it... Wes clapped Roark on the shoulder a bit awkwardly. He looked to Nat for help.

"We'll honor their life," Nat said. "I'll ask Liannan to help me prepare them for burial at sea."

Nat and Wes left the room together, Nat moving quickly and Wes following right behind. But he stopped, feeling a sharp tug on his sleeve. He looked down and saw Brendon. The smallman had a pinched, anxious look on his face and was wringing his hands in worry.

"Captain…"

"Just call me Wes," he said. "We don't go by formalities here."

"Wes, then." Brendon nodded. "There are more of us—more boats out there—filled with our people, headed to the same place. But during the ambush we were separated."

Wes nodded. He knew as much from seeing the slaughter on board their ship. "The ships that attacked you, did they carry this flag?" he asked, showing the red stars of the RSA.

The smallman nodded.

Wes wiped his brow. It was just as he'd suspected: Sniper boats were circling. "Look, I'd love to help out every pilgrim in this ocean, but we're running as tight as we can, and we can't take any more. We don't have enough supplies to feed ourselves, let alone you guys. We'll be lucky if we make it to the Blue before the goop runs out."

"Then they are lost," Brendon whispered.

Wes sighed. "How many ships?"

"Five...at most. We were following them toward the Hellespont, which is when the attack happened, and then we were separated by the trashbergs. We haven't seen them since, but we know they're out there. Some of them must have survived. They're lost and hungry and they don't have anyone. Liannan was leading us. They were following our boat."

This was why he never took these jobs anymore, Wes realized. It was too much—he couldn't save everybody—he couldn't even keep his soldiers alive, let alone in line. Daran was lost, and while the kid was a jerk and a lowlife, he had still entrusted his life to Wes and Wes had failed him. He couldn't keep doing this, there were so many... and he was too young to watch so many kids die. Now he was being asked to save a few more...for what? So that he could watch them starve? Or fall victim to frostblight? He blinked; his vision had gone black again, as if to remind him.

"Please," Brendon said. "Please...just give them a chance. That's all we're asking."

Wes looked down at him. They were called smallmen . . . maybe they had small appetites? He wondered how they would feel about eating bark. "Look, I'll see what I can do. We'll do one loop around Hell Strait and if we see anyone we'll pick them up, but that's it. I can't waste time circling this drain."

"Thank you!" Brendon said, shaking his hand vigorously. "Thank you!"

Wes handed him and Roark a few fried chicken wafers he'd been saving for a dire emergency. "What is it?" Brendon asked, staring at the foil-wrapped object.

"It's not the healthiest thing in the world, but it tastes good—share it with your brother."

"He's not my brother," Brendon said excitedly, but he was already tearing off the silver wrapper and inhaling the scent.

Wes's cheeks creased in a sad smile. So many promises he had made already. To take Nat to the Blue. Now to scour the oceans for more of the smallkind. He was soft, he'd always been too soft; it was his Achilles heel, his heart.

THIRTY-THREE

Liannan prepared the bodies for burial with the help of Brendon and Roark. Nat lent a hand as well, helping to wrap the white cloth around each one, folding and tucking the linen so the fabric did not bunch. The smallmen were somber, silent tears rolling down their cheeks as they accomplished the difficult task of caring for their dead.

"We're ready," Nat told Wes and Shakes, who were waiting by the doorway respectfully. Farouk had made it clear he wanted no part of this and remained on the bridge, watching. Together the boys lifted the body of the man first, then the woman, and laid them out on the deck. The small funeral party followed them upstairs.

"Would you like to say a few words?" Liannan asked the weeping friends.

"Yes." Brendon nodded. He folded his hands together and took a moment to compose himself. Nat thought he would not be able to do it, but finally he spoke, and his voice was strong and clear. "We say good-bye today to our friends Owen and Mallory Brown. They lived simple, brave lives and were taken from us too soon. We will forever honor their memory and cherish their friendship. We give them to the sea. May they rest in the light."

"May they rest in the light," Roark repeated.

Nat looked at Shakes and Wes to prompt them and the three of them echoed the smallmen's words. "May they rest in the light," they murmured.

The group looked to Liannan.

She moved toward the still, shrouded bodies. "Owen and Mallory, may the wings of the drakon guide you to the Eternal Haven."

The sylph nodded, and Wes and Shakes lifted the first shroud to the edge of the deck, then the next, and gently rolled them off the ship, giving the dead to the waves.

Three dead in one day, Nat thought. Daran was one of their team, but there had been no funeral for him. No words spoken on his behalf, no blessings, but then, perhaps he had not been worthy of any. The dead couple had given their lives for their friends, but Daran would only have brought death to his team.

Liannan, Brendon, and Roark stood at the railing for a long time, watching the sea.

Wes took Nat aside. "We'll put them in the crew cabin."

"Right." Nat nodded, understanding the plan. Space had opened up with Zedric in the hold and his brother lost.

"I'm going to move back, too," Nat said to Wes. "To

the crew cabin, I mean."

"Oh?" Wes said, taken aback.

It made sense, now that Daran was no longer a factor. "Is there a problem?" she asked, not meaning to sound brusque. But if she was going to nip this whole thing in the bud, she had to do it now, and quickly.

Wes shrugged. "Do what you want; it doesn't matter to me."

"Right," she said, and couldn't help feeling just a little hurt at his tone. Even if she wanted to push him away, she was irritated he had given up so easily. Just a few hours ago he had held her hand for a second too long when she'd saved him from the waters.

"I'll go, then," she said, her pride getting the best of her.

"Fine," he said, distracted, and walked off to the bridge to join Shakes.

Nat leaned against the wall. Well, that's done. She wrapped her arms around herself against an arctic draft, lonelier than ever.

She soon regretted the rash decision to move her belongings back to the crew cabin. She should never have decided to move. The captain's quarters were cozier, warmer, with a real bed. Now she was back to sleeping on a blanket on cold metal mesh.

She got the lowest bunk on the port side, and above her, Brendon snored softly, while above him, Roark's nose whistled like a high-pitched teakettle. At least Farouk, who talked in his sleep, was at the helm, on duty, or else there would be three of them in a nighttime symphony.

Liannan had taken the hammock on the other end of the room, next to Shakes, and Nat heard the two of them whispering quietly in the dark with a newfound intimacy. She missed Wes, missed knowing he was near. It wasn't really the noise that bothered her, she realized; in fact, she liked it, after living alone, to feel the comfort of people around her. She just missed him, missed him even though he was only a few feet away. Did he miss her? she wondered. When she finally drifted off to sleep, she had no dreams.

The next morning she awoke to hear Shakes yelling. She ran up to the deck and found him kicking at the rail. Wes was holding his hands to his own head in frustration.

"What happened?"

"Zedric. Farouk," said Wes, his cheeks red with anger.

"What did they do?" Nat asked, feeling a stab of fear.

"They're gone," Shakes said.

"Gone?"

"They abandoned us last night. Took one of the lifeboats and left. Farouk must have busted Zedric out," Wes explained. He was disappointed in Farouk; he understood Zedric's anger, but he thought the skinny kid was on his side, he'd thought he was loyal. It was difficult not being able to count on his crew, he thought. It wasn't always like that, especially not during the war. He and Shakes were the only survivors of Delph company, but there had been others: Ragdoll, Huntin' John, Sanjiv. All good men, all gone now.

"We're lucky they didn't kill us in our sleep," Nat said.

Shakes pounded the nearest wall. "They took the rest of the supplies, left us with nothing. Not even a twig to chew on."

"But why? They won't survive for long out there; why would they take that risk?" asked Nat.

"Snipers took out the crew of the other ship. Somehow, one of them must have noticed, and figured that they'd rather take their chances with the RSA than with us," said Wes.

"They're probably eating navy rations now, while we're going to starve," Shakes said moodily, lifting each bin and finding it empty.

The rest of the group was gathered around the galley hopefully, but there was nothing to be found. Brendon removed a few crumbly wafers that Wes had given him from his pocket and shared them with the group.

"Thanks," Nat said, smiling. Brendon was the same age as she, but with a wise man's face, and Roark a little older. They weren't brothers, but from the same tribe, it turned out. Distant cousins, maybe. The genealogy of the smallkind was too complicated for Nat to understand, although Brendon had tried to explain earlier. She bit into the cracker. "I haven't had these since I was a kid."

"I have never had one before," Brendon said. "It is a very interesting flavor."

"We're surrounded by water, and there's nothing to eat. Where we're from, we cut through the ice and fish," Roark said.

"Truly?" Shakes asked, curious. "All the fish I've ever had was some kind of replacement substitute. I thought the oceans were dry."

"Not our part of it," Roark said.

Nat shook her head. Why hadn't she realized it before? *Fish...the flash of the redback's tail beneath the water...*

Of course!

THIRTY-FOUR

"I don't know why I didn't think of it before!" Nat said, her face lighting up. "We can find food."

"Where?" Shakes asked. Even Liannan looked intrigued, although the sylph had explained that her kind did not require very much sustenance, which is why they were long-lived.

"Out there!" Nat said, pointing to the gray sea through the porthole.

Shakes shook his head. "Aw, man, I thought you had a real idea. There's nothing out there but trash."

"No, no," Nat insisted. "I was there—the day that—the day that we hit the trashbergs. With Daran and Zedric. We were looking out to the sea and we saw them... redbacks. There are fish out there."

Wes sighed. "There haven't been fish in the ocean since—"

"I'm telling you, we *saw* them. And Daran said he'd seen them before." It dawned on her now what the Slaine brothers had been doing that week before Daran had drowned, when they were sneaking off by themselves. They were fishing! They were *eating* and hiding it from the rest of the crew.

"If you're right, then I can do it," Roark said. "Donnie can help."

"Yes." Brendon beamed, glad to be useful.

"Too bad we don't have any poles," Wes said. "Or bait, for that matter."

Roark was undeterred. "Poles are not necessary for this endeavor. The essence of fishing is a good line. Something strong enough to hold the redback's weight, but light enough to allow the sinker to pull the line down. Any ideas?"

Wes smiled. Nat could tell he liked the way Roark thought. "I saw a spool of wires in the bilge, not the heavy stuff—it might be light enough to work." He nodded to Shakes, who headed down to look for the wires.

"Next to the starboard…" Wes called.

Shakes put up a hand. "I know where it is, boss."

"But is it safe to eat?" Nat asked. "With all the toxins in the black water?"

Wes shrugged. "It's not ideal, but we can take the risk. We need to eat."

Nat agreed.

An hour later the group had crafted two fishing poles, using metal tubing from the deck rails and the spool of wire Shakes found in the bilge. "There, that'll do." Roark nodded.

Wes made hooks from bent nails and handed them to Nat, who finished the poles by threading the spinners and hooks onto the long delicate wire.

Roark and Brendon grabbed the poles and got to work. Nat watched as they each cut a swatch of cloth from Brendon's shirt and tied it around the wire. The cloth would act as a marker just above the waterline. If a fish tugged at the line, the little red swatch would disappear below the water. Cool.

Nat turned to Roark. "What about bait?"

Wes sighed. "We've got nothing to spare. I might be able to pull a worm from somewhere under the decks, but that's about it."

"Again, that is not a problem," Roark continued. "Only the bottom-feeders like worms. We don't want to eat those anyway; they're full of lead and who knows what else. We'll be fishing near the surface where the water is a little cleaner. As for bait, we don't need food. Watch." Roark and Brendon whispered a few words, took a chunk of metal, and placed it on the hook.

"What are you doing?" she asked.

"Small magic," Brendon said, grinning.

"A little something to attract the fish," Roark said. "Once it's in the water, it will spin and dance just like a little minnow. When the fish start biting, there will be more."

Nat had been doubtful at first, but Roark's idea suddenly seemed real. Her hopes soared: Perhaps they would eat today after all.

"It's true, then, what they say about you guys," Shakes said excitedly.

"What do they say?" Roark asked, his eyes narrowed, obviously knowing the deadly rumors about the smallfolk among mortal kind.

"Only that you are cleverer than most," Nat said gently. "Isn't that right, Shakes?"

"I can help, too," Liannan said, as she leapt from the boat and onto the icy sea, her slender form light enough that she could walk on water. The group watched in delight, and Shakes looked downright worshipful.

The smallmen cast their lines and the sylph gasped. "They're coming!" she said. "I see them down below."

Liannan tiptoed back onto the boat and joined Nat in watching the little red dot bounce along the surface. Roark gave the line a little jerk, trying to set the hook. They didn't have reels, so they had to wind the wire around the pole as they raised the line. Halfway up he stopped. "He got away," Roark mumbled. He looked up from the ice at the disappointed faces of the crew. "Patience—we'll get him next time."

It took three tries before Roark finally hooked a redback and was able to pull the fish to the surface before it escaped from its crude hook. After the second catch, the two smallmen were shivering, and Roark handed his pole to the sylph, who cast the line far out into the water. Nat did the same with the second pole that Brendon had handed her, throwing the line as far as she could.

Nat kept one eye on the red cloth and the other on the horizon. The shadows seemed to stretch longer as each minute passed. She was ready to give up when she finally pulled her first redback from the water. "I got one!" she cried, and Liannan hurried to help her wind up the wire. The red fish went wild when it landed on the deck. Nat nearly had to jump on top of it to stop it from flopping back into the waves. She laughed out loud as she held the fish in her bare hands. Its skin was as cold as ice and slippery like oil. Its muscular body flexed forcefully against her grasp. Nat realized at that moment that other than the bird a few days earlier, she'd never held a wild animal before. The redback thrashed in her grasp and Nat's heart beat wildly. *Is this what we've lost?* she thought. *Is this what the ice has taken from us?* She wondered if that was what the Blue would be like, the redback so full of life that it was almost a shame to eat it.

Somehow, the redbacks had brought a warm current with them, a clean stream of unpolluted water. "What is that?" she asked Liannan.

"Water from the Blue," the sylph said. "The oceans are melting, the world is changing, returning to what it was."

The girls pulled two more redbacks from the icy water before the fish stopped biting.

Before they lifted their last one from the cold water, Shakes was already frying the fish. He and Wes had cleaned and prepared the day's catch, gutting them, pulling out the bones but otherwise keeping the fish whole. The stove in the galley was busted, so Shakes had rigged up an impromptu one by mounting a cylinder of propane under a flat metal plate. The propane burned wildly—it looked like he was searing the fish with a flamethrower—but it worked.

"Redback à la Shakes," he said cheerfully, serving up the plates.

The group gathered around the table with their plates of fish. Wes looked around at the expectant faces. "Well, what are you all waiting for? Eat," he admonished. "I told you, we don't stand on ceremony on my ship."

Nat was a little skeptical, seeing the skin was charred on the outside, but she changed her mind as she soon as she cut into it. The flesh was white and moist. She took a bite and smiled.

She couldn't remember enjoying a better meal. She remembered the small, silent meals at home, nuked fauxburgers while she watched a show on the nets. Even once she'd hired Wes's team she had eaten alone, feeling uneasy in the company of the Slaine brothers.

Brendon and Roark had found a rare jug of mead among the Nutri cans, and were pouring glasses all around.

"More small magic?" asked Nat.

Brendon nodded. "If only it had been enough to save our friends."

At the end of dinner, she saw Shakes and Liannan

moving slightly away from the group. Nat felt some relief to discover that the lovely sylph was more interested in the first mate than the captain.

"He's got it bad, that one," Brendon noted, motioning to the two.

"Aye, that was fast. But then, can you blame him? She's a sight." Roark smiled dreamily. "They're not called the Fair Folk for nothing."

"He's not bad-looking himself," Brendon teased as he took Roark's hand in his.

Ah. So that was their connection. Not brothers, after all. Not at all, Nat smiled.

Outside, on the deck, Shakes leaned closely to the ethereal sylph, and Nat could see that Liannan didn't seem to mind. Nat turned away from them to say something to Wes but stopped. The glow left her cheeks.

Wes wasn't there. His chair was empty.

THIRTY-FIVE

The new crew settled into place. Brendon was better at plotting a course than Farouk had been. Something in the trashbergs made the compass go haywire and swing out of control, something Farouk had never been able to adjust for, which was why they had run into the trashbergs and veered out of course. Now that everyone knew about the stone, there was no more pretense concerning their destination—the Blue. Nat would spend the mornings up at the helm with them while Wes consulted the map, holding the blue stone up to his eye while he made corrections on the navigational pad. Brendon made concessions for the compass and plotted their course on the back of a coffee-stained document he found in the engine room. If they had continued to follow the compass, as Farouk had done, they would have kept traveling in circles.

But with Brendon at the bridge, they kept to a straight line. He guided the ship deftly past the mounds of trash that cluttered the ocean. His small hands moved nimbly—

he seemed to have a natural feeling for how *Alby* would react as he turned the wheel. Whereas Farouk preferred to smash through the smaller piles of ice and trash, Brendon moved gracefully around the obstructions, swerving through the crowded ocean without ever once hitting the debris. It made for a much smoother ride— free of the constant scraping sound that the ship made when Farouk had sailed it through the ocean.

While Brendon kept them headed in the right direction, Roark commandeered the galley and the daily fishing. They were finally making good time and their fear of starving began to fade. It was a better crew than he'd ever had before, Wes thought. They worked as a team, like one unit, functioning smoothly. Some nights they were downright merry, with Nat leading the card games, and teaching them to play gin, whist, and snap, or poker if they were feeling punchy. The smallmen taught them the Layman's Code, a way to communicate by knocking, as well as games they knew: Smallman's Secret and Who's the Sprat. Liannan tried to teach them a game from her people, but it was too complicated and involved high-pitched whistling and singing no one could imitate or understand.

Liannan and Shakes tried to keep their budding romance under wraps, and aside from Shakes grinning like a maniac all day and Liannan blushing whenever he was near, they merely appeared to be very close friends, laughing over their cards, or teasing each other when the other had failed to guess the Smallman's Secret.

Wes was glad for Shakes, but he was also apprehensive for his friend; he had no idea what Shakes was thinking. In his experience, it was best not to get involved, but he was also a little envious of his friend's happiness. Nat had made it clear that she wasn't interested in him, and he respected her wishes, even if being so close and yet so far from her made him feel uneasy. The sooner he dropped her off at the Blue, the better for everyone. Then he could turn around and forget they had ever met.

That morning, she was standing too close to him again, helping them navigate through the strait. "Here you go," he said, handing her back the stone when the task was done. His fingers brushed her palm, but he had learned to ignore the electric feeling, and he walked away from her quickly.

Nat watched him leave the bridge, feeling troubled at his abrupt departure. It was all for the best, truly, since there was no chance of them being together. But when she found him by the railing a few hours later, she went to him without thinking. "Your sister?" Nat asked, looking over his shoulder to the picture in his hand.

"Yeah, that's Eliza."

He showed her the photo of a little girl in a puffy snowsuit, standing next to a snowman. He was in the picture, too, his chubby arm slung around his sister's shoulders.

Nat stared at it for a long time. "How old did you say she was when she was taken?"

"Let me see—I was seven."

"And so was she."

His eyes crinkled. "Shakes told you, huh?"

"Yeah."

"We were twins, but I came out first. She's always been my little sister."

"So what happened to her—really?"

Wes sighed. It was hard to talk about. He didn't remember much. "There was a fire," he said quietly. "Smoke alarms didn't work. It came out of nowhere and then it was everywhere."

A fire that came out of nowhere. Nat felt a chill in her entire body. No. It couldn't be true. "She burned?"

He gripped the picture tighter. "No, that's the thing… they never found a body. They said she must have disintegrated into ashes, but come on, there would have been something…something to identify her…"

Fire and pain. She closed her eyes and could see it. The smoky ruins…the child burning within the flames…

"She's alive. She has to be. She's out there somewhere," he said.

"I'm so sorry," Nat whispered. She was sorrier than he ever knew.

"It's okay." He echoed the words she had told him the other day. "It wasn't your fault."

Nat did not respond. She wanted to reach out to him,

but it was as if he were behind a wall of glass. He would hate her now. He would always hate her. She didn't need to push him away, she already had. *The fire. The child. The fire that came from nowhere. The child that was taken.*

"Wes, there's something you should know about me..." she said, her voice almost inaudible, just as Shakes burst from the helm.

"More ships!" he said. "Roark spotted them in the trashbergs; kid's got eyes like a fighter pilot."

Wes stood up straight. "RSA?"

"Not sure. Still too far to tell," Shakes said, as he followed Wes out to the deck.

Roark was climbing down from the crow's nest. He reported his findings. "They don't carry the flag."

"The engines are too loud, too," Wes said. He took out his scope and looked out at the distant horizon. He focused the glass and he could see them better. He could hear them, too.

There was the sound of gunfire and cannons.

Brendon walked off the bridge and stood next to Roark. "What is it?"

"A battle," Wes said, still peering at the ships through his lenses, watching bullets fly between them. "Between two slavers, it looks like." He recognized them by their silhouette. The two massive ships were so overloaded with junk, they looked more like shantytowns than ships. It was just as he'd feared when the navy ships left them alone.

"Slavers," Brendon whispered. "That can't be good."

Nat felt dread, thinking of the slavers from K-Town she had seen. Hard men, with flinty eyes and ugly tattoos.

"Looks like they're both Jolly's crew," Wes said, handing her the binoculars so that she could see the skull and bones painted on both of the ships.

"Who's Jolly?" asked Nat, returning the glasses back to him.

"'Jolly' Roger Stevens, otherwise known as the biggest icehole who's ever sailed the ocean gray," Shakes muttered.

"So why are they fighting themselves?" she asked.

They watched as the ships converged. One was clearly following the other, its crew preparing to board the smaller ship. They collided with a crash, and a moment later, the two crews were engaged in hand-to-hand combat. Men toppled into the sea. Gunfire mixed with grunts and laughter.

"Slavers rob each other all the time; it's easier than roaming the sea for pilgrims," Wes explained.

"With any luck they'll destroy each other," Shakes said. "Then we can just drift away…"

"Have we ever been that lucky?" Wes sighed. "But go back to the helm and try to get us behind one of the trashbergs. Maybe we can hide."

Alby moved toward a floating junk pile, and for a moment, Wes thought they might be lucky after all. But then the gunfire ceased. The scavengers stopped fighting.

Wes looked though the scope, studying the two ships, and realized why the attack had stopped—the slave cages on the defending ship were almost as empty as their attacker's—there was hardly any loot to fight over.

He zeroed in on the two captains, who were meeting on the deck of one ship. They shook hands and turned, seeming to look straight at him.

The slavers had spotted them.

And it was clear: They were next.

THIRTY-SIX

Wes calculated his odds. He had Shakes, a blackjack dealer, a sylph, and two smallmen on his side, and none of them except he and Shakes were experienced in combat. He told Shakes to stand at his side and ordered everyone else belowdecks to the lifeboats.

But no one moved.

"We want to fight," Brendon said bravely, as Roark nodded. "We're not going to run anymore."

"You're not getting rid of us this easily," added Nat.

Liannan was already scouting the slavers' approach. "If you have a plan, I recommend you share it with us now. They'll be upon us soon."

"Look, it's not that I don't appreciate your courage," Wes said. "But these guys are a rough bunch—Shakes and I have dealt with them before. Let us deal with them now. One wrong word and any of you could end up dead. Everyone get down to the lower deck; if we're boarded, take a lifeboat out—it has a small motor on it, it might give you guys some time, put some space between you and them," Wes said, taking out his gun. "Brendon, Roark—do you know how to use one of these?"

"We do not use iron," Brendon said, pulling out a silver dagger from his pocket. "But we are armed. And we have Liannan with us."

"She wasn't much help with the snipers who took out your old crew," Wes reminded.

"I did not see them," Liannan said coldly, as she appeared on the deck to join the group. "The ships are made of iron—which repels our power."

"Too bad." Wes sighed. "We could really use some help right now."

"I'm staying up here with you guys. I'm not leaving," Nat said. "I can fight." She locked eyes with Wes, until he nodded.

"Okay. But if we're boarded, we don't have a chance," he said.

"Then we'll die together," she said. It was all you could ask for, she thought.

"Boss—" Shakes said, turning to Wes. "Remember, if it comes to that, take me out, before they get here. I'd rather die here than in a cage. Shoot me first, okay?"

"Don't be stupid," Wes said, gritting his teeth, his heart pumping. "It's not going to come to that, I keep telling you."

"It's not?" Shakes attempted a smile even as his face was paler than the sail.

"Still want to stay up here?" Wes asked Nat.

She nodded. "That lifeboat is a death trap. I'd rather die fighting than starve in the ocean."

"Have it your way, but if we can't take them out, we'll take out each other," Wes said.

Shakes put out a trembling hand. "Deal."

Wes slapped his on top. Nat followed suit. "Done." Liannan and the smallmen added theirs.

Their deaths accounted for, Wes sighed. "All right, if you want to fight, start by staying out of sight. We need to conceal our numbers. Grab something heavy and hide." He motioned to Nat, pointing out a place behind one of the sidewalls where she could disappear. Brendon and Roark understood immediately and stashed themselves behind some clutter on the deck, disappearing completely. Wes looked around for Liannan, but she was already gone. Nat noticed his confusion and pointed upward. The girl had shimmied up the mast and was hiding among the sails, her slight, elven form almost invisible in the billowing fabric.

Nat crouched down with the boys. They waited, holding their breath, not speaking. She could hear the sound of the engines getting louder.

One of the slave ships sped toward their boat, the battering ram on its bow pushing ice and debris aside as it plowed through the water.

Wes raised a hand for quiet and motioned to Shakes, pointing toward the bow of the approaching ship. The soldier crawled to the back end of the big gun on the deck. The weapon wasn't much to look at, but it packed a whopping punch. Wes had welded the base of an old howitzer behind a metal shield. The shield allowed someone to aim and fire the gun and have some degree of cover. The short-armed gun was like a miniature cannon and fired rounds as large as baseballs. It would have been a formidable weapon if only they had more than one round of ammunition for it. Shakes checked to see whether the barrel was loaded and nodded to Wes.

They only had one shot, so they needed to make it count. Wes waited until the ship was close. If they could score a good hit, they might be able to sink the slave ship before it got close enough for its crew to swim to them. Even a good hit might scare them away if they thought he had more ammo.

Wes considered his strategy: He wanted to scare the slavers away before they could see how poorly armed his crew was, but the farther the slavers were from them, the harder it would be to hit the ship.

So he waited as long as he could and then nodded to Shakes.

His friend took his time aiming the big gun. The sighting mechanism was missing, so Shakes had to guess to hit his mark.

The ship was a mile away…half a mile…

Wes was about to yell at Shakes when the soldier finally pulled the trigger.

The cannon-size gun let loose with such a bang that

the whole deck shook, and the air filled with a thin cloud of smoke.

But when the smoke cleared, the slavers were still coming for them. The shot had gone wide, hitting a patch of ice thirty feet from the vessel.

Shakes cursed and Wes climbed behind the thick metal shield. "It's not your fault," he told Shakes, his eyes never leaving the slave ship. "The charge in that thing is decades old; it's a miracle that gun even fired."

The two of them watched, hands on their sidearms, as the ship moved closer. The vessel was like theirs, a run-down, put-together affair, but unlike *Alby*, which had been lovingly restored, the slave ship had a hodgepodge look. Its hull had been reinforced by car hoods, refrigerator doors, corrugated sheets of metal, a lumbering patchwork of junk. Smoke drifted from its chimneys. Wes spied several ominous-looking gun barrels poking through the metal maze.

The ship was so close now that they could hear the slavers speaking to one another.

Everyone huddled in their places and waited.

"What are they saying?" Roark whispered to Nat.

She strained to hear. "I'm not sure." The slavers' language sounded brutal to her ear, a corruption, all consonants and no vowels. Then she realized they were actually *speaking* textlish, a language that was only designed to be written, not spoken—even though she'd heard it in pockets of K-Town, and once in a while when she was a dealer in Vegas.

The slave ship was right next to them now; the mercenaries had tossed over a rope ladder and were boarding their ship. A raggedy troop of hard-looking boys and men climbed aboard, along with a few scary-looking women, holding guns and sharpened steel shanks. Nat counted thirty of them.

Across from her, Wes holstered his gun.

"What are you doing?" she asked, horrified. They had planned to fight. But now it looked as if Wes was just going to give up.

"If we fight, we'll die. There's too many of them, I thought they were only going to send a small strike crew, but we can't take all of them," he said. "It would be suicide. We have to surrender."

"But we said—"

Wes didn't let her finish. "I'm going to let them take us; maybe I can talk my way out of it—I know these guys. And if not, it'll give me some time to think of another way out."

"Another way?" Nat said pointedly.

"Don't worry—I would never give them your necklace," he said. "I promise. I would eat it first." He grinned.

Wes nodded to Shakes and the rest of the team. Slowly, he came out from behind the shield of the howitzer, raising his arms in surrender. The group followed suit. There was no argument, no debate. Wes marveled at that;

they were better at following orders than his old unit. The smallmen dropped the daggers they'd drawn for battle; Liannan descended the mast and walked regally to the front, holding her robes around her, Shakes hovering protectively nearby. Nat went last.

The slavers murmured and gestured to one another, as they surrounded the small group. Two of them took Wes. They bore the same scars, like scratches from cats or branches, on their cheeks. Wes knew that the lowest of the slaver clans cut their babies' cheeks at birth. The scars grew as part of their faces—forever marking them as people of the black ocean.

"That's it? That's all your numbers?" the largest one demanded. Wes noted that his face lacked the scars—this man had grown up outside of the slaver clans. He spoke the standard tongue, but his words were barely comprehensible. He stank like the sea and his clothes were stained and tattered; he would probably wear the rags until they disintegrated.

"Yes," Wes replied.

"Thought you ran a bigger crew than this, two soldiers and four passengers?"

"We lost a few," Wes said.

There was a murmur in the crowd, and the mercenaries quieted down, parting for the appearance of the ship's captain. Nat stifled a gasp. It was the familiar face of Avo Hubik, the Slob, the slaver from whom she'd won their ship. Just as in K-Town, Avo was sleek and handsome, his black eyes as deep as the night. Like the slaver who'd spoken, his smooth, handsome face was without scars, but he did sport a skeleton tattoo on his forearm. Nat noticed the scar above his eyebrow was almost the same shape and on the same spot as the one on Wes's forehead. Coincidence, she wondered, or something else?

Avo walked up on the deck with a smile on his face.

He stopped when he saw Nat and his smile broadened. "Ah, there you are. Just as I suspected, you were too cheap to be a proper trophy. I should have known you were working for this guy," he said, pointing to Wes.

Wes shrugged as if he weren't caught in a trap. He matched Avo's leisurely pose. Two old friends and adversaries meeting again.

"Slob, nice to see you again," Wes said with a grin. "It's been too long."

"Wesson," Avo said. "I have warned you many times not to call me that."

Wes laughed. "Let us go, Slob. You can have your ship back—but I'm warning you, don't touch my crew."

"I *have* my ship back, didn't you notice? Your dear old *Albatross* is aptly named," the slaver said, no longer smiling. "And as for your crew . . ." His eyes flicked over to the girls, lingering on Nat.

"Don't even think about it, pervert," Wes warned.

Avo laughed. "Don't worry, Wesson, your sloppy seconds aren't my style," he sneered.

Wes began to talk faster. "Hey, man, come on, be cool,

you know me, let me work for you. I've got a good crew here, you know I can double the area you'd normally be able to cover in a day. Jolly won't even have to pay me my usual fee—I'll take a cut as a favor." He smiled his easy, charming smile. Running another con, but this wasn't a safari guide or a lazy seeker team. This was the most feared scavenger in the black waters.

Avo laughed a short, nasty laugh. "Bradley said you'd turned soft, but I didn't believe it. Seeing you with a bunch of girls and dwarves, I guess he was right. Now I understand why you didn't have the nerve to take the job," he sneered.

"What's he talking about?" Nat asked, looking at Wes. "What job?"

THIRTY-SEVEN

Avo laughed again. "Tell her, why don't you? About how Bradley offered you good work, easy enough, hunting down pilgrims in the black waters. Cleaning up the ocean of trash. Lucky for us, you didn't take it. Looks like you decided to join them instead."

Wes sighed. This wasn't going as he'd hoped.

The second slave ship pulled up next to *Alby*. This one was similar to the first, with a long line of cargo containers dangling like cages from the edges of the deck. Its captain, a lean, bald, and surly-looking pirate, boarded the ship. His skin was pale and jaundiced, unlike the scavengers of old with their nut-brown sunburned faces. But the sun's rays did not reach the ocean anymore; it was as gray out here as it was anywhere else in the world, and so the slavers were as pale as any citizen of New Vegas. Like Avo, Wes noticed, the new guy was carrying a military locator on his hip.

The bald slaver was known as the Ear, Wes remembered now. Called that because he was missing his right one.

His ship was the *Van Gogh*. "This is all we got?" he asked, looking contemptuously at Wes's scraggly crew.

"Looks like." Avo nodded. "The boys checked it out. A lifeboat's gone, but that's all. They lost a couple along the way, Wesson said."

The Ear spat on the deck. It was clear he didn't think much of the ship. Wes noticed burn marks on his jacket and wondered whether the slaver had taken them from his earlier fight with Avo.

"Toss for it?" Avo asked, throwing a silver coin in the air.

"Heads," the Ear called.

"Tails," Avo showed him the back of the coin. He smiled and pointed right at Nat. "That one."

"No! Don't hurt her!" Wes yelled. "Avo, I swear to god if you—"

"Wait—wait—" Nat said, as Avo removed a blade from his back pocket and walked toward her. She cringed from his touch.

"Relax…" the slaver said, pulling up her sleeve. He marked the skin on her hand with a crooked *S*.

Wes struggled against the men holding him. "I need to warn you…she's marked!"

The slaver grinned. "Exactly. Marked but still healthy. Which is why I want her—she'll fetch a higher price at the markets. Vardick, take her to the *Titan*." He nodded to one of the mercenaries, who grabbed Nat by her cut hand.

"Wes—!" she cried.

"Nat! Don't fight them—don't—"

But Nat kicked at Vardick, and in turn he knocked her on the side of her head with the butt of his rifle, and she went down hard on the deck.

"Don't mess up her face," Avo said, annoyed. "They don't like when they're too beat-up looking."

Wes broke away from the grip of the pirates holding him and spun around, burying his fist in the nearest slaver's gut, breaking his ribs and sending him to the ground. The slavers had a lot of brute force, but none of them really knew how to fight. The man was twice Wes's size, but he'd hardly had a chance to move before Wes struck him. His military training proved handy in moments like this, and right now, with slavers on all sides, he'd take on the whole crew if he had to.

"Enough of that," Avo said, languidly raising his pistol. "Or I'll make you watch what they do to her."

Wes froze and surrendered. The pirate he'd defeated kicked him in the back and he fell to the deck.

"Next," the Ear said, "I'll take Vibrate over here."

Liannan shot Shakes a worried glance as the Ear's men took him to their side. Shakes didn't make a sound as they nicked his ear with a cut. Blood dripped from the wound.

Avo studied the rest of the group. "I'll take the sylph," he said finally. "Maybe Jolly'll want her for his collection."

Liannan kept her hands behind her back. She didn't

want to carry their brand. But it was useless, as a pair of Avo's men tag-teamed her, forced her hand open, and carved it.

"The smallkind." The Ear pointed. "I'll take them both, two for the price of one, eh?"

Like Shakes, Roark and Brendon did not cry or scream when their ears were cut. Wes was proud of his crew. He only hoped he had an idea to get them out of this. He hadn't lied to Nat, but the situation looked more dire than he'd thought. He had counted on all of them being on the same ship. But now that they were being split between two…it would be harder to rescue them all.

"What are you doing with the little ones?" Avo asked, curious.

"Outlaw territories—circus will pay a lot for 'em."

"I'll take Wesson here," Avo said languidly.

Wes kept a smile on his face as the pirate slashed his hand. "You'll regret this, Slob. I promise you. Remember that. Warn Jolly, too. I'll come for him when I come for you."

They were brave, empty words, he knew, but he hoped it would give his people courage. And he was glad that at the very least Nat was with him.

"Vincent!" Liannan screamed, as the two groups were dragged to their respective ships.

But Shakes didn't even look up. He had already given up, Wes thought, and maybe so should he.

THIRTY-EIGHT

The back end of the *Titan* served as a village for the captives, with cargo containers arranged in a horseshoe along the perimeter of the deck. The containers were mounted so that half of the box was sitting on the deck and other half was hanging over the water. The arrangement allowed for more space on the deck, but Wes guessed the scavengers weren't after efficiency. Left to hang in the cold ocean air, the cages would be doubly cold and any attempt at escape would likely land you in the black waters.

The only way in or out was through a heavy iron door locked by a bolt as big around as Wes's arm. There was a jagged hole in the middle of it, enough to let in some light. A gray-skinned scavenger pressed the point of his blade to Wes's back as he pointed to a cage's open door, and Wes walked in, Nat right behind. Through holes in the steel floor, they could see the dark ocean waters rushing below them. The loud rush of moving water echoed inside the box, making the two of them shiver. The cage felt ten degrees cooler than the ship's deck.

Hanging above the water, there was nothing to insulate them from the freezing ocean.

Wes smelled ripe fruit and nuts, and for a moment he forgot the cold as he looked around for food. But the cargo box was empty. He wondered whether there was something outside their door, but he saw nothing. He thought for a second that the cold was starting to play tricks on his mind. He panicked, then realized what he was smelling. In faded orange letters he caught sight of the NU-Foods logo on one of the walls. The company specialized in "New Foods for You"—food that didn't require refrigeration or cooking. You simply stored them in a cupboard and used them as needed. The foods were guaranteed fresh and bacteria-free for decades. *Stock up for a century!*—or something like that. He'd forgotten the tagline. Immortal food. The smell of NU-Foods remained strong. The smell would be here when the world ended. It was the cockroach of foods—indestructible even in its grossness.

Wes laughed and so did Nat. They were about to starve, smelling nothing but processed food products.

Her smile faded quickly. He could tell she had something on her mind. "Is it true? What the Slob said?" Nat asked. "About the job?"

Wes sighed. "Yeah. It's true. I was offered the same job he's doing." He told Nat about the mission he'd turned down. *This isn't work, it's murder*, he'd told

Bradley. "The RSA uses slavers to kill or torture its own citizens. They didn't care what I did with the pilgrims—as long as I made them disappear. If the Blue is real, they don't want anyone else finding it."

"You must have quite a reputation," Nat said thoughtfully.

"Yeah, well, I turned them down, didn't I? This is all my fault; I shouldn't have let you leave New Vegas."

"It was my choice," she said. "It's not your fault."

"It is exactly my fault, but I'm hoping Avo will listen to me. We have history together. He'll hear me out, at least. He's had his fun and his revenge; he's won already. I'm in a cage."

"You and Avo—you have the same scar on your right eyebrow. But you said Shakes hit you with a pickax. That it was an accident."

Wes grimaced, looking uncomfortable. "I'll tell you sometime."

"He was in the service with you, wasn't he? Avo Hubik. They said he's from New Thrace, but he can't be, he doesn't have an accent. I wondered about that when I won *Alby*. By the way, I always thought '*Alby*' was short for ALB-187, but Avo called it the *Albatross*."

"It's an old joke between us, that that ship's more of a burden than anything. You're right, he's not from Thrace; he's ex-army—we served in the same unit," Wes said. "Now he's a mercenary, just like me."

"What happens if you aren't able to persuade him to

show us some mercy just because of the good old days?"

Wes sat. "Well, if I know Avo, one of these days he's going to get distracted, or lazy, and I can bust us out, get all of us the hell out of here."

"And if that doesn't work? We'll be auctioned off as slaves, right? I mean if we're lucky, that's what'll happen. Because if no one wants us, they're going to sell us to the flesh markets, won't they? The outlaw territories are starving. And they'll take any kind of meat." She shuddered. She'd heard the dark rumors about the flesh trade—first they blinded the slaves with acid, then skinned them alive before butchering them for parts.

"It's not going to come to that, Nat. I won't let it. Remember our pact?"

Nat didn't answer. "But why did he say I'd fetch a higher price... What do they do with the marked?"

"I don't know." Wes wouldn't meet her eye.

"You do, you just don't want to tell me." Nat felt her stomach twist. Wes was trying to hold it together, but she saw the fear in his eyes that he was trying hard to hide, and she remembered how young he was then. How young they all were. He was the best at pretending. He kept his cool, made them believe he was older and in control. But he was only sixteen. He was still just a boy. All of them children and orphans. Slob was the worst of them, Nat realized, the meanest bully on the playground.

The cold seemed to nip at them from all directions. There were no distractions, nothing to see or do. The days and nights were unnaturally long, and always, there was the arctic wind, burning like a fire that offered no heat.

For the next several days they were kept in the cage with nothing to eat, nothing to drink but melted icicles that formed around the corners. Nat felt fine at first, but on the third day she felt too dizzy to even sit up. She was claustrophobic in the cage, drained of energy, hungrier than she'd ever been. She tried to sleep, but her body shook every time the wind whistled through the bullet holes. The frigid air would sweep across her skin, waking her from her sleep as it robbed her reddened cheeks of their last drops of moisture.

Nat heard a tearing sound and she thought for a moment that the crate was about to fall to the water below. She looked up and saw Wes ripping a long strip of fabric from the liner of his vest.

"What are you doing?"

He didn't answer; he just kept tearing another long strip from his clothes.

"You're going to freeze! Stop it!"

"Here," he said, handing her the longer one. "Eat it."

"What is it?" she asked, too weak to reach for it.

"It's Bacon Fruit. Tastes like fruit, looks like bacon. The military rolls them into these polyiso tubes. Poly's basically the stuff they use to make home insulation. The liner keeps the dried fruit fresh for years. Shakes and I discovered it makes for cheap personal insulation just as easily, so we stuffed our jackets with them." She watched as Wes reached inside the lining of his vest and tore a long strip of fabric from inside it.

"I was trying to save it until we really needed it. Looks like that day has come. I never actually thought I'd end up eating the stuff." He took a bite and smiled. "Tastes worse than it looks."

He was wrong. Nat thought it was the most delicious lining she had ever eaten. The hunger faded for a moment as she chewed.

In the morning, the guard pushed tin cups of gruel and water through the hole in the door. Along with the Bacon Fruit, it was enough to keep them from starving to death, but that was all.

Still, every time the door banged, Nat was sure it was Slob; she hadn't liked the way he had looked at her—she could almost see the watts in his eyes. But as the days passed and nothing happened, Nat began to think that maybe he had forgotten about her, or that maybe Wes had been able to talk him out of selling her for now.

What did they do with the marked? Why did they fetch a higher price at the markets?

Nat could hear Liannan in the storage container next door, which meant that the sylph was still alive. But what about Shakes and the smallmen? She wondered how they were faring, and prayed that they were still alive.

She fell asleep on Wes's shoulder, when she heard a soft voice call her name in the darkness.

"Nat? Nat? Can you hear me?"

"Liannan!" Nat said.

"I can't talk long, the iron is too strong, but I can project my voice a little. I'm scared, Nat."

"Don't be. Wes will get us out of here. He will, I know he will."

"It's all this iron," Liannan said softly. "If only there was a way to get out of this cage."

"Maybe there is," Wes said, piping up, "if I know these guys. By tomorrow they'll be bored and they might let us out of here. Which is good and bad."

"Bad how?"

"Because when slavers are bored, they make the slaves put on a show."

THIRTY-NINE

Wes was right. A few days later the slavers let them out into the open. Nat was glad to feel some warmth on her face, glad to be out of that small container. Her eyes had not seen daylight in nearly a week. Though the sky was its usual foggy gray, it burned for a moment like an ancient summer sun when they opened the cage.

The pirates singled out the marked prisoners. Nat was separated from Wes and made to stand with the others in the middle of a circle. The slavers kept iron spears, crudely forged from scrap metal, pointed at their backs in case the prisoners attempted to use their powers against them, although there was little chance of that happening, as the hunger and despair had sapped every ounce of hope from the captives' spirits. They performed as dutifully as trained monkeys.

Nat watched as fellow marked slaves levitated boxes, made the sails ripple, and knocked glasses around the deck.

"This is what they're for, right? Stupid parlor tricks," sneered a crew member holding an iron spear.

"You there—do one," another said, pointing to Nat. For a moment she was caught off guard. "Me?" she mumbled, and the slaver nodded, his mouth opening to reveal jagged set of yellowed teeth.

She didn't move. He poked the sharpened piece of metal at her, and Nat shivered. Her mind was empty. She felt less than human and knew immediately that was the slavers' intent.

"I can't," she said. "I can't do anything."

The slaver's jagged smile disappeared. He narrowed his eyes, his face contorted horribly. He made to bash her with the stick, and Nat cowered, ready for the blow, but none came.

She looked up to see the slaver turning red, his collar contracting around his neck, choking him.

She looked around—and a fellow marked prisoner was staring at the slaver with a focused anger.

The slaver began to sputter as the fabric continued to tighten, cutting off the blood. The man fell backward, his head crashing on the hard metal deck.

The slavers laughed at their fallen comrade. A second pirate—tall, burly, and stripped to the waist to show off his ugly tattoos—kicked the downed brute aside. "You've got to take charge of these animals!" he snarled. "If you give them half a chance they'll toss you in the ocean. Go belowdecks and make yourself useful." He walked past the row of marked prisoners. "It's my turn to have some fun."

"You like to play, huh?" he asked, pointing to the young boy who had choked his comrade. He gestured to a row of cages. "Hold those up for me!"

The boy seemed uncertain what to do next.

"DO IT! OR I'LL STICK THIS THROUGH YOUR ROTTING NECK!"

The marked slave closed his eyes. He had a dotted patch of raised skin on his temple, the most common mark, which meant he had the power of telekinesis—he could move things with his mind. Slowly, ever so slowly, the row of cargo containers rose from the ground. They floated a few inches, then a foot, then three feet, but the effort was too much and the slave collapsed on the ground, along with the cages, crashing on the deck.

"OY! WAKE UP!" the pirate yelled, kicking at him.

"He's dead. You killed another one. Slob will be pissed. Traders are coming. You know they pay more for the marked ones."

"What they want with ice trash is beyond me. In a month they'll all be thrillers."

"Besides, he's not dead," the other one said, throwing a bucket of black water on the poor boy's face. "But I'm sure he wishes he was."

They were marched back to their cages, Nat too weak and too scared to talk, even as Wes tried to console her by rubbing her back. So that was what Avo wanted the marked for—to use them for amusement—for sport until they could sell them. The slavers would toy with them, a form of torture, like pulling wings from a fly, until they were sold.

That night Nat heard a faint fluttering sound outside her cage.

"What is it?" she asked Wes, who moved toward the door, looking through the tiny hole.

"Don't worry, it's not the guards," he said. "Look."

Nat peered through the slit. A flock of multicolored creatures surrounded their cage—they looked like large butterflies or birds, but were not either—they were flitting and flying, as their marvelous blue, pink, purple, gold, and silver feathers lit the night like a rainbow.

"Can you hear them?" Liannan asked, her melodious voice echoing through the darkness.

"Yes—I can—I can even understand what they're saying!" said Nat in wonder.

"What are they saying?" Wes wanted to know.

Nat tried to explain—it wasn't so much that she could hear them speak words or sentences, it was that she was filled with their emotion, their spirit.

"They're saying...they're saying...there's hope. There's hope for us. Hope and welcome."

There was a noise from the food slot. Nat cried out in surprise as small nuts, seeds, and fruit began to fall through the hole. She took Wes's handkerchief to catch them.

Hope, she thought. *We will survive this.*

Thank you, she sent to the birds. *Thank you. Please, we are not the only ones here. Bring food to all.*

They ate their meal, and Nat could hear cries of delight murmuring through the slave quarters.

Nat picked several berries and shared them with Wes, their lips turning red from the juice.

Afterward, Nat found she still had her deck of cards that she always kept in her pocket, and they played card games, using seeds as chips. "Fold," Wes said disgustedly as he threw his cards down. "Where did you learn how to play?"

"It's one of the first things they teach us at MacArthur. How to play cards. They size up our abilities that way. See who can use their powers to predict things, read minds, stuff like that," Nat said, shuffling the cards and dealing the next hand.

"So that's how you win," he said with a wry grin. "Not fair."

She looked at him and shook her head. "Not at all. I can't do anything like that, I'm just good at it," she said, a little annoyed. "Is that so hard to believe?"

Wes grunted. He assessed his hand. "Fold!"

She laughed.

He pushed a cup of seeds her way and she knew he would have given them to her anyway. "So, card sharking is just part of the training?" he asked.

"We move on from the poker table to number games,

patterns...like the one at the fence." She picked up a card from the stack. "What about you? You never told me how you ended up a mercenary or why you left the military. I know you said you didn't want to go career, but still, wasn't it easier being a soldier than having to do this sort of thing? I mean, look where we are."

"Truthfully, being a hired gun is a more honest life than one in the military," Wes said, as he studied his hand.

"How's that?" she asked, putting a pair of cards facedown on the floor.

"You were never in the service—so you don't know half the things they ask us to do, in Lower Pangaea, New Rhodes, Olympia. It's their way of guaranteeing the soldiers' loyalty. They make us all complicit in their crimes. Once you've done it, you don't think twice about saying yes the next time, since you've already crossed the line." He discarded a few cards, picked up two more.

She was silent for a moment. "Is that what happened... in Texas?"

He brooded on that. "Yeah." He didn't look her in the eye. "The rebels wouldn't surrender, we had them cornered, but they wouldn't wave the white flag. The town was empty; no one knew where the Texans were hiding their people. I found out by accident. I got caught on a run, hauled in, and tortured. That's how I got this scar. Avo too. But we didn't break. They thought we were dead. We managed to escape, and we even caught one of their people...he was marked..." Wes sucked in his breath.

"You don't have to tell the story if it's too hard."

"I didn't want to do it, I wanted no part of it...but I couldn't stop him either. Avo, he..." Wes looked agonized.

"He tortured him."

"Yeah." He closed his eyes. "He had a mark on his cheek, a brand...like a serpent. Avo figured out he could... he could..."

"Hurt him by touching it," Nat said softly.

"Yeah."

"He would push on it, and it would glow...and the guy just kept screaming...and finally, he broke. The Texans were hiding their people a few miles inland. Hidden in the snow. They'd moved them into one of those old arenas. I thought we'd surround them, you know, like a siege. But the orders came. Bomb the entire place. Kill their kids, their wives, everyone. Get them to surrender."

"It wasn't your fault. You didn't do it. You didn't torture him and you didn't give the order."

"But I couldn't stop him either. Their blood is on my hands and I'll never be able to wash it off." He took a shaky breath. "I left the service after that...I didn't want to be any part of that..."

"Wes—you're not a bad person," she said, putting her cards down, the game forgotten.

Wes did the same. He shook his head. "It was war—but it wasn't right. We were no better than the slavers. Worse, maybe."

FORTY

The next morning, the slavers were intent on discovering why their prisoners were not starving and listless as they had been. A team of guards searched every cage and stripped down every captive but found nothing. The cages were empty. Every crumb and every seed had been eaten.

Nat was worried the pirates would punish their captives, but the arrival of a new batch of pilgrims focused their attention elsewhere.

That was the routine: Every day the slavers scoured the surrounding area in a small black inflatable. Some days they returned with captives, some days, none. Nat, Wes, and the rest of the prisoners were on deck, watching as the next batch of victims arrived. From afar, the captives—a group of smallmen—looked strangely peaceful, hopeful even, but as the boat neared the slave ship, they began to react violently. One drew a dagger from his pocket, while two others attacked the slavers, kicking and punching.

The pirates quelled the little rebellion soon enough, throwing one of the smallmen overboard to drown so the rest fell into line, the sight of their sinking comrade taking the fight out of them.

Nat learned how the slavers worked; in the morning they filled the inflatable boat with food and supplies. They sent out their better-looking men, clean-shaven and decently attired. They would circle the dark ocean until they caught sight of a pilgrim boat.

The slavers would coast alongside the pilgrims, greeting them warmly, offering aid and guidance. More often than not, the pilgrims had been lost for days and were likely starving. The slavers would tell them they were from the Blue, and were there to offer them safe passage through the strait; all the pilgrims had to do was ditch their boat and climb on board theirs. The doorway was not far, they told them.

It was only when they reached the hulking slave ship that the pilgrims realized they had been lied to, and that far from finding the refuge of the Blue, they had been turned into prisoners, and enslaved. Hence the sudden violence.

The smallmen were hustled onto the ship, their faces pale and frightened, noses broken as well as their spirit. Two of them were placed in the cage on the other side of Nat and Wes's.

Later that night, Nat knocked on the wall. There was a tentative knock back.

They knew the Layman's Code! Just like Brendon and Roark did.

Where did you come from? she knocked.

—We are from Upper Pangaea. There were more of us.

—*Yes. We know. We picked them up. Brendon Rimmel and Roark Goderson.*

There was a long pause and then:

—Brendon is our son. Is he safe?

—*He is alive. As for safe, we do not know. He is on a different slave ship. We were separated upon capture.*

—Thank you.

With new captives to torture for their entertainment, the slavers didn't bother with the rest. "How do you think they're doing—Donnie and Roark and Shakes?" she asked.

"Shakes will take care of them as best he can," Wes said. "He won't leave them."

Nat nodded. That sounded about right.

"Another game?" He yawned.

"Sure."

They played poker for a while, Nat beating him easily. "Your scar moves when you have a good hand," she told him. "That's your tell."

He wiggled his eyebrows. "Tell me more."

"Wes, I do have something to tell you," she said. "I just… I haven't been honest with you." She had to do it. She had to tell him, even if it meant he would hate her, even if it meant they could never be friends again.

He rubbed his eyes. "Yeah, what is it?"

"The night your sister was taken…" She couldn't do it, she thought she could, but she couldn't tell him.

Wes raised his eyebrow. "The night my sister was taken…?"

"When I worked for Bradley, I… I was part of a repatriate team…we would take things…without anyone knowing…secrets, weapons…but our specialty was people."

He clenched his jaw and tossed his cards to the floor. "No. No. Don't tell me that. You had nothing to do with Eliza!"

"I'm a monster…I…hurt people…your sister…"

He shook his head, tears coming to his eyes.

"Your sister is dead, Wes. Because of me. I killed her."

"No!"

"The night you described, the fire that came from nowhere, the fact that there were no remains…Oh god, Wes, the things I used to do…the things they made me do…the things I *can* do…"

"NO, NAT, NO! You had nothing to do with that!" He took her hands in his fists. "Look at me. Listen to me! It wasn't you. You had nothing to do with that!"

Nat was sobbing now, and Wes was holding her so tightly. "They would send us out—to do exactly what you described—to take children! When people wouldn't give them up to the repo men, we would take them, to keep everyone in line. To remind people they couldn't break the rules. If that guy hadn't dropped Shakes like he had...they would have sent a team for him. I did it! I know it was me who took Eliza. I'm so sorry, I'm so sorry," she cried. "I didn't know. But when you talked about it—it all came back...everything...we would destroy things...bomb things...the fires..."

"No," he said miserably, releasing her from his grip. "No. Listen to me. It wasn't you, Nat. You might...you might have done those sorts of things in the past...but you didn't kill Eliza."

"How can you be so sure?"

"Because I know what really happened that night." He leaned against the wall of the cage and closed his eyes. "Because the fire was Eliza's idea. She was behind it all along," he said quietly. "Eliza was marked. She had blue eyes, and a spiral on her arm."

"A weaver."

"Is that what you call it?"

"She could create illusions, couldn't she?"

"Yeah. She...made this fire...I still don't remember what was real and what wasn't. But here's the thing about Eliza...she wasn't...she wasn't..." He sighed. "She wasn't very nice. She was...scary sometimes. I don't know where she is or what happened to her, but I need to find her, Nat. So I can save her...from herself."

Nat stared at Wes.

"It wasn't you, okay? I know. Because... I know my

sister. And all those things you did…they're in the past… you couldn't help it…you were just a kid. They used you. They use all of us," he said.

She didn't know what to feel then. Relief?

It didn't seem like enough. She just felt empty. Even if she hadn't been the cause of Eliza's disappearance, she still felt guilty.

"Hey, come on now, don't look like that," he said. "Come here."

She leaned against him and he folded her in his arms.

"So your sister was a monster," Nat whispered, feeling safe as she leaned against him, their bodies creating a small space of warmth in the cold room.

"I didn't say that," he said, his nose almost in her hair, his soft breath on her ear.

"She's a monster…like me."

"You're not a monster."

"There's a voice in my head, and it's the voice of a monster."

"You mean like the way you understand animals?" he asked, and she could feel him smiling.

"No, it's different."

"Do you know what it is?"

She shook her head. "All I know is that it was the voice that told me to escape, to go to New Vegas, and go to the Blue. And it sends me dreams. Dreams of fire and devastation, dreams of flying, like it's preparing me somehow."

"What's it saying now?"

"Actually, it's been quiet for a while." Since the white bird was killed, she realized. There was something more. Since she had fallen for Wes, it had been silent, angry somehow. She remembered the anguish of the wailer, and its large shadow on the water, its anger as it tore their ship apart.

"What else can you do?" he said, hugging her closer to him.

"Not much," she said, as she snuggled against him. "It just comes and goes. I mean, when bad things happen, it saves me—I jumped out the window at MacArthur and it carried me, but I can't make it do anything unless... I feel something strongly, then it just comes out. I've never been able to control it. Except..." She hesitated, shy all of a sudden. "Except when I pulled you from the water. It was as if I could hold it, I could use it." Crystal clear and in control, that was how she had felt, when she had saved him.

"Huh." Wes thought it over. "I think you're afraid to use it, and that's why it's unpredictable. I think you have to embrace it. You can't fight it. Don't resist it."

Resist it? It was true. She had resisted it. She had tried to hide from it. Tried to outrun it. But it was there. It was always part of her. *The voice is mine. I am the monster.* Hadn't she known that from the beginning? Why was she fighting it?

Wes spoke directly into her ear, his strong arms around

her, and she had never felt safer. "You have to accept who you are, Nat. Once you do, you can do anything you want." He chuckled softly. "Or maybe, to tap into your power, all you need to do is think of me."

FORTY-ONE

Nat felt shy the next day, when she woke up lying next to Wes, his arm still slung across her torso. She picked it up gently, trying not to disturb him. She heard the sound of far-off gunfire and she walked to the door, to look through the slit to see what was happening. Wes woke up and stood next to her. "What's going on?"

"More captives, it looks like. More smallkind," she said. She moved away from the window so he could see. "And the Ear is back. His ship mustn't be too far from ours."

The smallmen were shivering on the deck of the ship. Their hands were unbound; they wore no chains or ropes. There was no need—the slavers had simply removed their coats, exposing them to the cold. The frozen air was its own shackle, crippling the smallmen, forcing them to obey.

There was a barrel full of ice and slurry, and it looked like the slavers were playing one of their favorite games: making Popsicles. They threatened to dunk anyone who dared to disobey their orders. At this temperature, the water would immediately freeze on the skin, and death would not take long.

Wes prayed that the smallmen would obey, and then looked away; he'd seen too much already. He tried not to listen, but there was no way to block out the Ear's braying laughter as it carried over the sound of screaming. The bald slaver was joking with the Slob that now he had enough for a tiny circus.

The next few days were the same, and the weariness and the claustrophobia began to take its toll. There were no more new captives, and the mercenaries became restless and frustrated, taking their rage out on the prisoners. The small cups of gruel that had arrived once a day disappeared, and Wes noticed the bitter joy the slavers took in the cries of the young and old among them.

They were down to their last Bacon Fruit, Wes's jacket was almost flat, and although he tried not to show how cold he had become since they had resorted to eating his clothing, Nat could see the blue flush on his cheek, his frostbitten fingers. He spoke less, and when he did, his words were slow and calculated as if each syllable was a struggle.

The weather had worsened as they made their way toward Olympia City, the center of the flesh markets. Sudden showers of snow poured from the sky and a constant fog filled the air. The water was rougher as they neared the outlaw territories, and trashbergs swirled around the ship.

Wes was visibly trembling and, more than once, he asked Nat if it was day or night—his eyes were bothering him. He had chosen to eat rather than to be warm. Nat tried to make him wear her coat, just for a minute, but he adamantly refused.

Nat knew she had to do something before they plunged into despair. Wes was deteriorating before her eyes. "Liannan," she called. "Tell us a story about the Blue."

The sylph's voice carried over. Her voice was weaker than the last time they had spoken, and Nat knew that the imprisonment was taking its toll, the iron slowly sapping the strength from the lovely being. "It's beautiful. Everything they say about it is true. Your throat does not burn when you inhale; the water is as clear as the air. The sun still shines in the Blue...and the grass is the green of emeralds."

"How do you know? You've been there?" Wes challenged.

"I am from Vallonis."

"So why are you here, then? Why leave?" he asked. Nat wondered why he was being so aggressive. He had never acted that way toward Liannan before.

"The Blue is part of this world, it has always been part of it, and once, very long ago, it was this world. A shining civilization: Atlantis, a world where magic and science existed peacefully together. But the promise of Atlantis died during the First Breaking, and the Blue faded into the mist, until the Second Attempt in Avalon. But Avalon died as well, and the world of magic was closed to this land. When the ice came, it is said among our people that the Return was finally upon us. That the Age of Science was over, and the Third Age of Vallonis had finally come. Our people have returned to this world, but…"

"But?" Nat prompted.

"Something went wrong. This world is killing our magic and killing us, causing what you call the 'rot'…and so we sent scouts out, to bring our people back to the doorway, back to the safety of Arem. But it will not be enough to hide in the Blue. Our worlds are colliding, becoming one again. The Blue must cover the land once more and magic have its proper place."

Nat frowned. "Or…?"

"Or everything will be poisoned, not only this world, but Vallonis as well…until everything is lost. I was sent to the gray lands to find the source of the sickness. I chanced upon the pilgrims and thought to lead them to safety first, but afterward, I must resume my search."

"See? She's not giving up," Wes said, finally a ghost of his former smirk appearing on his drawn, handsome face. "So you don't either."

She smiled back at him, but the smiles left their faces when the door to their cage opened with a bang and the guard pointed to Nat. "You're up."

"Hold on!" Wes said, sticking his foot through the

door before the man could slam it closed. "What's going on?"

"What do you think?" The guard smirked. "Traders are here. Shopping. Get ready."

Nat glanced at Wes.

"No, hold on, hold on now," Wes said. "Avo said he wouldn't harm my people in any way…"

The guard laughed. "And you believe that, lover boy?" He kicked away Wes's foot and slammed the door. "They'll be here in five!"

Wes clenched his hands into fists. "When he comes back—listen, when he opens the door, I'll hide behind the shadows, and I can deck him from behind, then we'll get out of here, get Liannan out, get to the lifeboats. I think I know where we are—we can't be far from the port at New Crete."

"No, Wes," she said slowly. "It's too dangerous. There are too many men out there. You don't have a gun, we don't have a ship—if you fight him, they'll kill you."

Wes shook his head. "No—listen to *me*, Nat. I'm not going to let them take you!"

"It will be all right," she said bravely. "Maybe…maybe they won't want me."

"NO!"

The guard opened the door and handed her a metal collar linked to a chain. "Put it around your neck, just in case you try anything funny."

The collar was tight against her skin; it was made of iron, dull and heavy.

"Come on now," the guard said, tugging at her chain. "Come on, get a move on. Say goodbye to your boyfriend."

Good-bye? Then she realized—if the traders took her—this was it. She would never see him again. This might be their last moment together. It came upon her so suddenly, and seeing the stricken look in his eyes, she couldn't help but tear up as well. But what could they do—they were trapped here. She didn't want him to fight them, she didn't want him to get hurt, and so she would go quietly and say good-bye. "Well, I guess…good luck, then?" she said, trying to appear nonchalant even as she swallowed the lump in her throat and walked toward the door.

"Nat, wait…" Wes said, and before she could take another step, she felt Wes's hand reach for hers. He turned her toward him, his dark eyes burning.

Without a word, he leaned over and kissed her.

Nat was startled, but she raised her mouth to meet his, and as his lips pressed on hers, she felt his arm encircle her waist, pulling her close, as if it were the most natural thing in the world, as if they fit together and always had. She could feel his heart beating in his chest, the heat between them—and the desperation. She ran her fingers through his soft hair—something she had yearned to do since they'd met. His kisses turned hard, passionate, and as she inhaled his sweet scent—felt his body against hers, she felt the strength in him. She could keep kissing him forever, she thought…

Why had they waited so long for this? There was so much she wanted to say but so little time to say it. She fluttered her eyes open.

Wes had a hand on her cheek, looking at her with so much feeling. "Nat—" he said, in a strangled voice.

"It's okay," she whispered. "Whatever happens, I can take care of myself."

"So you keep telling me," Wes said, his voice strained and hoarse, as the guard pulled her away. "But see, the thing is, it doesn't matter that you don't need me, because…I need—"

But before he could finish his sentence, the guard pulled her away from him. With a great roar and a look of deep and unfathomable anger on his face, Wes kicked the gun from the slaver's hand and pummeled him with his fists, sending him sprawling to the ground.

"Nat, run!" Wes yelled.

A group of slavers were upon him, and Wes fought ferociously—ten of them were heaped on the deck, bloody and bruised, but he couldn't take on the whole ship, and as strong as he was, they outnumbered him until he was lying in on the floor, blood streaming from his eyes, nose, his face raw.

Nat screamed but there was nothing she could do, and so she continued screaming all the way through the length of the ship. Even as he lay broken and bloodied in the cage, Wes could hear her cries.

FORTY-TWO

They tossed her back into her cage. Wes was still lying in a crumpled heap in the middle of the floor, and she ran to him. She was so afraid of what she would find that she could hardly breathe.

"Ryan!" she cried, turning him over.

His face was bruised and bloody, but he was breathing, and she ripped her shirt to wipe blood from his forehead. The slavers had been brutal, but they had left him alive, and for that she was thankful.

Wes opened one eye. "You're back," he croaked. "Thank god. I'm still going to kill him," he said. "I'm going to kill him with my bare hands. Tear him limb from limb. What happened? What did they do to you?"

"Shhhh," she admonished, wiping his face gently. "Shhh..." She shook her head. "No. No. I'm okay. I'm okay. Nothing happened."

Wes groaned. "What do you mean?"

"Traders didn't want me. They said I wasn't marked and they wouldn't pay, said I was worth nothing. Avo

311

was furious, but he couldn't talk them out of it."

"But how?"

She whispered into his ear. "Look at my eyes."

He opened the other eye and stared up at her.

Her eyes were gray.

"Lenses?" he said.

She nodded her head.

"Well, I'm still going to kill him," Wes mumbled. "That promise I'll make sure I keep."

Nat smiled, remembering his lovely kiss. "Okay," she said, as she continued to clean him up. He would look pretty banged up for a while, his handsome face swollen and cut, but he would be all right. His wounds would heal.

She kissed his forehead and held him close. "You know what?"

"What?" he asked.

"I remember now why you look so familiar. You're a death jockey, aren't you?"

"Used to be."

"The night I escaped from MacArthur, I walked right into the race. Do you remember?"

He sat up and opened his eyes. "I remember. You... you kept the car from hitting me, and from hitting you. You were the girl. The girl on the tracks. I looked for you, you know. I wanted to make sure you were okay."

"I'm okay."

His eyes crinkled. "What happened to your shirt?"

"You're wearing it as a bandage."

"Is that right?" he smiled wickedly. He looked at her again, and she saw that he was looking at the mages' mark on her skin, the flame that she always kept hidden, right above her bra.

"So that's it, huh?" he said.

"Yeah," she said, grimacing. "That's my mark."

He reached his hand to it, and she recoiled, preparing for the pain, but when his finger touched her skin, she was warm, so warm, and there was no pain, only…peace. "It's beautiful, like you, like your eyes," he said. "Now cover up, you're going to get cold."

That night, when Wes had fallen asleep, Nat spoke to Liannan through the walls. Nat told her friend everything. The traders' arrival. How the traders had made the marked prisoners stand in line for inspection.

"What did they want with us? Do you know, Liannan?" she asked. The head trader had been garbed in priestlike robes. Their skin was coated in white powder, and their hair dyed to match. She described the way they had culled the marked prisoners, and those who were showing signs of rot—sallow pallor, yellow eyes—had been dismissed.

"I've heard stories about the white priests," the sylph said quietly. "They believe that they can transfer the powers of the marked to their own bodies. It's a lie. They're butchers. False prophets. Fakers. They pretend to have power, but all they have is their mad religion."

"Transfer our power...how?"

"In a ritual...a sacrifice."

Nat shuddered. "They had some specialist with them, but she said I was nobody, that I wasn't marked so they didn't want me." She told Liannan about Wes's kiss and the miracle of her safety. "My lenses...they came back. I don't know how...I'm a lucky girl," she said.

"Luckier than you might guess; only a spell could provide such protection to hide your true nature," Liannan told her.

"Oh, I don't think so," Nat protested. "I had an iron collar on, I couldn't do anything. Maybe the trader just didn't know what to look for."

"No, don't you see? When Wes kissed you, he blessed you with a protection spell. One that even iron could not restrain."

Nat was taken aback. "But how?"

Liannan did not answer for a long time. But when she spoke, her words were light and almost teasing, "He must like you very much, Nat, to have woven one as powerful as that."

FORTY-THREE

The next afternoon, as they were gathered in the circle, Nat noticed the guards were distracted. Suddenly there was a great screeching noise, and the ship listed to the right—and then picked up speed. "What's going on?" she asked.

"We're headed somewhere else, looks like," the smallman next to her said.

Wes whistled for the nearest guard. "Hey, man, what's happening? Aren't we going to the markets?"

The guard laughed, showing his broken teeth. "Don't worry, mate, it's still the auction block for you all. But before then, the boss has been called to do something else."

"What?"

"Now, why would I tell the likes of you?" Then he whacked Wes on the head with a blow that would have killed a weaker man.

* * *

The answer came the next day, during preparations for the circus. The slavers went from cell to cell pulling out marked prisoners for another show, but the cold had taken its toll. The prisoners had reached a turning point and had neither the strength nor the will to perform anymore. The pirates would have to look elsewhere for amusement.

They didn't accept this revelation very well. A particularly ugly pirate sneered as he kicked open the door to Nat and Wes's cell to find them sitting on the floor, weak from the cold. "All of you who were looking for the Blue—well—by tomorrow it will be just another occupied territory. Maybe they'll call it Nuevo Asul."

Nat raised her head in horror. "What do you mean?"

"Navy's zeroed in on the location of the doorway. We're shoving you lot off on the Ear's ship so we can move faster; Jolly wants us travelin' light so we can pick up any bounty. They owe us for the work we did," he said, as he shined a flashlight into their irises and grunted his approval.

"He's checking for frostblight—can't sell us if we're too far gone, can you?" Wes explained.

The pirate nodded. "Yeah, whaddaya know, the land of unicorns and honey's real after all. Fresh air and food for everyone, right? As if." He snorted, and left them to their cell.

The Blue.

Vallonis.

The military was on its way to the Blue, so that the RSA could take it as a territory, just another extension of its borders, imposing its will and dominion over the land.

Wes stared at Nat. "The stone...you're not wearing the stone," he said softly, the horror dawning on his face. "Why aren't you wearing the stone?"

"Because I gave it away," she said quietly.

"You what?"

"I gave Avo the stone."

"But why?"

Nat shook her head. "Before the traders and the white priests came, Avo took me to his room."

Wes gripped her forearms. "What did he do?"

"No...it wasn't...that wasn't what he wanted."

She remembered the slaver's smug smile.

Avo had put a hand on her collarbone, caressed her jaw. "Exquisite," he had whispered. He was talking about the stone. She had unhooked the chain and given it to him without a fight.

"The voice in my head, it told me to do it." She looked up at Wes, and there were tears in her eyes. "I tried to resist, but I couldn't stop myself. I told you, I'm a monster. There's something wrong with me, Wes. I gave it away. I gave away the stone." Rage and ruin. Devastation. She was the catalyst, she was the key...What did she do? Had she given up hope? Had they turned her into something? Was this something they had programmed into her at MacArthur? But she couldn't stop, had given up the stone as easily as a trinket, as if it were nothing. As if the Blue were nothing to her.

She sunk to her knees. "There isn't any hope. Everything will be lost. Just as Liannan said."

"Stop it! Let me think, okay? Just stop! Didn't you hear what he said? They're moving us."

"Only to another cage," she said bitterly.

Wes put a finger to his lips. "Hold on! Do you hear that? I think those are *Alby's* engines. They must have fixed the old bird. Listen, I think this is it. This is our chance. Remember what you told me? About never giving up hope? We can still work with this."

"But how?"

"No one's going to die, and they won't take the Blue." He smiled.

"You're crazy," she said. "Getting cocky again."

"If I am, it's because I'm betting on you."

PART THE FIFTH

INTO THE BLUE

I'll find the havens fair and free,
and beaches of the Starlit Sea.

—J.R.R. TOLKIEN, BILBO'S LAST SONG:
AT THE GREY HAVENS

FORTY-FOUR

"Okay," Wes said, shaking Nat awake in the morning. "You know what to do?"

Nat blinked her eyes open. "Yeah."

"Tell me."

"They're dropping us off at the other ship."

"And?"

"They'll be distracted, everyone will be out of their cages, and they'll want to dump us as quickly as possible, which means they'll let down their guard, hustling us out. When we see an opportunity, we need to take it."

Truly, it wasn't much of a plan, but it was all he had. They had knocked out the strategy to the smallfolk as well. He only hoped that Shakes, Brendon, and Roark were still alive and on the Ear's ship. He would need their help when it began. Wes felt better than he had in days; his color was high and he felt his blood pounding in his ears.

"You love this," she said to him, watching him prepare for battle, as he wound strips of cloth around his fists.

"I won't deny it." He smiled. "We get out—and we beat them—or we die trying."

"But if I can't..." she said. So much of his plan hinged upon her ability to use her power and she wasn't sure she would be able to. She didn't trust herself—she had given away the stone—she was worse than a monster. She was a traitor to her own kind.

"You will. I know you will," he said. "You won't let me down."

It was another miserable morning. Around noon, the prisoners were marched out of their cages and brought on the deck for another round of cruel amusements.

"You, boy," the fat pirate with the worst mean streak said, singling out a small child from his family. "Come here."

"Please no!" his mother cried. "No—take me instead—please!"

"Take 'em both," another suggested.

"Why not?" the first one agreed. He looped a rope around each of their necks, making a noose. The other slavers brought out a bucket and a barrel for the mother and son to stand on. Then they tossed the other end of the ropes over one of the sails.

A skinny pirate with a chipped tooth pointed to the father, whose mark was shining on his cheek. "See if ye can save 'em both, eh?"

The fat pirate laughed. "See who ye love better." Then

he kicked both the bucket and the barrel and the wife and the boy were hoisted into the air, their legs kicking and their faces turning bright scarlet as they fought to breathe.

"Save him!" the mother gasped. "Save our son!"

The father of the boy held out his hand, so that his son floated higher than the rope around his neck, but the energy it required was killing him. And as he held his son from death, his wife began to lose consciousness, the noose cutting into her throat.

Nat buried her head in Wes's shirt, stifling a scream. Wes trembled with fury as he held her close.

"Ear's here—he'll want them all alive! They're no use to him dead!" a voice snarled; it was the first mate, and in quick succession both the boy and the mother were cut down from their gallows.

The boy lived, but the woman did not respond, and both father and son were weeping over her lifeless body.

"Get up, get up," the fat pirate yelled, kicking at them. "Get 'em all out!" he screamed, ordering the rest of the prisoners lined up to board the Ear's ship.

The *Van Gogh* pulled up next to the *Titan*; the Ear's crew amassed on its deck, awaiting its newest cargo. They had slaves on hand as well to help with the new prisoners. Wes was glad to see Shakes among the slaves. *Alby* was floating by the *Van Gogh* as well. They must have been using it as a scouting vessel, just as he had hoped. Maybe this plan would work after all. He caught Shakes's eye and gave him a signal, the military code that meant "prepare for escape."

Shakes flashed two fingers to indicate he'd received it.

Next to him, Nat squeezed his hand. "Remember our deal," she said. *I would rather die at your hands than at theirs.*

He shook his head. "It won't come to that."

Nat looked over the row of prisoners waiting to board the *Van Gogh*, and spied Liannan's sleek blond head among them. Wes had gone over the plan with her the night before as well. Liannan looked as beautiful as ever. Her eyes sparkled. She had seen Shakes on the other ship, alive.

Brendon's parents, Magda and Cadmael, were among the smallkind waiting to board. Magda had Brendon's curly red hair and Cadmael shared Brendon's shy smile. Nat hoped no harm would come to them.

The wind started to howl and the two ships rocked unsteadily as the ocean kicked up black waves. The two slave ships were only twenty feet apart, but the water was too rough to pull the vessels closer. If they were roped together, the two ships would bump each other, and neither seemed sturdy enough for that.

The Ear sent a smaller boat, two men on an outboard motor, from the *Van Gogh* to ferry the slaves from the *Titan* to his ship. When it arrived, Slob's men threw a makeshift rope ladder down to the smaller craft. The slaves would have to climb down to the Ear's ferry.

Nat looked over the edge at the small metal boat as it bucked violently in the rough waters. This was not going to be an easy transfer.

She was right.

Hands bound, the first slave to attempt the ladder stumbled midway and then plunged headfirst into the dark waters. It took the two scavengers to pull him out and one nearly fell in. The Ear's men called up to the *Titan*: "Unshackle them for the climb. If we don't free their hands, we'll lose half the slaves to the ocean."

Wes nodded to Nat. *This is our chance.* He'd counted on a little improvisation to get through this, but now he knew exactly what to do. It was just as he'd hoped.

One of the brutes walked up to Nat, who was next in line, and removed her cuffs. As he turned the key, the slaver looked down at the ferryboat. "I'll throw these shackles to you. As soon as she gets down there, we don't want to leave these slaves unshack—"

He never finished the sentence. Hands still cuffed, Wes rammed the guard from behind, and the pirate tumbled off the deck, almost smashing into the motorboat as he plunged into the water.

The remaining slavers focused on Wes, drawing out their knives.

"Nat!" Wes yelled. "Now!"

FORTY-FIVE

Wes swung against the pirate holding him, and a crowd of slavers fell upon him. Nat screamed, but there was nothing she could do. She couldn't break the iron bonds holding the rest of the slaves back. Useless. Useless. More slavers joined the fray—Wes was outnumbered—they would beat him until he was dead, make an example of it to the others.

She tried to focus, but she was dizzy with fear and hunger. A pirate fired his gun, and there were more screams, more confusion. Children crying...

The slavers were killing Wes...they were angry and would not stop until he stopped breathing...

If she did nothing, they would kill him... She struggled as the pirates held her...she was weak...she was powerless... She heard Wes cry out in pain, and it was his voice that echoed in her head now. *I think you have to embrace it. You can't fight it. Don't resist it. You have to accept who you are, Nat. Once you do, you can do anything you want. Or maybe, to tap into your power, all you need to do is think of me.*

She smiled at that for a moment.

With all her strength she smashed every iron cuff that held every prisoner.

In a moment, everything changed. Freed from their shackles, the slaves outnumbered their guards two to one.

Without planning or coordination, the freed slaves took up a collective war cry as they went to work on their former tormentors. The marked sent steel crates flying through the air. Tools and buckets became weapons they sent directly at their guards. Daggers were used to stab their owners. A slaver's gun exploded in his face. Another found an iron cage smashing him against the mast. The mighty steel pole in the middle of the ship flexed with an awful groan. A marked family stood below it—eyes closed, the life pouring from their bodies—as they bent the mast at its base. Eighty feet of steel crashed to the deck. Cages were smashed, the deck was torn apart, and *Titan* listed in the water. The slaves fought hard—they had nothing to lose.

Their victory was short-lived. Bullets peppered the sky and Nat saw freed slaves stumble and cower as the scavengers aboard the *Van Gogh* began firing on the *Titan*. Smoke filled the air along with the sound of gunfire. A grenade exploded behind them, and the back half of the *Titan* roared into a mighty blaze.

"This way!" Wes cried, pulling Nat up from where she

had fallen. Liannan was behind him. "Shakes has the boat!" she told them.

They ran toward the end of the deck. Wes stopped. Shakes, Roark, and Brendon were on board good old *Alby* with Farouk. Wes stopped short, glancing from Shakes to their former comrade.

"It's all right," Shakes told Wes as he boarded. "Farouk was the one who helped us out of our cages."

There was no time for questions. Wes nodded to the boy and then turned to help Nat aboard.

"Donnie—your family is here!" she said as soon as she saw the smallmen.

"Where?" Brendon asked. "They're alive?"

"Yes, they were in the line with us—"

"Come on!" Shakes was yelling, helping Liannan on board.

Wes was at the helm; he started the engines and pushed the throttle to its limit.

"We can't just leave them!" Nat yelled, and she meant all of them, not just the Rimmels. The slavers had begun to retake control. They were running up and down the deck, executing prisoners one by one.

Wes swung past the *Van Gogh* as they headed for open sea. The way was clear. They were safe. He glanced back at the slave ship. Avo had made it to the *Van Gogh* and had taken charge of the revolt. "WHERE DO YOU THINK YOU'RE GOING?" he screamed at the prisoners.

"BACK IN YER CAGES! BACK IN YER CAGES!" a fat pirate bellowed as he fired into the air.

"Wes!" Nat called.

"I know, *I know*."

Wes turned the wheel hard and *Alby* groaned as it swung around in a tight arc to face the slave ship. The *Titan* was awash in fire, and its crew had followed Avo to the *Van Gogh*, where they now seemed to have the upper hand. Most of the pilgrims were in the *Titan's* lifeboats, paddling or motoring as best they could to escape. The *Ear's* scavengers, lined up along the bow, were taking shots at the unprotected lifeboats as they tried to escape.

Wes had grown attached to *Alby*, but as he powered toward the slavers, he realized it might be the last weapon in his arsenal. Wes told his crew to hold on and then rammed the *Van Gogh*.

There was enough smoke in the air that he caught most of the scavengers off guard when the two vessels collided. Wes just needed to buy time for the escaping slaves to get out beyond the range of the slavers' guns. The ocean was thick with ice and trash—it wouldn't take long for the small boats to find cover.

When they collided, *Alby's* bow made a temporary bridge between the two crafts. Wes leapt up onto the bow and boarded the slave ship, Nat and Shakes at his side, leaving the smallmen, Farouk, and Liannan behind. Half the scavengers were tossed overboard from the impact, and the rest were throwing ropes to their fallen comrades.

Wes grabbed a pistol from the hand of a fallen slaver and pointed it at the men. Shakes and Nat followed.

"Time to go for a swim, boys. You can paddle over to that raft of junk and hope some pilgrims find you."

Wes put a slug through the shoulder of the biggest scavenger, nicking a chunk of flesh from his arm. He'd survive, but the wound would smart for a few weeks. The slaver glared and began to climb down, followed by the last of his men. "You'll be fine." Wes smiled as he tossed the ropes overboard. His joking words hid his anger. He had to force himself not to fire on them again.

Brendon's parents were among the smallkind who had commandeered one of the small motorboats. They pulled up next to Wes's ship.

"Donnie! Donnie!" his mother cried.

"I'm all right, Mum, come on, I'm okay." Brendon laughed.

"Take the lifeboat to the port of New Crete. My people will find you, and lead you home," Liannan told them.

"Right then, hop on board, boys," Cadmael said.

"We're going with our crew," Roark said.

"Don't worry, Mum, we'll be right behind, I'm their new navigator," Brendon shouted. "I can't leave my ship."

"What!" his mother cried, but his father looked proud. "We'll see you in Vallonis." He nodded. "Magda, let's go."

Roark and Brendon helped the rest of the team

scramble back onto *Alby*. Nat stumbled as she fell on board, Shakes revved the engine, and the boat began to pull away.

"Wait!" she cried. "Where's Wes?" She turned to see Wes still on the deck of the *Van Gogh*. He'd stayed behind to make sure everyone got on board safely.

"Shakes! Turn back!" Nat yelled. "Wes is still back there!"

She saw Wes making a run to leap on board when someone grabbed him from behind and he fell back. Avo Hubik and a dozen other slavers surrounded him. Seeing *Alby* return, the pirates began firing on them, bullets whizzing through the air, pummeling the ship's hull.

Brendon yelped as a bullet grazed his arm, and another plugged Shakes in the shoulder. Wes's crew tried to return fire, but they were badly outnumbered.

"WHAT ARE YOU GUYS DOING? GO! GET OUT OF HERE!" Wes yelled, even as Avo held a gun to his temple.

The slaver laughed. "Surrender, or I will make him eat his own fingers when I send him to the flesh markets."

Shakes hesitated and killed the engine, unsure what to do.

"GET LOST! TAKE THE SHIP AND GET OUT OF HERE! NOW!" Wes screamed in fury, as the bullets continued to fly, one dangerously close to hitting Nat in the head. There was little cover on deck from the shower of gunfire.

"We can't save him," Farouk said. If they stayed any longer, the slavers would overtake them, and they would be back where they began, but in worse circumstances. The slavers didn't take too kindly to slaves who tried to escape.

"No," Shakes said. "No! We're not leaving him."

"But we'll all get captured."

"SURRENDER!" Avo screamed.

"GO ON! MOVE, YOU IDIOTS!" Wes yelled again.

That did it. Shakes tugged at the wheel and gunned the engine.

Nat remained on deck, her eyes fixed on Wes, surrounded by slavers.

"Bring the acid. Get him ready for the knives," Avo ordered.

Wes shook his head at her. "Remember our deal," he mouthed.

She knew what was in store for him. The flesh markets. The flaying. He would die slowly and horribly, as they skinned him alive, as they stripped the skin from his body; they would force him to experience every second of his own terrible death.

Nat felt tears spring to her eyes. *No. No.*

The slavers were upon him now. Three of them held him back as he stood on the deck, while another brought the bucket of acid to blind him, the beginning of the torture.

Alby was pulling away as the slavers kept firing on the

ship. Nat had only a moment to act, a moment to decide.

Wes kept his eyes on her the whole time. "What did I say, Nat, I told you it wouldn't come to this." He smiled. *There are worse things than getting shot, worse things in the world than dying quickly.*

She knew what he was asking her to do.

But he was right. She wouldn't let it come to this. There was a way she could save him and save them all.

Nat grabbed a sidearm from one of the boys. She remembered what Liannan had said the other night. She could feel the otherworldly strength rushing through her spirit as she locked eyes with Wes.

Her eyes filled with tears of hope.

"Do it," he mouthed. "Hurry."

The slaver held a bucket of acid over his head.

There was no time and no other way to find out.

Please, let this work. Please let them have been wrong about me.

Then she shot Wes through the heart.

FORTY-SIX

Chaos exploded on the deck of the *Van Gogh*. Avo Hubik stared at the fallen body of Ryan Wesson as if he couldn't quite believe what had happened. The slavers looked stunned, and the pirate holding the bucket of acid dropped it on his own foot, causing more confusion.

Aboard the *Alby*, Nat collapsed to her knees, shaking, and the smallmen howled in grief. "What happened? What happened?" Shakes yelled.

"She shot him—Nat shot him—" Brendon whispered.

"WHAT?" Shakes turned white. "WHAT DID SHE DO?"

Farouk stood next to him, stunned. "Wes is dead?" he whispered.

"ICEHOLE!" Avo said, kicking Wes's body overboard. "WHAT ARE YOU MORONS WAITING FOR—GET THEM!" he yelled, and the slavers reloaded their guns and resumed firing on *Alby*.

"Help me," Nat said. Wes's body was floating facedown in the water by their ship, and she leaned over to reach for him. The smallmen lent a hand, holding on to her as she pulled him out of the water.

"Got him?" Shakes yelled.

"Yes," Nat said, cradling Wes in her arms. He was already cold and stiff. "Let's go, Shakes!"

The team ducked for cover, and it looked like the slavers would take their boat, but Shakes finally got the engine running and they sped away.

When *Alby* was out of range the slavers' gunfire stopped, and the *Van Gogh* headed back toward its course to the Blue. On the deck, Nat cradled Wes's body in her arms. "Wes, wake up, wake up," she whispered. "Wake up, come on, wake up!"

"Wake up? You shot him in the heart! He's dead!" Farouk exclaimed.

"No," she said. "No," she whispered when Wes did not stir. He was so very cold. "This wasn't what was supposed to happen."

Liannan knelt next to her and put a hand on her shoulder. "I think he's gone," she said quietly. "I'm so sorry."

"NO!" Nat screamed. This was not the way it was supposed to end. No. Not like this. Not now. Not after everything they had done to survive. After everything they meant to each other.

"Let's get out of here," Liannan told Shakes. She looked sorrowfully at Nat. "It wasn't meant to be."

"What's going on?" Shakes asked.

Liannan shook her head. "I'll explain later."

Nat held Wes in her arms and continued to sob. She'd believed she could save him. She had thought she could save them all. She hadn't meant for this to happen... She hadn't meant to *kill* him...She had thought...she had thought she was saving him...that she was saving them all...

They were right about me, then, she thought dully.

Subject has no heart.

That's what they told her at MacArthur.

She was only a weapon, a vessel for fire and pain. She had no heart. There was a cold, dead space where it was supposed to be. She was not human. She was marked. She was a monster.

Subject is unable to love. Unable to feel. Subject is perfect for our needs.

She had believed they were wrong. She had believed her feelings for him were real, that what she felt for Wes was true...

She had believed she could save him as he had saved her. When he had kissed her before the traders came, when he had saved her from the white priests.

But she was wrong.

Subject unable to love. She did not love him and so she could not save him.

Brendon handed her his handkerchief, and Roark put a hand on her shoulder. Both of them were crying quietly.

Nat felt numb.

She thought she had been so clever. She had gambled and lost.

And now Wes was dead.

A few minutes later Shakes walked out of the bridge and knelt by his friend. "I kept telling him he'd get himself killed one day."

"Shakes—"

He brushed off her hand, too upset to even speak. *Don't worry, I've never lost him yet*, he had told Nat in the Trash Pile. Her fault...this was all her fault...she was such a fool to think...to think that she was different... and to hope that she could...

They brought Wes down to the captain's quarters and laid him out on his bed. His face was gray and the bullet she had put in his chest left a neat, round hole.

Shakes staggered out of the room, as if he had no more strength even to walk. The smallmen followed after him.

Liannan entered.

"I killed him," Nat whispered. "This is my fault."

"Better that you had, or the slavers would have killed him and his death would have been worse than a thousand agonies. Plus, if it's any consolation, you saved the rest of us. Can you do this?" she asked. "Get him ready for burial?"

Nat nodded and wiped her eyes. Together, the two of them wound his body in a sheet, wrapping him and blessing his forehead with oil. She put a hand on his cold cheek. He was so handsome and so brave.

"We will keep him here for a little while, let everyone have a chance to say goodbye, before we give him back to the ocean," the sylph said.

Nat nodded. She walked back out to the bridge. There was no more sign of either the *Titan* or the *Van Gogh*.

The lifeboats were bobbing in the sea, on their way to the port at New Crete.

She found Farouk at the helm, looking lost and confused, his eyes red-rimmed from crying.

"Where's Shakes?" she asked.

"Dunno," the young soldier sniffed. "He looked like he wanted to murder somebody."

From below, they could hear Shakes pummeling the walls of the cabin. Liannan joined them on the bridge. "I think we need to leave him alone for now. He doesn't blame you, Nat, but he's angry. He's angry that he couldn't save his friend."

Brendon and Roark huddled with them as well. "None of us blame you; you did a brave thing," Roark said.

Her heart was broken, but Nat held herself together and fought the tears back. Getting away was only one part of the plan.

"What do we do now?" Farouk asked.

"The same thing we did when we set out from New Vegas," she told him. "We need to get to the Blue. The RSA is heading there. We need to stop them from entering the doorway. Liannan, you know the way?"

The sylph nodded. "Yes. Brendon, help me—we need to plot a course."

FORTY-SEVEN

It was dark when Nat entered the crew cabin. Shakes was sitting on a hammock, bent over, his head in his hands, while Liannan rested her head on his shoulder, murmuring softly. The sylph looked up when Nat entered. "Nat is here," she said softly.

"I can go," Nat said.

"No, it's all right, she can stay," Shakes said, motioning for her to take a seat.

Nat could barely stand to meet his eye. "Shakes," she said. "I'm so sorry."

"Don't apologize," he said finally, looking up from his hands and attempting a smile. "Liannan told me what you hoped would happen. You did right. Besides, I hope I would have done the same."

"I know," Nat said. "You're a good friend."

"So are you." He nodded.

They sat together in silence for a while, then Shakes told her about their time on the Van Gogh. They had been put in cages as well, but the Ear's men hadn't starved them, since they were going to be sold to the circus, which fetched a good price. Their cages were located down in the hold, so at least they had been warm.

On their second night aboard the *Van Gogh*, they saw Farouk. He wasn't in a cage. The slavers could barely navigate or maintain their own ship. When they'd found out Farouk could do both, they pulled him from his cage and put him to work. When the rebellion started, it had been Farouk who let them out of their cages.

"Turned out the whole thing was Zedric's idea. He'd escaped from the hold when Farouk caught him. He tried to persuade Zedric to stay, but Zedric refused. He forced Farouk to help him, since he didn't know how to navigate. He was going to try and make it to the port at New Crete. But they got picked up by the slavers, and when Zedric resisted, they shot him on the spot." Shakes raked his fingers through his hair. "I told Wes those Slaine boys were trouble, but he always did have a soft spot for Santonio survivors."

"He told me what happened there," Nat said.

"Did he?" Shakes nodded. "Bet he didn't tell you he tried to save them, did he—tried to get the Texans to sign the treaty, that's why he got captured and tortured, but it was too late. They gave him a medal for the 'victory,' but he left the service anyway."

Liannan returned and sat next to Shakes and put his hand in hers. "You should rest," she said.

Nat left them alone and went to the captain's quarters

to check on Wes, covered in the shroud. Roark was sitting with him, keeping the body company. Tomorrow they would give Wes to the sea. She sat with them for a while, until Brendon urged her to lie down—he would sit with the body. She went back to the crew cabin and when she finally slept her dreams were full of fire.

The next morning, she woke to the smallmen talking excitedly. They were standing by her bunk.

"Get up!" Roark said happily.

"Come see!" Brendon said, tugging on her sleeve.

Nat followed them to Wes's cabin, where Liannan and Shakes were hovering by the doorway. The two of them were smiling so intently, it was as if they were almost shining with happiness. Nat felt the first stirrings of hope in her heart.

"Go. He wants you," Liannan said.

As in a dream, Nat walked into the room.

She found Wes sitting up in his bed. His face was no longer gray, but pink with life. His chest was bare, and the wound right over his heart was merely a scab.

"Hey, you." He smiled, putting his shirt back on and buttoning it up. "I thought I was a goner when I saw you pull that trigger. I'm lucky you've got such terrible aim, huh?"

Nat fought a smile. She remembered that when she had raised her gun, she had hoped for this outcome, had wished for it with everything she had.

"Seriously though, I felt that bullet rip me apart. But I'm here."

"You are," she said with a laugh, feeling giddy with happiness. *They were wrong about me*, she thought. *They told me I didn't have a heart. They told me I would never love anyone...and look...look at him...look how beautiful he is...how alive...*

"You knew this would happen?" Wes said. "But how?"

"It doesn't matter how," she said. "You're here, and that's all that matters." *A powerful protection spell. I must like him so very, very much*, she thought.

"Nat," he said, taking her hand in his. "I wanted to say something to you before...I don't know if you want to hear it...and I don't know what's going to happen when we reach the Blue...but...maybe we can...after you find what you're looking for . . . if everything's okay . . . maybe we can..."

"Yes," she said. "Yes." Whatever happened, the answer was yes. Yes!

His eyes lit up with joy. "Yes?"

"Yes." She leaned down, but he was the one who pulled her to his lap, his strong arms surrounding her, and then they were kissing, and kissing, and kissing, and his mouth was on hers, and they were together, where they belonged, and she buried herself deep into his arms, and he kissed her everywhere, her nose, her cheeks, her neck, her mark, and she was laughing with happiness.

"All right then," Wes said, squeezing her tightly, his old grin returning, happy to be back on his ship with his crew. "What did I miss?"

Nat was about to reply when Roark burst into the room. "We're here...at the doorway to Arem. But Donnie says we've come too late."

Ahead of them, on the distant skyline, they saw the battleships approaching the small island.

FORTY-EIGHT

The navy fleet had surrounded a tiny green island, almost invisible as it was hidden so well by the gray frozen ones around it. It was in the middle of the archipelago, a small green gem.

"Supercarriers," Wes said with a frown.

"Missile destroyers, frigates, missile cruisers. It's a full drone army." Shakes whistled, peering through the binoculars. "They're serious about this."

Liannan paled. "They must not be allowed to enter the doorway. My people cannot defend themselves against this firepower. If they are allowed to enter, it will mean death to Vallonis. If only we still had our drakonrydders…"

Nat was startled out of her paralysis. She had been overwhelmed by the size of the fleet, helpless against the magnificent array and might of the country's massive military machine, commanded by soldiers somewhere in bunkers, hidden far away where they could not be stopped. She had done this. She had given away the stone, and now it was too late—there was nothing they could do now, nothing they could do to stop it—but something Liannan said struck a chord in her.

Drakonrydders.

"The drakon," she whispered. "The monster in the sea. The wailer. You called it a protector of Vallonis."

"Yes, but it is missing its rider and it is uncontrollable without one, a wild animal; otherwise it is our greatest defense."

Nat felt as if she were waking up from a deep and dream-filled sleep, as the memories she had long suppressed returned to her all at once.

The voice she heard inside her...that had ceased to speak because it was speaking in other ways...

The song of the little white bird...

The creatures that came to feed them...

They all said the same thing...

You have returned to us.

Bless you...bless the drakon...bless its rider.

The voice had stopped speaking to her after the death of the white bird. The wailer had been grieving. The wailer was the drakon.

She was not alone. Never alone.

I have been searching for you, but now it is you who must come to me. Journey to the Blue. The Haven needs you.

It is time we are one.

Don't resist your power. You have to accept who you are, Wes had told her.

She was part of the drakon. She was its familiar, its shadow. When the ice came, the universe was split in two, so that when the drakon was born sixteen years ago, it was split as well, its soul born on the other side of the doorway. The drakon had been looking for her ever since.

She had no heart.

Because she was the drakon's heart, the drakon's soul. She and the monster were one and the same. Torn from the other, lost, alone, and only complete, together.

She walked out to the deck, watched as the navy made its way toward the green island that held the doorway to the other world. This was why she had journeyed to the Blue, because the Blue needed her as much as she needed it.

"Nat—what are you doing?" Wes asked, running out to the deck where she stood by the railing, her arms outstretched. "You're going to get killed!"

She stepped away from him, as she felt her power surge within her, wild and free, unchained; she let it wash over her, let it cover every part of her body and her soul, felt its fury and its delight at being unleashed. She did not cower from it, she did not hide from it, she let it run over her, take over her spirit, she accepted the force of its magnitude.

It scared and exhilarated her.

The awesome power within her, that had kept her alive, that kept her safe.

She was a drakonrydder. A protector of Vallonis. They

had kept the land safe for centuries upon centuries. She was the catalyst for destruction. She had been preparing for this all of her life.

She knew now why she had given the stone to Avo, and in turn to his commanders.

She was drawing the RSA to the doorway, drawing its entire fleet there, its entire might to one location, so that *she could destroy it*. Her dreams had prepared her for exactly this moment. Everything in her life had led up to this, so that she could answer the call, could perform her duty when the time came.

Fire and pain.

Rage and ruin.

Wrath and revenge.

Valleys full of ash and cinder.

Destruction.

Death.

She had brought the war here, had brought the war to the edges of the earth, to rain vengeance on her enemies, to protect her home. This was what she was made for, this was her purpose, her calling.

She turned to Wes and blinked back angry, happy tears. "I know what I have to do now. You were right, Wes, I can fix this thing."

Then Nat raised her arms to the sky and called for her drakon.

FORTY-NINE

DRAKON MAINAS, ANSWER MY CALL. HEED MY WORD.

ARISE FROM THE DEEP AND VANQUISH OUR ENEMIES!

Nat was the drakon, she was its heart and soul, she was its master and its rider.

The sea parted, and a blackened creature rose to the surface. Its skin was the dull color of coal, rippling and studded with spikes. Its eyes were the same shade of green and gold as Nat's, the pale green of summer grass, the gold of a bright new morning, and it carried the mark of the flame on its breast, the same one that was on her skin. Its massive wings fluttered and folded, a curtain, an umbrella. It was huge, almost as large as a ship, a wonder to behold, terrifying and beautiful.

"DRAKON MAINAS!"

"ANASTASIA DEKESTHALIAS," he rumbled.

Her real name. Her immortal name that had come to her in a dream. Natasha Kestal was *Anastasia Dekesthalias*.

Resurrection of the Flame. Heart of Dread. Heart of the Drakon.

The creature fixed upon Nat and Nat felt something inside her transform, as if she were opening her eyes for the first time. The world around her grew brighter, and the smallest sound resonated in her ears. Even her mind seemed to expand. She stared into the creature's eyes and in a flash, the two of them were linked.

Nat's chest burned; she could hardly think as a new and intense pain washed over her body.

What was it?

Fire. She was breathing fire.

She was made of fire, of ashes and smoke and blood and crystal.

She was burning, burning.

Nat could see everything the drakon saw, felt everything it felt, sensed its anger and its rage.

The drakon rose into the air and the sky exploded with gunfire and missiles as the ships targeted this new enemy, but the drakon was faster and flew higher.

Destroy them! Vanquish our foes! Rain death upon our enemies!

The drakon roared. It zeroed in on the smaller ships first, pounding their hulls, tilting them against the waves and rolling the men into the water. Its powerful wings sent tsunami-like splashes of toxic water onto the ships' decks. The drakon used the black ocean as a weapon. The frigates swayed and bobbed, and soon toppled over.

The black ocean became thick with smoke.

Nat watched as the drakon dove beneath the dark water, disappearing into the depths only to emerge a moment later beneath one of the ships—lifting it up above the waves and breaking it in half as if it were a child's toy. With a mighty screech, it grasped another ship and tossed it high into the air. When it fell, it slammed it into another boat, sinking them both.

The surviving soldiers beat a retreat into their lifeboats, and other ships begin to follow.

We've won, Nat thought, as the armada scattered and ships began to turn away from the green island. But a fresh volley of gunfire exploded from the two massive supercarriers. Their guns fired in elaborate patterns, guided by computers that tracked, plotted, and anticipated the creature's course as it dove and wound through the sky.

Hide, hide, Nat sent urgently, and the drakon rose upward, its ashen underbelly blending with the dark clouds. But the gunfire continued its relentless rhythm. Red and orange flares sparked through the smoke.

The drakon was nowhere to be seen.

Nat panicked until the creature reemerged. The clouds disappeared into steam as flames shot down from the sky, dissolving the fog like mist meeting the morning sun. The drakon's fire lit the dark ocean with a light that the black water had not seen in a hundred years.

Its flame as bright-white as day, its wings tucked

behind its back, the drakon descended like a bomb towards the middle of the nearest destroyer. Its fire engulfed the ship, and the air reeked of burnt plastic and molten steel. The ship collapsed into the waves, its hull crumpling like twigs before flame.

Another supercarrier released an array of missiles directly at the drakon. The creature rolled away, but the ship's guns met their mark. A rocket shell tore the drakon's wing and the clouds glowed a fiery red once more.

Down below, Nat collapsed on the deck.

FIFTY

"Hit! I'm hit!" she whispered, holding her arm.

"Nat!"

Wes was by her side. "Nat!"

"The guns! You have to stop their guns!" she told him.

"Right—what was I thinking—just waiting for you guys to save our skins—Shakes! Farouk! Roark! Brendon! The guns!"

They'd never match the naval firepower, but Wes guessed they wouldn't have to. Not with that thing—Nat's drakon—on their side. A few of the remaining ships had open gunners on their decks. The soldiers sat behind heavy artillery shields, but he could still see glimpses of them as they trained and rotated their guns to follow the creature.

Wes grabbed his sniper's rifle and climbed to the highest point of his ship. He motioned to Shakes. "Hold my leg and try to steady me; I need to get a clear shot at these guys."

"But, boss, you'd be totally exposed."

Wes knew he was right, the gunners were distracted by the drakon, but as soon as he fired, they'd turn their attention to him and he'd be a sitting duck. But he needed the height to get a clear shot and he'd just have to take his chances afterward.

Wes turned to his targets. He aimed low on the first shot and put a bullet through the hand of the first gunner. The second gunner spun toward Wes. He was manning a gun big enough to obliterate anything within a yard of him. The soldier smiled at Wes, wanting to let him know he was going to enjoy cutting him into shreds.

But Wes didn't respond; instead he fired, and the bullet pierced the man's armor before he could reach for the trigger. *There's always just a fraction of a second between life and death*, Wes thought. *Take every second you can.*

With the sky cleared of gunfire, the drakon reappeared beside *Alby*. Its wing had healed, and it was beating glorious waves of air as it hovered above the water, its torso casting a jagged shadow before it descended to the deck.

The ship tilted as it received the creature's weight. The drone of battle faded, and for a moment the crew stood, captivated by the drakon.

Its breath was like a whirlwind, raspy and strong like a hundred men sucking in air at once. Deck plates buckled and screws unwound from their fastenings—the creature was as heavy as stone. It drew in its mighty wings and lowered its head with a thud that shook the deck.

Nat knew what came next; she just needed the nerve to go through with it. The moment was surreal and stretched for what felt like minutes. She looked at the crew, who smiled at her hopefully. Liannan nodded, and Wes was the one who offered his knee for her to step on, to climb.

He took her hand and hoisted her up. "Give them hell," he whispered in her ear, his eyes shining with admiration.

The drakon turned its neck, and Nat climbed onto his back, digging her heels against its side. When she reached his neck, the creature's thick shoulder muscles adjusted to her weight, giving her a seat upon its mighty spine. She gripped its hard scales, and the drakon pushed off with a force that nearly tore her from its back.

Smoke filled her eyes as they soared upward. The cold wind rushed at her cheeks and in a moment they were above the battle. In one glance she could see the whole scene, laid out like a photo on a page. She saw the remaining ships rocking in the great black waters, the long sea of ice, and the brilliant fringes of the small green island.

From this height, the earth looked different—flatter, and even the noise from the battle was muted. They were so high in the sky they were invisible to the ship's guns. The gray smoke covered them, and Nat held on tightly. She felt the drakon's muscles contracting with each flap of its mighty wings.

The creature inhaled a mighty breath—its long

muscular torso flexing beneath her—and her lungs, too, filled with fire once more.

"To battle!" Nat screamed, and the drakon surged upward so quickly that her hands ripped away and she fell from its back and she was flying.

She was airborne, just like that night at MacArthur when she had jumped out of the window. This was the same, and as she glided through the air, she felt no fear.

She could do this. She could fly.

She called to her drakon again and willed it to come to her. She caught it by the neck but they were moving too fast and her fingers gripped his scales for the briefest moment before her momentum pulled her away. She fell downward, but once again she was not afraid.

Drakon Mainas, to me, she urged, as the sea rose up to meet her.

Just as she was about to fall into the water, the drakon appeared beneath her and she slammed into its back. She righted herself and dug her feet into its hide.

They circled for a moment, then plunged toward the remaining ships.

Breathe deeply. We will need all our strength. Now exhale, Drakon Mainas directed.

Nat felt the same dark fire suffocate her throat, but she did not fight it, she breathed it in. Drakonfire. As she exhaled, a wild blue flame burst from the drakon's mouth, covering the largest supercarrier in a swirling iridescent blue blaze.

They turned to the stealth cruiser next. Its surface was perfectly smooth and sleek, and the drakon bathed the entire ship in a flame so hot that the oxygen around the ship ignited in a wild orange fireball. The ship's armored exterior contracted like shrink wrap—the hatches fell inward, the guns warped, and the windows slid from their frames.

The drakon roared its joy and flew higher and faster. With Nat directing its movements, when it flew back down to attack the remaining ships, it was able to evade the torrent of gunfire with a new and surprising agility. Nat held on with all her might, and the drakon's spikes cut into her hands, but she felt no pain.

They exhaled together once more, and the blue flame bathed the final warship in a blinding cone of fire. The dark water boiled, clouds vaporized, the air crackled. As the ship sunk, its myriad guns let loose with a final volley. Shells sprayed in all directions.

A single explosive round cut through the drakon's chest, piercing not just the creature's flesh, but Nat's as well.

The two tumbled, falling toward the sandy beach as the last warship sank into the fiery sea.

FIFTY-ONE

Wes's crew cheered as the final cruiser sank into the ocean. The smoke began to clear. The drakon had done its work. Wes scoured the sky and the sea for the drakon but saw nothing. They had stopped the armada, but at what cost?

The waters surrounding them swirled with blue flames as the ocean's chemical sludge caught on fire.

"Where is she? Where's Nat?" Wes demanded.

Shakes held up the binoculars but shook his head.

"Come on, take us to the shore," Wes ordered.

They docked the ship by the green island, and Wes made his way to the coast. The air was cloudy with black smoke. Wes coughed. He thought he could see the drakon lumbering in the distance, but the sky was dark and his eyes were watering. The water was filled with wreckage from the battle, and those who survived were swimming to lifeboats.

From the shadows of the green forest, a few sylphs appeared. Like Liannan, they were clad in white raiment.

They looked at Wes with somber faces.

"Where is she? Where's Nat?" Wes asked.

"The drakonrydder was shot from the sky," the nearest sylph replied. "She is gone."

No way. No way. Wes kicked at the sand, unwilling to accept it. He knelt on the beach, his hands to his face, and stifled a scream of rage.

The waves lapped on the shore, and when he looked he saw a familiar-looking black boot.

He ran to the body and turned it over. It was Nat, still in her black coat and jeans.

In the distance, the drakon nodded its head. Wes wondered whether it had laid her down there for him to find.

"Nat! Wake up!" he yelled. Her flesh was cold from the icy water. Dark burns covered her skin. He laid his head down and put an ear to her mouth. She wasn't breathing. He began to pump her heart, just as he had been taught. Three quick pumps, then he held her nose and breathed into her mouth. Nothing. He did it again and again. Nothing happened.

Liannan walked over the waves toward him. "I can help, please, bring her—follow me," she said, leading Wes deeper into the island.

He lifted Nat in his arms and carried her, running after the fast-moving sylph as the crew followed behind him.

Liannan led them up the coast, over the burnt sand, and into the island's interior. Wes looked around in wonder at a dense forest, with trees arching into the shape of a doorway. He had never seen trees before other than in pictures or on the nets, and these trees were like unlike anything he had ever seen. The branches curled with inch-long thorns, and roots reached up out of the soil. He laid Nat on the ground. He looked around in wonder at the green grass, the sky filled with life, birds chirping and fluttering, the buzz of insects, the smell of grass. The Blue was alive, alive as their world used to be.

The crew gathered around Nat's still form.

Wes put his ear to her chest and listened for a heartbeat. There was none.

"We're here, Nat. We're here. We reached the Blue. Now wake up," he ordered, his voice hoarse from crying.

He waited.

Finally Nat opened her eyes. She smiled at him.

Wes grinned. "You owe me ten thousand credits. Hand them over."

FIFTY-TWO

Nat laughed, sat up, and looked around. It was the Blue. Her home. Vallonis. There were no more clouds, no snow or fog. Just brilliant sunshine falling on her skin, warming her face. It felt like nourishment, as if the sun were giving her sustenance she'd been denied her entire life. Her ears filled with the sound of birdsong and the buzzing of insects. A soft, warm breeze fell on her face and tickled her cheek. The smell of blossoms, intoxicating and sweet, filled the air.

But nothing compared to the sky. The endless blue sky—there was no more gray, just a majestic blue. So this was why they called it the Blue. How could you name it anything else? She could feel the strength return to her body. The joy of breathing clean air. She was whole, she understood now, whatever rot had threatened to destroy her was expunged completely. She could return to New Vegas. She looked in wonder at the array of creatures passing through the doorway.

A dark-haired sylph was talking intently to Liannan,

who was shaking her head sorrowfully.

Liannan returned to the group. "This doorway has been compromised; my people have no choice but to close it. It is too dangerous. We had hoped to leave it open for those of us who had been born in the gray land. But they must seek another way home.

"I must return to my task, to search for the source of the sickness. I have much more to do still, but the rest of you must cross before it closes," she said.

"I'm not going anywhere," Shakes said, taking her hand.

She smiled at him tenderly.

"What about you, boss?" Shakes asked.

Wes shook his head. "I can't, you know I can't. I've got to go back for my sister." He stepped away from the green forest door and back toward the smoky beach. "Eliza needs me. She's out there...somewhere. I have to find her."

"Right." Shakes nodded. "Don't worry, boss, we will."

"I can help; I think our goals may be linked in some way," Liannan said. "If you'll have me."

"We will, too," Roark said.

Brendon nodded. "We will help you find your family. You saved ours, and so we will do the same for you."

Farouk was the last. "I'll come, too—to earn your trust again."

His team was assembled. This was his family now, his crew. There was just one person missing. Wes looked back at Nat, who stood alone by the doorway. "Nat?" he smiled, reaching out his hand for her to take.

She had said yes. They would be together. Always.

Nat felt tears coming to her eyes because she knew the answer she must give him. Drakon Mainas was in her head. *You know you cannot go with him. We are pledged to Vallonis, we must protect what our enemies seek to control. This doorway will close, but they will return, and when they do, we must be ready. You and I are the last of our kind. We are all that is left. You cannot forsake me.* She realized then that another cause for the drakon's rage was its anger when it felt her falling for Wes. Falling in love was not part of the plan. Wes was a barrier to their reunion. The drakons and their riders did not love; they only served.

But she loved Wes. So much.

He was waiting for her to take her hand.

But she could not. She *must* not.

This was it.

The separation that could not be averted.

The ending she knew was coming.

This was the goodbye she had dreaded from the moment she had met him. She had fallen in love with him from the start, when he had stepped up to her blackjack table so long ago, in another lifetime, when they were strangers, a mercenary and his client, a runner and a dealer, a boy and girl.

"I can't." Nat shook her head. "I'm so sorry, Wes."

She had said yes before, but that was before she knew what she was…before she understood her place in the world… She had answered his question with a lie, a lovely lie. A lie that she had wanted to believe, that she had wanted to be real. But it was a dream. Fire and pain. Rage and sorrow. She was made of this, her cold heart of dread.

Wes nodded, holding his bluff, not letting her see what this was costing him, his blank poker face. "Well, good luck, then," he said, holding out his hand.

"Good luck," she said, and shaking his hand, placed the last two platinum chips in it.

The crew came to surround Nat, to hug and kiss her goodbye. Then it was time to go, and Wes turned back toward his ship.

Nat watched him walk away and then ran after him. Hot tears fell down her cheeks. "Ryan!"

When he heard her call his name, his face was so full of hope that it killed her to say what she needed to say. "*I love you*. I love you so much, but I can't. *I can't*. I love you but I can't go with you."

"I understand," he said softly, and stepped back toward the beach.

She put a hand on his arm and turned him toward her, just as he had done to her that night on the *Titan*, when the traders had arrived. But before she could kiss him, he swept her off her feet and kissed her, dipping her low and holding her close.

"I'll come back for you," he whispered. "This isn't the

end for us. I promise." Then Wes kissed her again. More slowly this time.

Nat watched him walk away from her, her heart breaking and healing at the same time. *There is hope*, she had told him once. She would believe it. The feel of his kiss lingered on her lips. She hoped it would be soon, that he would return to her soon. That they would be together one day. She would like that very much. She would trust him with all the treasures in the universe. She would trust him with her very heart.

Then Nat called for her drakon and together they flew through the doorway, into the Blue.

ACKNOWLEDGMENTS

Mike and Mel would like to thank the awesome TEAM FROZEN: our amazing, lovely and brilliant team of editor and publisher Jennifer Besser and Don Weisberg, for believing in the book from the beginning and putting their whole hearts into it. Our super-agent and partner-in-crime, Richard Abate, and Melissa Kahn at 3 Arts, for all the support. Everyone at Penguin Young Readers Group for their dedication and enthusiasm, but especially Marisa Russell, Elyse Marshall, Shauna Fay Rossano, Emily Romero, Shanta Newlin, Erin Dempsey, Scottie Bowditch, Felicia Frazier, Courtney Wood, Erin Gallagher, and Anna Jarzab. Theresa Evangelista for the beautiful cover. Lynn Goldberg and Megan Beatie from Goldberg McDuffie for spreading the news to the world. Our film and TV agents Sally Willcox, Michelle Weiner and Tiffany Ward at CAA for navigating the crazy world of Hollywood for us. Our wonderful friends in life and letters Margie Stohl, Alyson Noël, Aaron Hartzler, Ally Carter, Rachel Cohn, Pseudonymous Bosch, Deborah

Harkness and James Dashner for being comrades-in-arms. To our extended family, especially our brother-in-law and beta reader Steve Green for loving our stories. To our number one girl: Mattie, one day you'll be in the family business as well and we look forward to that day with so much love and excitement!

Lastly, to all our readers who have followed our books from Blue Bloods to Wolf Pact to Witches of East End, thank you for letting Nat and Wes into your hearts. We hold you in ours.

Much love to all,
Mike and Mel